ALSO BY *Wm. Stage*

Ghost Signs: Brick Wall Signs in America

Mound City Chronicles

Litchfield: A Strange & Twisted Saga
of Murder in the Midwest

Have A Weird Day:
Reflections & Ruminations on the St. Louis Experience

The Practical Guide to Process Serving

Pictures of People 1982-1993

Fool For Life

BY *Wm. Stage and Margaret Stage*

The Painted Ad: A Postcard Book of Vintage Brick Wall Signs

To My Best Pal Nick May

NOT WAVING DROWNING

You will recognize

[STORIES]

Many characters within

Cheers!

Wm. Stage
BACHELOR OF PHILOSOPHY

ILLUSTRATED BY **BEN TEGEL**

floppinfish

FLOPPINFISH PUBLISHING COMPANY LTD
ST. LOUIS, MISSOURI

FOR PETE BASTIAN who has some pretty good stories of his own

LIBRARY OF CONGRESS CATALOGING IN PUBLICATION DATA
Stage, Wm. [1951-]
Not Waving, Drowning
—Literature: fiction / contemporary

ISBN 978-0-9629124-9-8

Cover photograph: ©2010 Wendi Wirawan
Cover and Interior Design: Michael Kilfoy, Studio X
www.studiox.us

"Bertie DuBois on the Ivories" was originally published in the
June 1984 issue of *St. Louis Rehabber* magazine under the title
"Cold-Hearted Night."

The WWII reminiscences in "Charlie Shaw for the Defense" were
excerpted from *The Unguarded Moment*,
the unpublished memoirs of Charles M. Shaw, Major, U.S. Army Air
Force, courtesy of Tom Shaw.

The author wishes to thank Tom Karsten, Sally Jackoway,
Mary Stage, and Rob Corley MD for their help with this book.

Printed in the United States of America
Set in Adobe Jenson Pro
First Edition

On the title: "Not Waving but Drowning" is a short poem by British poet Stevie Smith, originally published in 1957. As the title implies, it describes a man whose frantic thrashing in the sea causes beachside onlookers to think he is not in distress but waving to them. I have borrowed this pithy phrase from Ms. Smith, as it fits in with the theme of these stories—people who are in over their heads.

On the stories: At least one character in each of these stories represents someone I have known, casually observed, or heard about. The common thread among these characters is that they have arrived at a junction in their lives where they either are in trouble or caus-ing trouble. With this as a starting point, I make up a story around them. For instance, there really is a female beggar who stands at the 7th Street off-ramp, but her name is probably not Tammy and I have never seen her with a dog. A scale-train engineer really did perish in a freak accident at the St. Louis Zoo, but so far as we know his body was not nibbled by hippos. You get the idea. Charlie Shaw did, in fact, defend Tom Burnham on charges of murder. And, yes, an acquaintance did take a strike from a highly venomous snake in his collection. However, in my versions, the lead-up to these events, as well as the way they happen, strays imaginatively from the intractable facts of reality. Moreover, many minor characters in this work may be found in real-life as well—Rabbi Rovinsky, J.R. Moore, and Charlie Hoessle to name a few. My high school English Comp teacher, Peggy O' Shaughnessy, urged us to "write about what you know." The stories are set in St. Louis, my home since 1978.

Contents

*"Fortune makes us blindly play her terrible game,
and we never see beneath the cards."*

—VOLTAIRE

NOT WAVING
DROWNING

RANDALL KOCH
SEX OFFENDER

THE FUNNY THING IS HE WAS TRYING TO BE DISCREET. He drove along the alley until he found a spot that was out of sight of any houses, the view blocked by garages and tall weeds. Six-fifty, the sky just beginning to lighten. He braked the Subaru, cut the lights, climbed out, and stood between two Dumpsters to relieve himself. Zip. The urine streamed out with considerable force, audibly splashing against the side of the Dumpster. Three coffees since five and he'd been holding it now for the last hour. As his bladder began to empty he spoke to himself, as he often did when alone, whispering, "Oh, this is good, so good, what a glorious feeling." Nearly finished, he heard some muffled conversation coming his way. Just as they rounded the corner of the garage, he turned and they saw him exposed, pissing away. The man clutched at the girl, spun her around, saying, "Don't look, baby." And then he stood there, glaring at Randall, asking him, demanding of him an answer to what the hell he thought he was doing out here, using his alley for a toilet. "You're no better than some dirty animal," the man told him.

Randall couldn't believe he'd been caught in the act, the two sneaking up on him like that. He shook off the last drop of urine, zipped up, offered a very sincere apology along with the excuse that he had to go really bad and there was no gas station anywhere nearby with a public restroom, which was the truth, and that surely he, the dad, had been in a similar strait in his life and he should know how it is: "When you gotta go, you gotta go."

With that, he walked past them, got into his car and drove off. No need for extended discussion. He looked in the rear-view and saw them still standing there, watching. "Of all the trash-littered alleys in St. Louis," he muttered, "I've got to pick the one with people creeping around." He continued on his rounds, driving around North City, knocking on doors, a Special Process Server trying to serve papers. He had good luck in the morning, finding people at home. By eleven-thirty he had served four summonses, two adult abuse orders of protection, and a subpoena for records. He would go back out again after having lunch at home, a century-old, two-story wood frame in a decent neighborhood on the far southwest edge of the city limits. Walking from the car to the house, it was hard to miss the white business card taped to his front door, confronting him like a merciless bully. The embossed insignia of the St. Louis Metropolitan Police Department, the name Det. Joe Oldenburg with two phone numbers, office and mobile, and the hand-written message above the name that said, CALL ME TODAY, BUCKO—DO IT!

His life would change that day and not for the better.

Not just Laurice but the kids, Max and Felicia, noticed the change in Randall in the weeks leading up to the trial. He seemed distracted, off somewhere in the clouds. He still shot hoops with Max in the driveway, still took Felicia to Girl Scout meetings, still helped Laurice prepare dinner and made love to her every third or fourth night, but he executed these and various other tasks without his usual gusto. The family worried for him, he saw that. Hell, he worried for his own self, chewing his fingers bloody over the possible outcome of the trial. Sadly, the once-merry Koch household had become infected with gloom and vexation.

The fortuitous thing in all this was that, as an independent contractor, he served process for more than twenty lawyers, busting his ass day-in, day-out for these people. Any of them would be happy to take his case. He knew right off who he'd call—Mayer Rubin, an affable and successful lawyer who hung his shingle in the county seat of Clayton. While other lawyers just left the papers with the receptionist for him to pick up, Mayer often made time to personally give him the papers he was to serve. His practice was about fifty percent criminal and Mayer enjoyed discussing this or that pending case, often using Randall as a sounding board for the strategies he hoped to employ. Unlike other lawyers farting around at the last minute before trial, Mayer's subpoenas were always ready well in advance of the trial. He worked weekends, he wore tasteful yet conservative attire, he visited his clients in jail if they couldn't make bond. Yes, Mayer Rubin would do a bang-up job for Randall's case. The question was: Could he make it all go away?

The trial of *State v Koch* started out on a sour note, the judge mispronouncing Randall's name as "kotch." Randall, standing before the bench occupied by this august person, found himself blurting, "It's Koch, Your Honor, like the popular soft drink. You may have been thinking of the former mayor of New York. Honest mistake. Same spelling, different pronunciation."

The Honorable Titus P. Mead glared at this miserable specimen of humanity standing before him and replied, "I don't give a horse's patootie how it's pronounced. You, sir, are on trial here."

The bailiff read the charges: Sexual Misconduct by Indecent Exposure, a second degree misdemeanor. It was a bench trial, no jury, and Mayer Rubin had only to convince the judge that his client was a straight arrow. A family man, a churchgoing man—alright,

Temple, on occasion—and a member in good standing with the Missouri Botanical Garden. Indeed, an upstanding citizen with no previous record and that this unfortunate incident was, well, just that, the sudden, urgent beckoning of a full bladder and, thinking he was alone, seizing the opportunity to relieve that pressure. Moreover, earlier that morning Randall had taken hydrochlorothiazide, a diuretic pill prescribed to him by a licensed physician for treatment of high blood pressure. Surely this was a mitigating factor. In summation, Randall was not some depraved flasher, merely a man heeding Nature's Call.

The judge nodded at Mayer's delivery as if he were sympathetic. This was a miscue, for he then went into a diatribe about the breakdown of society being caused by people like his client who felt they could urinate wherever they damn well pleased and in view of decent-minded citizens simply going to their car. The judge shifted in his seat, cleared his throat, and shocked Mayer Rubin by asking, "You've read the Bible, have you?"

"I'm a Jew, Your Honor. Jews read the Torah."

"Well, if you were a Christian and had read the Good Book you would have come across a passage that is pertinent to this case, one that is found in Kings One, Chapter Fourteen—the Old Testament—and which tells how God will smite anyone that 'pisseth against the wall.' Those are the exact words, and we know that smiting can be fatal because God goes on to say that, after he kills them, their dead bodies will be eaten by dogs. That's if they live in the city. If they live in the country, birds will devour their carcasses."

"It sounds like they were in need of some public health codes. But how does this relate to my client? Do you want to smite him?"

"Well sir, at this very moment the State *is* considering smiting him, in a manner of speaking. I use that salient passage to illustrate how public urination was seen as a serious offense in ancient times, a slap in the face of civility. But as heinous and unsanitary as that act may be, the attendant offense of indecent exposure is worse. You are well-versed on the law, Mister Rubin. How does the statute read? Please tell us."

Mayer Rubin was well aware of the language of the statute. He didn't have to look it up; he recited it by rote: "The crime of sexual misconduct is committed when a person willfully and deliberately exposes one's genitals in such a way to cause affront or alarm."

The judge brought his fingertips together and formed a sort of geometric design. He pulsed a beat with his fingers, a spider doing pushups on a mirror. "Yes, yes, that's the crux of it," he said, looking down on Mayer Rubin with all his judicial might. "Pray tell us, sir, did your client willfully and deliberately expose his genitals?"

"You have to, Your Honor, otherwise you'd be peeing in your pants."

"Irrelevant! And pray tell us, did your client's action cause affront or alarm?"

Mayer Rubin shrugged. "I can't speak for the state of mind of those who happened upon the scene."

"Well, it just so happens that I have sworn testimony from both the father and his daughter. Let us see what their state of mind was like."

Randall, sitting at the defense table, cringed. This wasn't going well.

Judge Mead harumphed and began to read. "'When we first saw the man, he had his back toward us. He could have finished his business, zipped up, and then gone on his way. Instead, he turned to face us, his penis hanging out of his trousers. He made no attempt to conceal his privates and he even shook it at us. I remember him grinning. It made me sick to my stomach.' That's the father," clarified the judge.

"Now, the daughter, age thirteen. I quote, in part, 'He was holding it and waving it around like he was really proud of it and it freaked me the way that thing looked, kind of like a zucchini,'" Judge Mead chuckled, saying it was cute, the girl's spelling of zucchini as z-o-o-k-e-e-n-i, then continued, "'kind of like a zucchini, but not green. It was so gross I can't even describe how gross it was and I still think about it every day, pretty much.'"

Randall cringed even more demonstratively. Somehow the story had changed from Randall merely being caught pissing to him brandishing his rude, erect member in front of the girl.

"There you have it," said the judge. "Being freaked out"—and he held up two sets of waggling fingers to indicate quotation marks— "is no different than being affronted and alarmed. The criteria have been met. Therefore, I pronounce the defendant guilty and sentence him to sixty hours of community service along with supervised probation for a period of three years. In addition, because the offense involved a minor, he will register himself as a sex offender."

Mayer Rubin could scarcely believe it. "With all due respect, Your Honor, that's a pretty stiff sentence. Couldn't we arrive at something less draconian? I will remind you that my client is a Special Process Server, in essence, an officer of the court. Surely, that merits some professional courtesy."

The judge sneered at this proposal. "I don't give a horse's patootie if he's a Supreme Court Justice, that sentence is well within guidelines. It could be even more stringent! If I were you, Mister Rubin, I would stop while I'm ahead. Case closed."

The incident made the papers, not the highly-read Law & Order section of the *Post-Dispatch*, but strangely enough, it earned an entry in the inglorious Chomo Club Perps & Pervs section of

The Evening Whirl, "An Uninterrupted Crime-Fighting Publication Since 1938." This dog turd of a mention came to Randall's attention by way of Eddie Williams, a black attorney that he worked for and liked a lot. One day, about two weeks after the trial, he showed up at Eddie's downtown office to pick up some summonses and there was *The Whirl* placed neatly atop the stack. It wasn't the current edition, but Eddie had evidently seen the report and thoughtfully saved it for Randall, having highlighted the salient passages. Accountable to no journalistic standards, *Whirl* writers employed colorful phrasing and bold assertions. The headline was bad enough: WHITE BOY CAN'T KEEP HIS MOUSE IN THE HOUSE; HOPED TO IMPRESS YOUNG GIRL. This was followed by an account of the crime, including such fabrications as "When the girl's father threatened to beat his freakish ass to a pulp, Koch fled the scene in a cowardly manner." It even reported his sentence, adding that, "Community service is yet to be determined, but as far as we're concerned, licking the toilets clean at the Greyhound station would be appropriate." It was the last line, however, that really stung him: "Koch, a noted Special Process Server, had better keep a close eye on the lawsuits he serves—one of them just may be for him."

Eddie walked in the room, caught Randall going over the summonses. "You know what a chomo is?" he asked, pumping Randall's hand in a soul shake.

Randall shook his skull in exasperation. "Yeah, it's a guy who can't seem to get a break lately."

Eddie grinned. "Nah, it's prison slang for child molester."

"Go fuck a duck," said Randall.

"Hey, I'll fuck anything that walks, but you're my man through thick and thin," assured Eddie. He may have been Eddie's man, but, sure enough, some law firms dropped him.

Although his canvas bag was no longer bulging, he kept on serving what papers he had, pretending as best he could that everything was still okay. And he was good at pretending like that. If things were crashing down around him he could convince himself it wasn't really happening, even though he knew it *was* happening. It didn't make sense, he knew that: It was his secret paradox. One thing he couldn't escape was the Sexual Offender Registry, a grim reality if ever there was one. Before he walked out of the courtroom that day, the clerk handed him a phone number and said he had three days to register. It took him all three days to make the call, the stigma getting in the way. Finally, when he did make the call, it was mundane, like making an appointment for a tire rotation.

A drab office on the fifth floor of the courts building. He walked up to the window, the clerk asked him why was he here. A tough one right off the bat. Why *was* he here? To get branded a sex offender, to pick up his shackles and manacles, to join the rest of the merry crew on the good ship *Depravity*. I'm here to register, he told her. Sign in, she told him, visibly bored, and an officer would be with him shortly. There were two guys in the waiting room, staring at the floor. He took a seat as far from them as possible. Minutes ticked by, the others were called. At last a short, dark-complected guy came out and acknowledged him. "I'm Paul Lauria," he said, the hint of a twinkle in his eye, "I'll be your contact officer." He led Randall down a hallway to a small room with only a table and two chairs. Bare walls, fluorescent light, a manila folder on the table. His file. They sat facing each other two feet distant. Lauria took a pen from his shirt pocket, loosened his tie, and began.

"I don't know what happened in that Northside alley that morning. You could've simply been in the wrong place at the wrong time. Bad luck happens. I'm not here to judge, I'm here to make sure you know the law and comply with that law." This put Randall at ease, the guy treating him like a person. Lauria began to write on a steno pad as he continued. "Because your crime was sexual in nature, involving a person under the age of eighteen, you are required to register as a sex offender and this registry is public record—anyone may go online and view it. That's how it is. And before you leave today, I will take your picture, take your fingerprints, and swab the inside of your cheek to get a DNA sample. These identifiers will be forwarded to the Highway Patrol, which maintains the database. That's how it is. In addition, you are required to report to this office every ninety days and sometime during the month of your birthday, and, coincidentally, you share the same birthday as me. Cancer, the crab. Tenacious, stubborn. You too? Well, continuing on here, you will also inform this office any time you change employment, anytime you change your address, anytime you change your underwear."

"What!"

"Kidding!" said Paul Lauria, laughing lightly. "Relax, but we do need you to report change of address, change of employment, change of the vehicle you drive. That's how it is. You will not be in the presence of a minor unless there is another adult around. And by around, I mean within view. This does not apply to your own children—I see you have two—but to children that are not your own. Their friends, for instance. That happens, there should be a big red flashing danger sign in your head, yes? Lastly, you may not live within a thousand feet of a school or daycare. Do you presently live near one of those?"

No, Randall said, he did not. "Well, that's the nuts and bolts of it," said Paul Lauria. "Now, we'll talk in general and I'll answer any of your questions no matter how frivolous."

An hour later Randall left the building. He got into his Subaru and drove aimlessly for a while, zig-zagging through city streets, alone with his thoughts, dour and self-pitying. He felt like one of those cartoon characters that walks around with a black cloud over his head, this thing just getting worse and worse. He found himself coming up on a residence where he had a summons to serve, two days left on the paper, but he kept right on going. What did it matter? He switched on the radio, catching the snippet of a commercial: "Call now to help give sewing machine training to widows in Asia ..." Then he decided some music might help. He fumbled through the CDs in their case beside him on the passenger seat. Cowboy Mouth? Too exuberant. Pat Metheny? Nah, more for the highway, windows closed. How about this one with a demon-snake on the cover? Steve Earle. Yeah, songs about guys getting in trouble, guys going to jail. He put in the CD, cranked it up and drove on, feeling solidarity with Steve Earle and the hard luck guys he sang about.

Grudgingly Randall became accustomed to his situation—what other choice did he have? Laurice, however, was not the understanding wife she could have been, and over time her displeasure with his misfortune became more transparent. Always attuned to the feelings of others, it was she who sensed the disapproving looks of neighbors who had learned of Randall's offense. It was she who felt the prickly unease of their letter carrier, a once jocular fellow who no longer made chit-chat in her presence but seemed to hasten away as fast as he could. Even the greaser hunk at the Jiffy Lube no longer was all over her when she brought her Lexus in for an oil change. Real or imagined, she took it all in and it was tearing her up. She took it out on Randall, chiding him for all sorts of peccadilloes. Not putting away all the dishes, parking his car too close to hers, premature ejaculation—they were still doing it, but Laurice was having second thoughts. The sex offender's wife, that was not an attractive appellation. She deserved better.

To make things even worse, a letter appeared in their mailbox one day, about two months into his probation. Neat, concise handwriting on the envelope addressed the letter to Randall Koch with the word Personal underlined twice. Laurice opened it without hesitation. "Dear Mr. Pervert," it read. "We know what you did and we are watching you. One false move with any of the neighborhood children, even so much as a pat on the head, and you are back in jail for good this time. P.S. We always thought there was something strange about you. Normal people don't mow their lawn on a Sunday morning. We also notice that your eyes are set close together. You might check the abnormal psychology texts to see what this means!" Laurice stood there, a cascade of emotions washing over her. Who was this guy she married? Why had she not seen his true nature before now? What would he do next to bring shame upon their family? And it was true, she had known it all along, his eyes were set close together.

When he came home that afternoon, she had the letter laying open on the kitchen table. "How was your day?" she asked rather coldly. Actually, she didn't give a rat's ass how his day had gone. She'd been stewing over this thing and was at the boiling point. He replied that he had served two subpoenas and four summonses by noon and then put in two hours serving lunches to the homeless at St. Patrick's Center, working to fulfill his community service commitment.

"Those people can eat," he told her. "Lots of them came back for seconds, and some for thirds! They had turnips as the vegetable. Or maybe it's a tuber. Are tubers vegetables? Why don't we ever have turnips, honey?"

"Shut up, will you?" She motioned to the letter. "That came for you today. Read it."

He read it at a glance and dropped it back on the table as if it were afire. "That's just plain mean," he said. "Do you think it's the Engels or the Barlows?"

"What does it matter who's behind it?" she shrilled. "What matters is that now we—your family—are involved in your problem. *We* have to suffer, *we* have to endure ostracism, all because you can't keep your dick in your pants!"

Randall got a hurt look on his face. "Aw, honey, settle down. Don't let the mean-spirited actions of busybodies get to you. Please? This thing will blow over in time and everything will be back to normal." He started moving toward her, conciliatory, intending to put his arm around her. She would have none of it.

"Don't honey me," she said, slipping out of reach.

The Koch household had the ambiance of a rendering plant. Laurice became aloof around Randall and this caused resentment which, in turn, fueled the estrangement. Max and Felicia, knowing their father was going through a terrible time, tried to be understanding, but every time a classmate would throw out a taunt— "Hey, Max, you seen your dad's wiener lately?"—Randall, ever the good father, would lose that much more esteem. When he took Felicia to Girl Scouts, the other parents shooed their children away from him as if he were some cankerous leper. This took its toll on Randall as well, and he found himself knocking off work early, mid-afternoon, and holing up in various bars around the city. He'd come home after six, three sheets to the wind, eat whatever was left of dinner, mutter a few half-intelligible sentences, and hit the sheets early, often before sunset, lapsing into stupefied slumber.

One morning, after the kids left for school and Laurice had gone on some errand, he went to his office and turned on his computer. He'd heard of Family Watchdog, a website that listed sex offenders, posted their pictures, their addresses, and what they'd done. It was all legal, the creators of Family Watchdog couldn't be sued for invasion of privacy. As a sex offender, you had no privacy. Unlike counterfeiters, batterers, manslaughterers, and common thieves, your particular sex crime was out there for anyone to see. It was the modern version of the Scarlet Letter.

He got to the home page. Find Offenders by Location or by Name. He chose location and typed in his own zip code. A graphic suddenly materialized, the Registered Offenders Map, with little colored squares showing where they lived or worked. The map included the surrounding zip codes but, boy, there were a lot of little colored squares, 801 all told. A red square meant that person had committed an offense against children; a yellow square, rape; a blue square, sexual battery; and a green square, "other offense," whatever that might mean. He clicked on a red square. It took a second to load, and up popped a mugshot, name, and address. Rita Kessler looked to be in her fifties and lived only two blocks over. Not particularly attractive, looked like an IHOP waitress or a grocery store clerk, but hadn't he seen her at the PhilMart buying cigarettes and lottery tickets? What had she done? He clicked on convictions and got the answer: Statutory Sodomy 1st degree. "Probably serviced some hormone-crazed teenage boy," he whispered to himself, for he was alone. "He got off and she got caught." The conviction was in 1996. "Wow, fourteen years later and she's still doing the perp walk—virtually, online, but still."

Another red square quite near his own house. He clicked on that and a startling image appeared. White guy, shaved head, goatee, jug ears, malevolent black eyes, penetrating gaze. Sexual Abuse, his crime, but this one dating to 1987. What the hell? He clicked on one more red square from the vicinity. This produced the image of a light-skinned black guy, late twenties, shaved head, slight smile. Child Molestation 1st degree, dating to 2003. Guy looked like he was shit-faced when the mugshot was taken. There were more, lots more, mostly guys with various charges that spurred the imagination: Indecent Liberties, Lewd Act with a Minor, Endangering the Welfare of a Child—hell, that could be something as blasé as driving around with your kid in the back seat unbuckled—Deviate Sexual Assault, Possession of Child Pornography, Obscene Performances, Rape, Stalking, and Being a Creepy Pervert in General.

Of course, he had to go there. Wasn't that why he was here, on this voyeuristic website? He took a breath and clicked on the little red square that was his residence. His own face materialized and he was surprised at how benign he looked, not at all scary like the others. "That's not a bad picture," he told himself. "You can tell this guy's alright. You could even invite him over to your kid's birthday party. He's not going to get out of line, do anything lewd or lascivious. The poor schmuck. Look, he's got this silly smirk as if the whole thing were some sort of ridiculous joke." At the bottom of the screen he saw his name and address displayed, along with the charge Sexual Misconduct With a Child.

"Yeah, some child," muttered Randall, conjuring the visage of the girl. "Give me a break, she's probably seen plenty of dicks in her day. Child, my ass—if it weren't for her." He'd had enough. He closed out Family Watchdog and traveled through cyberspace to a more pleasant pastime, namely Get 'Em Drunk And They'll Do Anything-dot-com, his current favorite porn site.

Time passed. There was caution in the house, a holding back of civility, a stifling of normal human emotion, Laurice showing more affection to Chachka, the family bow-wow, than to Randall. The kids begging off his suggestions of things they might do together. The neighbors still glowering in his direction, treating him like a pariah. There was a rumor going around that he had gone to the ER at Barnes-Jewish for something—some small animal, possibly a hamster or a gerbil—that had to be extricated from the badlands of his colon.

There were days, in fact, when Randall sensed it was all hanging by the merest thread. He had completed his community service. Thrice he had dutifully reported to Paul Lauria, who stressed avoiding situations that could get him in trouble. He was no longer trying to pretend this wasn't really happening; he was just trying, as Lauria stressed again and again, to keep his nose clean and get through this thing.

One day there was a knock at the door, a curious knock, someone tapping out the old ditty "Shave and a Haircut–Two Bits." Someone familiar. He opened the door and there stood Rabbi Rovinsky, all 285 pounds of him, beaming, arms outstretched, ready for a hug. "Randall, you mensch, you! I was on my way to a bris and I thought I'd stop to rattle your cage. It's been so long, you know? So, how are you? You look great, I'll say that."

But Randall was circumspect and declined to hug. He hadn't seen the ebullient Rovinsky for probably two years. This was no random visit, the guy had an agenda. "Hey, rabbi," he said, "good to see you, too. I'd invite you in, but I'm painting the rec room. Big mess right now."

"No, no, I'm just here for a minute. Listen, I want to extend an invitation to you to come to Temple." He wagged a fat finger like a metronome. "Don't say no, say you'll think about it. You quit coming and I never knew why, but in light of your recent troubles I firmly believe it's time for you to come back. We are a very welcoming group."

"My recent troubles?"

"It's no secret. You got caught with your schlong hanging out. It happens, and now you're in the penalty phase. You're questioning your role in society, you're anxious over the perception of your

image—tawdry, jaded … um, soiled, perhaps. You think life is unfair. You need the company of understanding people, of a faith community. You need a lift, brother."

Randall saw that Rovinsky would go away if he gave the right answer. "I'd like to come, rabbi. Let me find my yarmulke, get it dry-cleaned."

"Such a kidder, you! We hand out yarmulkes at the door, you know that. Take your pick, black or blacker—ha, ha! Seriously, four o' clock, Saturday. Be there and better yet, bring the family. Temple Rodef Shalom, Reformed Judaism at its best. And, as a special incentive, I've written a homily with you in mind. It's titled 'Why Me, God?' Come hear it, Randall, the words as balm for your wounds. Do that for yourself."

"I'll talk to Laurice. Maybe you're right, maybe it is time to come back."

"I'll see you there," said Rovinsky, gleaming.

Randall shut the door and went to the window, making sure the rabbi departed. "Why me, God?" He spoke the words to himself softly and chuckled. He was alone in the house and his supplication became bolder, louder. "Why me, God?" He began to cackle. "Why me, God?" Laughing uproariously now. "Why me? Why me?" Then, he composed himself and pretended that God was answering him. Mustering his best basso profundo, "Why you? Why you? Because, Randall, you are a fucking idiot—that's why!"

It was only a few hours later that the doorbell rang again. He was having dinner with Max and Felicia. Laurice had left that morning and not returned. "Whoever it is, they can come back," he said to the kids. "We're not having our nice dinner disturbed."

"It's just Ramen noodles," said Felicia. "I'll get it." And before Randall could say no, she'd left the table. She was back in a minute, saying, "It's for you. Some guy, looks nasty."

Of all the people Randall could imagine at his door, Ronald DeClue was the most improbable. DeClue, his rival in the process serving business, always going around behind his back, trying to wrest his hard-earned clients from him. Underhanded, mercenary, and so unkempt that he could fit right in with a band of mendicant monks. The guy was a real bummer.

"Hey, Randall," said DeClue, trying, and failing, to sound friendly. Instantly, Randall knew that DeClue was here to serve him—the summons sticking out of his coat pocket—but serve him with what? DeClue made a fawning gesture and remarked how he'd never thought he'd be serving a fellow process server, "and even one that I admire. But, you know, the more I thought about it, the more it dawned on me that it's actually a good thing. Because, hey, if it wasn't me, it'd be some other guy and he wouldn't be as nice. Here you go."

Randall took the papers, his eyes going directly to the upper left corner of the summons, to the style of the case: *Laurice Y. Koch v Randall F. Koch* – DISSOLUTION OF MARRIAGE W/ CHILDREN.

"Okay, well, mission accomplished," said DeClue, backing off the porch. "Got to go, got a Show Cause Order over in Lemay. These lawyers, man, they keep you running. It never ends, but you know how it is. Good luck with that."

Randall was engrossed in reading the complaint attached to the summons, contemplating the phrase "irretrievably broken." He hardly heard DeClue's goodbye. "Hey, Randall," DeClue called from halfway across the lawn, loud enough for the neighbors to hear. Randall looked up. "That thing about you flashing a whole busload of school kids? I don't buy it. And even if you did do it, you had your reasons, I'm sure."

Randall considered this speck of flyshit for a moment and said, "Ronald? Go away."

The next morning Randall received a call from Meredith Bakewell, Laurice's best friend and recent author, having written *Touchy-Feely: How To Flourish As A Warm, Caring Being*. Meredith was extremely cordial over the phone and believed she was doing a good deed by asking Randall to turn his world inside-out. "Now that you've been served and you know that the divorce is going through, Laurice feels it's best that you pack what you need and find another place," Meredith said, her voice dripping with empathy. "She's staying here for now. Of course, she'd like to come home, but she won't do that until you're out of the house. I know it's hard to leave everything you know and love, but these things, tragic as they are, happen. And when they do, we all must make sacrifices."

"What sacrifice is Laurice making? May I talk with her?"

"She doesn't want to talk right now, and she's not even here. She's so distraught that she's spending the day at the spa."

Randall, the dutiful, soon-to-be ex-husband, decided to go with the program and moved into the Archview Guest House on Watson Road. There he lived and worked out of a 12 by 16-foot room that smelled of dirty socks and had a shower with the water pressure of a leaky faucet. He was not one to overly fret over negative experiences. Sometimes, as mentioned, he would simply pretend that the bad thing wasn't happening to him and thus, anxiety would be kept at bay. Other times, and this was one of them, he would acknowledge the bad thing, but go directly to a fallback plan. In this case, the plan was forget Laurice, find an apartment, get a lawyer who'd see that he got his kids on weekends, and start dating again. He was thinking of getting a tattoo as well. He believed he would find an apartment in short order so he waited to call in his change of status to Paul Lauria. No sense in doing it twice.

One night, there was a knock on his door. He was awake watching TV, drinking scotch and bourbon from little airline bottles that he'd thought to take with him. He peered through the peephole and saw a girl standing outside. She knocked again. He turned the knob.

"Oh, hi!" she said, seeming surprised. "I wasn't sure if you were there."

"Oh, I'm here alright. Who are you?"

"I'm Janelle. I live three doors down, been here almost two weeks. I just thought I'd come say hi. It gets lonely around here."

"I'll bet it does," he agreed. "Nice of you to drop by. So where's the rest of the Welcome Wagon?"

"Huh?" she said, suddenly looking past him. "Hey, is that Conan on the TV? I love that show. Mind if I come in and watch it with you?"

Randall was no bumpkin. He suspected that this girl, wearing a lavender tank top and short shorts with paw prints on the behind and the words KEEP YOUR PAWS OFF, suspected that she might be playing him. She likely had some secret motive, robbery perhaps, or a boyfriend lurking nearby, ready to club him, take his wallet and car keys. Or, she might just be a nymphomaniac.

"What is that sparkly stuff on your chest?" he wondered.

She glanced down at her cleavage. "Oh, that's spray glitter. Do you like it?"

"You look pretty young to me," he said. "I don't want to get in trouble."

She laughed at this. "Yeah, I know. I still get carded for cigarettes, but I just turned twenty last week. It's up to you, of course. I mean, you seem like an interesting guy and I'm just looking to pass some time."

In his inebriated mind he recollected what Paul Lauria had told him, the thing about the flashing danger sign when faced with choices like this. And yes, the sign was flashing now—red, DANGER, red, DANGER, but then it turned yellow–CAUTION and, finally, green. He leaned out the doorway, looked up and down, checking to see if anyone was watching. "Okay, just for a little while," he told her.

He found a place within two days, a modest apartment on the second floor of a four-family flat in the Dutchtown neighborhood. There was a Hispanic market on the corner and a bar, Roy's Ratskeller, two blocks down. He wasted no time calling in to report his change of address. Paul Lauria wasn't available, so he left the information on his voice mail, mentioning the pending divorce and the sudden departure and saying call me if you have any questions. Then he went to work.

For the first time in months he had a full load, plenty of papers to serve in every direction. Some of the addresses were out-state—fifty-sixty-seventy miles away—and he relished those drives through the countryside, windows open, music playing, the smell of manure in the fields. He was starting to feel good about himself, starting to imagine life without a probation officer, without having to assess the potential risk of every social interaction. And to sweeten the pot, there was a woman in his life. Well, she didn't yet know that she was in his life, but he was about to make an overture. Donna Gianino was a single mom whose daughter was in his daughter's Girl Scout troop. Anytime they were together, a cookout or just standing in the parking lot watching the girls run amok after a meeting, they seemed to hit it off. She likely knew about his troubles, all the other Girl Scout moms did, and it didn't seem to matter with her. She was nice and pretty and smart; Randall thought he would give it a shot.

He drank four Budweisers and a vodka tonic to get up the nerve to dial her number, a number that was not listed but which he'd gotten by calling the phone company and providing his process server security access code, which was supposed to be for official business only. She picked up on the second ring. He took a breath. "Donna? Hey, it's Randall Koch from Girl Scouts. How are you?"

"Fine, Randall. What a surprise to hear from you. How did you get my number?"

"Oh, I saw it written on one of the activity sheets and it just stuck in my mind. I can't help it, I have a photographic memory like that."

"The mind is a camera, true. What can I do for you, Randall?"

"Well, I don't know if you've heard, but Laurice and I are no longer. I've moved out and live in the city. I'm starting a new life."

"If you're happy, then I'm happy for you," she said.

So far, so good, thought Randall, then he took the plunge. "So, I don't know that much about you, like whether you have a boyfriend, but if you *are* available I'd like to ask you out. Maybe a concert or a movie, what do you say?"

"That's a nice offer. I'll consider it."

"You're so easy to talk to and you have the greatest smile. And the Rice Krispies Treats that you bring to the meetings are dynamite! I thought, Well, give it a try. She might just say yes. And you did—well, at least you didn't say no."

She laughed lightly. "Slow down, Don Juan. I'm not used to so much flattery. There is a concert coming that I want to go to. Have you ever heard of The Pixies?"

Randall had not heard of The Pixies. "Yeah, they're great! Whenever that is, count me in. I could pick you up early and we could have snacks before the show. Get to know each other better."

There was a silence on her end. "Donna?" he said.

"I'm really disappointed that you took me for a cheap thrill," she said, cooly. "Disappointed and hurt. As if I would do something like that on a first date."

"What are you talking about?" he said, instantly regretting the irritable tone. Then he understood there had been a horrible misunderstanding. "Oh, you thought I said sex before the show. That's so funny! I meant to say appetizers. At a restaurant, you know?" But he finished his sentence talking to the dial tone.

He wasn't due to report for another three weeks, but Paul Lauria called him in early, like, "Get down here now." This isn't good, Randall told himself on the way downtown. He imagined himself being scolded for something like a little child. "And if there's one thing I'm really good at," he said sub-vocally, chuckling to himself, "it's being scolded." By the time he walked in the Sex Offender office his anxiety level was off the charts. Immediately after signing in, Paul Lauria came out to get him. Once in the interview room, Randall got an earful.

"You know, I was wrong about you," said Lauria, looking him straight in the eye. "What I mean is, there are two kinds of sex offenders. Those that made a mistake, who see the folly of their actions, and are highly motivated not to make that mistake again. They keep their nose clean and assimilate back into normal society. And then there are the repeaters, those that are doomed to commit sex crimes again and again, because no matter what consequences are dangled before them, they just can't help themselves. It may be five years down the road or it may be five months, opportunity presents itself and they go for it, like an alcoholic going for his drink." He shook his head sadly. "Thing is, I really thought you were someone who was in the first category."

"I *am* in that category," protested Randall. "I've been good."

"Oh really? Then why did we get a report from the County STD Clinic of a seventeen-year-old girl, diagnosed with gonorrhea, naming you as a sexual contact?"

"Was her name Janelle?"

"How many seventeen-year-olds have you been with?"

"Okay, alright. I'm not hiding anything here. It was consensual. She came to my room at the Archview Motel. I didn't seek her out. We watched TV, it was innocent—for a while. Anyway, she's twenty. I saw her driver's license." This last statement was a lie.

"That's right," said Lauria. "The Archview Motel. You were there a couple days, in transition to your present location. And did you report this temporary abode to this office?"

"I know I should have, but—"

"There are no buts," snapped Lauria, his face turning a shade of crimson. "You knew the rules, you signed off on them. There are no gray areas, no clause that says 'You don't have to report a new address if you don't entirely unpack.'"

He was quite exasperated, Randall could see that. "It won't happen again, I promise."

"That is such a feeble response," rejoined Lauria. "Do you understand what's happening here? Let me tell you what's happening: You're *making me* fuck you up. That's right, your little interlude with a minor and your negligence in reporting a change of address are causing me to have to report this to the prosecutor's office. Which means jail time, brother."

"I don't think I could handle that," said Randall.

"You know, you seem like an alright guy who's been a victim of circumstance. At least some of the things that have happened to you could be attributed to bad luck. And I could almost forgive these new transgressions—almost—if it weren't for this other thing, far more serious than the others."

"What is that? What now? What?"

"Ever hear of Angie's Tiny Tot Daycare?"

"No, should I have heard of it?"

"It's just down the street from you. Six doors down in fact, and well within the thousand-foot perimeter of your forbidden zone. This constitutes a flagrant violation of the primary condition of your probation, that you not live near a school or daycare."

"That's crazy," exclaimed Randall, eyes bugging out. "I checked the neighborhood for schools and daycares before I signed the lease. There was nothing like that. No sign of any daycare."

"She runs it out of her home. The sign is in the window. If you had been more observant of your surroundings you would have seen the moms and dads dropping off and picking up their kids."

"Oh, come on! I had no idea anything like that was nearby. I'll move out. Today."

"You'll move out alright, but it won't be to another apartment. Three strikes, you're out. You're looking at some prison time. Sorry."

Rabbi Rovinsky phoned just as Randall was boxing up the last of his things. "Hey there, it's me. Your rabbi for all occasions. How's it going?"

"Not very well," said Randall. "I'm due to report to prison tomorrow morning. The dread is overwhelming."

"Yeah, I heard. Tough break, that's for sure. Is it a local facility? I hope so, because then we can come visit, myself and any others that want to come along. We are a very welcoming group, you know."

"Unfortunately, it's a medium security prison in the northeast corner of the state. I was hoping for the Workhouse out on Hall

Street, nice view of the slums and all. But that's a short-term joint, mainly a holding facility for those awaiting trial."

"You'll be in with some hardened people. You'll need moral support. They let you use the phone? We can talk after you get settled in, get some good behavior under your belt. Put me on your visitor list. I enjoy a nice drive every so often. How are the kids taking this?"

"That's a question I don't feel like answering right now, thanks for asking."

"Fair enough. Say, what is your shirt size? The knitting club wants to know, they're making you a sweater."

"Rabbi, that is so nice of them to do that. Tell them I'm very grateful, really, but tell them to give it to someone else. You have to wear the clothes they give you, which I believe is an orange jumpsuit with Department of Corrections written on the back."

"Well then, we'll send you a prayer shawl. They won't confiscate that, I'll bet."

"Sounds like a plan, I'll be looking for it. Got to go now. You're the best, rabbi. Know what? I wish I had come to Temple like you asked. I was too wrapped up in my problems, and now look where I am."

"You'll get through it and be a better man for it. That's a promise."

Well, looky here, we got us some new meat," called a prisoner named Jenks as Randall made his debut in the exercise yard. A new prisoner was cause to galvanize the population; his mettle would be tested that first day and, often, his place in the pecking order would be established. There were scores of guys milling about, looking for any break in the monotony, and several of them walked over to inspect this new meat.

"Look at his hands, he ain't no tradesman," said a large white guy with Woody Woodpecker tattooed on his bicep. He spat on the ground. "What's your line of work, boy?"

For an instant Randall thought to pretend that this wasn't happening, but no; they ask you a question, they expect a reply. "I'm a bakery truck driver," he lied, thinking correctly that they probably hated process servers almost as much as they hated cops.

"*Was* a bakery truck driver," said a ferret-faced guy named Pito. "In here, until we give you a handle, you're just New Meat and we'll fuck with you any time we please. Ain't that right, Waco?"

The large white guy nodded affirmatively. "That's right, any time we please. We say 'Get us a sody,' you get us a sody. We say 'Lick our boots,' you lick our boots. So what's your name, New Meat?"

"Randall Koch."

"Coke? Why not Pepsi? What the fuck kinda name is that?" said Jenks, feeling as though he needed to contribute to the hazing.

"I'll tell you what kind of name it is," said a muscular black man stepping out of the semi-circle that had formed around Randall. He was Pliny The Elder Junior, a self-proclaimed prophet-philosopher that Randall would come to know all too well in the coming years. Pliny The Elder Junior walked up on Randall, so close that Randall could smell the sweet potatoes he'd had for lunch.

"I read the papers, I heard of you," said Pliny The Elder Junior, poking Randall in the sternum with his stout index finger. Randall kept his arms at his side, trying to hold his ground. He was expecting the blow anytime now. "You're that process server who likes to show his pecker around, especially to little girls. Do me a favor, take a few steps to your right."

Randall did as he was told. "You see there?" said Pliny The

Elder Junior, quite pleased with himself. "It walks like a chomo. And if it walks like a chomo and talks like a chomo, then it must be a chomo." The others laughed wickedly at this, but Randall just smiled. He had the advantage on them, because he already knew what that word meant.

TAMMY JOHNSON
PANHANDLER

ONE OF THE FEW THINGS TAMMY REMEMBERED HER FATHER TELLING HER when she was a little girl, before he left home one day and never came back, was how people are just people, all over the world. Same basic concerns of food and shelter. Same stresses over fear of loss of job, loss of loved ones, meteors striking the planet and so on. He had been in the Navy and seen lots of people in his travels, and that was the sum of his observations. A strapping Swede was essentially the same as a Pygmy Bushman, both plucked from the same roiling cauldron of humanity, just shaped and colored differently. Tammy, by now a cultural anthropologist of sorts, believed her father's theory, but with one addition: Yes, people were essentially the same—all a bunch of bozos.

This day in January she was freezing her tits off, panhandling on the 7th Street off-ramp, when a guy rolled down his window and called her over. Hey, tell me a joke that makes me laugh, I'll give you some money. Tammy thought for a minute, conjured something she heard in fourth grade: Why does the ocean roar? I don't know, answered the guy, liking this, why *does* the ocean roar? Tammy took her time responding because this one could really tickle your funny bone and she didn't want to give it away too easily. So come on, already, he pressed, growing impatient. Why does it roar? Tammy gave him a deadpan and said, You'd roar too if you had crabs on your bottom. And then she cracked up, showing her big teeth and gums, laughing so hard at this dumb joke. The guy just stared at her, incredulously. That's not a joke, he said, it's a riddle and it's not even funny. She said, If it's not funny then why the big grin on your puss? The guy checked himself in the rear-view and said, I'm not grinning, I'm grimacing. He tossed out a few coins, which fell to the pavement, and peeled out.

She stooped to pick up her earnings, two quarters and a nickel. Big whoop. At least he didn't try to proposition her like so many others. That was the problem with being a female beggar, all the guys think you're really a hooker. How many times had she been invited to have drinks at one of the many bars that seemed to be on every corner around here? Some guy leering out the window, cajoling, Come on, take a break, would ya? We'll have a drink and talk about your situation. Real nice and reassuring—yeah, right. Her rule was never get in a car with a strange man even if he looks clean and well-off and seems mannerly.

This rule somehow didn't work very well, for it wasn't that long ago when she reluctantly let a guy take her to his place, a tidy ranch house in Affton. And actually, he did make her a nice lunch; he did make her hot chocolate after she turned down the cocktail; they did gab and he did seem interested in her situation. And while he was showing her his wind-up toy collection, he politely asked her to insert peanuts into his rectum. Not the ballpark kind, he emphasized, not the ones with shells, as if that made a difference in her decision. Then she was scared, alone with him in this house that smelled of boiled cabbage, worried to death he'd lock her up in the basement, keep her as another amusement or something. But he wasn't that kind of freak. When she declined, he took her back to her spot near the highway, the ride in strained silence.

A woman driver gave her the nod. Tammy walked over. Here's a dollar, she said, studying Tammy up close now as the crumpled bill changed hands, exhorting Tammy not to spend it on anything foolish. Tammy cringed inwardly. *Did you have to say that?* But she kept it to herself, instead telling her benefactor, Oh, no, ma'am. It's going toward food, nutritious food. The woman drove off, feeling good about herself. Tammy knew she was lucky to have this plum spot just south of downtown, the cars and trucks getting off I-55, having to stop for the light and, unless they were turning right, there was about a four-minute wait for the green. Plenty of time for interaction, be it chit-chat or eye contact, which could, and often did, lead to raking in the coin.

She inherited this spot from Stumpy Joe, another homeless person who did well flashing his hand-lettered cardboard sign with his left hand, making sure that the sleeve of his amputated right arm was pinned up and visible to passing motorists. The sign read DISABLED VIETNAM VET PLEASE HELP! Stumpy Joe took a shine to Tammy and made her his understudy. Stumpy Joe's sagest advice: Look needy and always have your hand out. One day after work, over beers at Phelan's, he confided that he had lost his arm only a few years back in an industrial accident—"You don't take a dare with a hydraulic punch"—and that he'd never even set foot inside a barracks. He told her that it was okay for panhandlers to fabricate a sob story if they didn't have a good enough one of their own.

"Fact, it's obligatory," he insisted, his tired blue eyes meeting hers, "because people need their heartstrings tugged. People are burdened with guilt over any number of things and charity is the balm that soothes a troubled soul. We, the ragtag society of beggars and bullshit artists, exist to relieve them of their guilt. Besides, we're carrying on a noble tradition." And by way of illustration, mournfully, plaintively, he cried, "Alms for the poor! Alms for the poor!" prompting a guy on his way to the toilet to drop a dollar on their table. By turns philosophical, theatrical, brilliant, Stumpy Joe was all of that; the guy could have been the president of IBM, he just didn't want to be. By the fourth beer, she was spinning from hearing the details of his checkered life when he up and said, "Well, I'll be off now. I'm heading to Florida, retiring from the panhandling racket. I'm going to take up marlin fishing."

"Just like that?"

"Just like that," he affirmed. "You can have my spot. Never take it for granted, you'll make fifty bucks on a good day. Now give me a kiss goodbye."

She gave him a kiss and wished she hadn't, the halitosis nearly making her retch. That, and the fact he'd casually mentioned earlier how he suspected he had tuberculosis. But truly it was a small price for all Stumpy Joe had done for her, including getting her in the St. Benedict Joseph Labre Shelter over on 9th Street. That was another stroke of luck, finding that. For one thing, they allowed women, putting them up in their own separate area, apart from the gang of vagrant men—unkempt, unshaven, always scratching something, guys who'd probably sneak into your cot in the middle of the night if they could. Stumpy Joe was one of those men, always saying how he'd "jump her bones" if she'd give him a chance. Truth was, she didn't think of herself as sexy or even having the means to arouse a man, so she never took him seriously. Still, she cared for him in a kind of maternal way and it would be a long day without having him around.

She watched him walk out of the bar, swiping a couple bills, unattended tips, from a tabletop on the way to the door. She settled back in her chair, told the waitress just a water this time, and took stock of herself. Once she had a job, a home, friends, led an ordinary work-a-day life. How did it come to this? There was nothing

specific she could point to and say, Well, if only that hadn't happened. No, it was a series of misfortunes beginning with the lay-off last summer. CitiGroup—even the thought of the place made her want to puke—is a major financial company out in Ellisville, something like two-thousand worker bees sitting in cubicles, half-comatose, staring at computer monitors, entering data, keystroking hour after hour, day after day. Definitely a soulless outfit. Strict time limits on bathroom breaks, that sort of nonsense, but it paid the bills. She did that for just two years until they downsized and she got the ax. Laid off by email. She went on the dole for a while, looking for work, at first casually, being somewhat picky. But as time went on and her savings dwindled, she grew more desperate and willing to accept almost any kind of work. There were odd jobs with a temp service, delivering the new phone books, giving out sample packets of antacid to shoppers in the mall. But they didn't last, and before long she was back to pinching pennies and worrying about her welfare. Then, she couldn't pay the full rent on her apartment. The landlord, a corporation, was not sympathetic, the woman in the leasing office nixing her proposal, telling her they don't do week-to-week leases.

She had to leave her apartment in the suburbs and move in with a friend, Iris, who lived in the city. "Just temporarily," she told Tammy, "I'm really not a roommate person." She found work finally at a car wash, the kind where a gaggle of people wash and wax and detail your car, but it turned out she was allergic to one of the soaps they used and she had to quit. Meanwhile, Iris was growing intolerant of Tammy, said she needed her space back, even though Tammy had pitched most of her stuff in the move and didn't take up much space at all, living there on the sofa. Tammy was down to thirty-four dollars and in dread of the future, taken to chewing her fingers much of the time. She began to wander the neighborhoods around the Southside. She kept to the alleys and found the

Dumpsters fascinating, seeing that people threw away some pretty good stuff. She found herself foraging for rummage; it was something to do.

It was mid-September when she finally got the boot, Iris telling Tammy it was for her own good and besides, it didn't look right to the neighbors, two single women living together. At least she still had Tillie, her Chevy Cavalier, beat up as it was, the tank all but empty, the plates and insurance both expired. She took her last few bucks, bought a couple gallons, and drove to a spot at the end of a desolate street in a questionable neighborhood, parked it, and settled in to her new digs. By day she would roam the alleys, do a little Dumpster diving, grab some free hors d'oeuvres at the supermarkets until they caught on, clean up at gas stations, and hang out at the libraries where she could use the bathroom.

She lived out of her car for two months and it wasn't so bad except for the time teenagers came while she was away and stuffed a dead possum into the undercarriage. She realized right off something smelled awful, but it took a couple days to find the rotting carcass and, by then, the stink was living in the car with her and she had to leave the windows open permanently. To avoid even worse pranks, Tammy cranked up the Cavalier and, running on fumes, relocated to another neighborhood, slightly more upscale and definitely more cheerful. After only a week there, concerned neighbors had called the police. The police, in turn, called the health department. One morning early, while she was clipping her toenails, a guy came by and said she was in violation of several health codes including the lack of a waste disposal unit. "Where's your toilet?" he asked, dubiously. She showed him the wide-mouth pickle jar, half-filled with a yellow-brown liquid that certainly didn't look like brine. He said that wouldn't do and wrote her up liberally. When he said he'd be back, she knew she had to move again. She tried to make it to the pumps a few blocks away, but old Tillie pooped out halfway there, in the street. She pushed it close to the curb, left it at a crazy angle, and set out to find a gas can. When she returned four hours later, carrying a little red plastic container holding eighty-three cents of fuel, her car had been towed with all her stuff inside.

If Tammy had been worried sick about being on the verge of homelessness with winter coming on, she was actually relieved when it finally happened. Now that she'd hit rock bottom, there was nowhere to go but up, theoretically. During her tribulations, she'd been thinking of the words to that song, Janis Joplin singing in that cigarettes-and-whiskey voice, "Freedom's just another word for nothin' left to lose." Well, now, at last, she was as free as they come. The question was, could she enjoy it while shivering through the night under a viaduct?

She migrated to Soulard, hearing that there were shelters there and various charities that offered services to the homeless. There she found Stumpy Joe and the ensemble of misfits that would become her pals—well, as long as there was something in it for them. St. Labre, with its kitchen and makeshift dormitories in the basement of a nineteenth century Catholic church, became home and, actually, it felt right to Tammy. There was a catch, of course: Your stay was limited. At the end of three months, even if you had nowhere to go, you had to leave and not return until another three months had passed. Sure, you could go to the Harbor Light Mission run by the Salvation Army, or Rev. Larry Rice's New Life Evangelistic Center, but they weren't near as nice as St. Labre. And besides, the caliber of clients, as the residents were called—didn't lawyers and stock brokers have clients?—the caliber of clients in those places was sketchy to say the least. Drug dealing at the dinner table, head lice, schizophrenia, and lord-knows-what-else in the bunk next to you, fights breaking out, nose-picking. She'd heard stories. She got into St. Labre in mid-December, just in time to fend off Old Man Winter.

The other catch, and it was a doozie, you had to disappear by day. Mornings, they all ate together—a decent breakfast, your choice of cereal, eggs, bacon, oranges or apples, cinnamon buns, and coffee—and then it was out the door by six and don't come back until check-in twelve hours later. Dinner and a cot were there for you but you had better not be late, because the food stopped being served at six-thirty and the big heavy-duty doors to the shelter closed at seven-thirty and no amount of pounding and yelling would open them. It was kind of like having to live with really strict parents.

What you did during those twelve hours was your business. Those first days she wandered Soulard with its stately churches and red brick houses, taking in the sights like a tourist would. On the third day, on a whim, she took a cardboard box from a Dumpster behind Soulard Market, tore off a flap, and with a Sharpie borrowed from a produce vendor she wrote: DOWN ON LUCK - ANYTHING WILL HELP. She did not put GOD BLESS like other panhandlers, some of whom also brandished those little green New Testaments, the ones they give out at the shelters—what a bunch of hooey that was. And when she finished with her sign, she went to the most trafficked corner in Soulard and became a beggar.

They knew at the shelter that she panhandled during the day and they tried to discourage her, saying things like "Some day you're gonna get into a situation you can't get out of," or "You're making yourself really vulnerable, standing alone out there. Some serial killer drive by looking for his next victim—that's you." One of the workers at the shelter, Reggie, gave her a police whistle, told her to blow it with all her might if something went down.

But Tammy was hooked on panhandling, freeloading, mooching, whatever you wanted to call it. For one thing, it was interesting, putting yourself out there, a human scarecrow, an object of attention, knowing anything might happen. Then too, she had the sort of temperament that did not get bored standing in one spot for hours at a time, nor did she get terribly frustrated when people ignored her. Sometimes the anthropologist in her came out and she saw herself as a kind of modern-day Margaret Mead, studying these drivers, potential donors, as if they were members of some primitive tribe. In fact, she started making notes almost from the beginning, jotting down musings and observations in a four-by-six notebook she carried. Her first entry read: "If someone gives you even a dime they feel they have to say something about your situation, and people say some dumb things."

Case in point. Not even an hour ago, a white guy, face like a jack-o-lantern, driving a late-model Continental, front bumper about to fall off, called her over. "Just yesterday I gave some money to Robert," he told her. "He's over on the Gasconade exit."

"I don't know him," she said, wondering why was he telling her this.

"Tall guy, long brown beard, wears a Cardinals cap? Carries a sign, says, 'Homeless, Not Clueless.'"

"We don't know each other," she stated emphatically. "We just keep to ourselves and try to get through the day. You start socializing with some of these people, next thing you know you're in trouble."

"Yeah, right, don't blame you. Trouble follow you 'round like a dark cloud if you let it." He handed her a shiny gold-colored coin. "That's a Sacagawea dollar, you know. She was a Shoshone woman who helped Lewis and Clark get to the West Coast."

"Like a travel agent?" She was funning him now.

"Yeah, something like that," he laughed, and drove on.

Forty-seven more vehicles came to a halt near where she stood, waiting for the light—yes, she counted cars, it was something to do—and the forty-eighth gave her a friendly toot. She walked up to the driver's window, saw a prim-looking guy in a tweed jacket.

"Where's your family?" he asked right off the bat. "Ain't you got no one to help you out?"

"My family's scattered all over the country, not that it's any business of yours." She could be brassy when she wanted.

"My family is eight-thousand strong," said the man. "You ever hear of Rising Son Church?"

"Where is it?"

"Festus, just down the Interstate."

"Nah, I don't get down that way. No car."

"I could take you there this Sunday. Tell me where you stay, I'll be there. These folks'll take care of you, you'll see."

"I'm doin' alright on my own."

"We all need a boost. Have you accepted Jesus Christ as your personal savior?"

"Maybe, depends on what I need to be saved from." A car behind in the line began to honk, the light had turned.

He handed her some change. She looked at it. The honking amplified, drivers incensed that they might lose their green.

"Now promise you won't buy any drugs with this money, okay?"

"I don't do drugs," she said, "but I do know you can't get much for sixty cents."

Then there were the overheard comments, offhand dialogue coming from the idling cars, the weather decent enough to have the windows open. Idiots, they talked about her as if she couldn't hear them. Each remark, cutting or otherwise, she wrote down in her notebook.

"Mommy, is that lady a hobo?"

"Look a that, she probly makes a hunderd bucks a day just standin' out here. I'm gonna get me a sign and try it. Hell, I can look as pitiful as the next guy."

"She's a hooker, betcha—looks like a crack whore, don't she? That homeless act is just to fool the cops. Wonder how many tricks a day she does?"

As a matter of fact, standing out here in plain view, a woman alone, that was an open invitation to being solicited. Already, in just a few weeks, she'd been propositioned by gold-toothed black guys, snaggle-toothed white guys, old coots, teenagers, greasers, drunks, truckers, mailmen, various women, pimps who wanted to put her to work, lunatics, head-bangers, sad sacks, and a doctor in a lab coat with a stethoscope around his neck who offered to give her a "thorough examination." She turned them all down with a smile and a pat response: "No, I don't do that, but thanks for asking."

One day in late January, bitter cold with a stiff wind, her resolve softened. A guy about forty, in a Dodge Ram, big toolbox bolted to the truck bed, probably in the trades, stopped at the light, opened his window. "It's too cold to be out here," he said, looking her up and down. "I thought you white girls had more sense. What'd you do, lose a bet? That's it, right? You lost a bet."

"Ah, it ain't so bad once you get used to it." Truth was she was on the verge of frostbite. Fingers, toes.

"Well, look here," he said, big grin, "maybe we can help each other out." He showed her two twenties. "I could really use a knobjob, that is, if you're up to it."

She moved a step closer to the cab, put her hand on the open window. "Nah, I can't see puttin' a guy's thing in my mouth. It might give me indigestion. Besides, I'm a vegetarian."

He laughed and it was genuine, gleeful, and that served to endear him to her. He took away one of the twenties. "Okay, then how about a little hand action?"

Hmm, she hadn't been with a guy for a long time, and never with a black guy. Plus, twenty bucks was what she made on a good day and this day she wasn't even going to hit five.

"What's your name?" she asked.

"Tom," he said.

"Well, Tom, alright. But I'm warning you, my hands are cold."

Just this once she told herself, and when she climbed into the pickup he already had it out.

It kept her up that night, lying in her cot thinking of what'd happened. The main thing was the size of it. Honkin' big, like a summer sausage and firm as a Louisville Slugger. He'd driven to a nearby alley behind the MotoMart, parked in the loading dock of an old warehouse, a hand-painted sign there on a brick wall NO DUMMING, which they'd both chuckled over. She started out, didn't feel a bit shy, surprisingly, and she took her time, wanting it to last as long as he did. Hunkered down out of sight, she played with it, a kid with a new toy, stroked it this way and that, base to head, stopping every now and then when she thought the sap was rising too fast, and then went back to it, teasing it, throttling it, tracing the path of the veins popping out, almost forgetting he was connected to it until she heard him moan and groan, saying, "I'm there." And when he came, he laughed, the stuff just spurting out all over, his pants, her coat sleeve, even got some on the dash, and him laughing *A-hah! A-hah! A-hah!* like he'd just heard the funniest joke. Life was strange, that was for sure. So it was done, and she wasn't going to make a habit of it, but it was kind of interesting, handling that thing, and it made her think what a long time it'd been since she had a man of her own.

She tossed fitfully, tried lying on her left side then her right, the cot not wanting to conform. Belly-down was out of the question. She could only lie on her back, staring at the pukey, pea-green ceiling, with its brown water stains. At least she could stretch out, unlike in her car when she had to lie fetal-position, legs cramping the next day. Her mind wandered through a tangle of thoughts and finally came to rest on her immediate condition. *Alright, okay, I am grateful for this cot, this place, as crazy as it sometimes gets. It's fine for now, but it can't last—you know that. Where do I go from here? You got any long range plan, or are you just gonna turn any way the wind blows?* At last, she got up, grabbed her pack and shuffled to the lavatory. She found a clean stall, made herself comfortable, and in the flickering fluorescent light, she got out her notebook and pencil. At the top of a clean page, she began to write.

THINGS I GOT GOING FOR ME:

1. not too horrable in appearence
2. decent figure
3. clean my plate pretty well
4. law abiding for the most part
5. can multiply numbers in my head
6. never had no social dizease including head lyce or gonnaria
7. once petted a dolphin at Sea World
8. good with animals specially dogs
9. nice to old people and handycapped
10. can almost touch the tip of my tung to the tip of my nose

She thought about this last one, whether it really belonged on this list. So what if she could do that? It wasn't going to advance her station in life. It wasn't even good enough to get her in a circus sideshow. She made a decision to cross it out and in its place she wrote "even dispozishn, mostly good natured."

She studied her list for a while and decided that, yes, she did indeed have a lot going for her and guess what? She was going to have even more going for her, because starting tomorrow she was going to improve herself. How exactly, she didn't know, but she had a lot to give so why not spread it around? Okay then, that was settled. She took a piss and went to bed.

The next day she was up-and-at-em, folded her bedding and placed it on the shelf, hit the head, wolfed down her breakfast, and was out the door even before the early birds. It was a pretty morning in February, cold and clear. She began to walk briskly, swinging her arms, building momentum, feeling electric in the moment. At one point, she stopped to talk to a squirrel in a tree. "Boy, I wish I had me a bushy tail like yours, I'd be switchin' it all day long. Feelin' good today, yessir, feelin' fine!"

She was heading for the off-ramp, but on a whim she thought to change her sign. Behind the MotoMart she found a cardboard box and ripped off the flap. By now, she had her own Sharpie and she wrote BE HERE NOW, which was the title of a book that she'd once seen at someone's house. She'd always liked that message, saying so much in just three little words. Now she was going to broadcast it to passing motorists, see how that would fly. Well, it really flipped people out. She appeared to be panhandling, but her sign said otherwise. She wasn't asking for anything. She was telling, but what exactly did it mean? Was she a prophetess? A roadside oracle? People were practically throwing money at her and by eleven-thirty she'd collected thirty-two bucks, a Canadian looney, some slugs, a flattened penny with the Our Father in tiny print stamped on one side, a yo-yo without a string, an overripe banana, and a music box that played "Brahm's Lullaby."

This was the best score to date and to celebrate she went straight to Rally's, walked up to the window and got a Mushroom Swiss Double-Stack and an order of onion rings. Then she walked another block down Broadway to Stadium Liquors and bought a 24-ounce Busch from the guy behind the counter, a guy she'd seen around, known as Blue. This liquor store was unique because you could buy one beer and drink it right there at the counter, gab, joke around with whoever happened to be there or just watch TV on the far wall. It wasn't a bar and she guessed it wasn't legal to be drinking in there like it was a bar, but it happened. A little party it was, different characters throughout the day, and if the owners didn't care, why should she?

She stayed for a while, that first beer tasting so good that she had another and another, her and Blue yukking it up, watching some cowboy movie on TV, rooting for the bad guys, swapping stories about growing up in the sticks, he in the tapped-out mining town of Number Nine, Illinois, and she in Clover Blossom, Missouri—"a fine place if you like cows and Southern Baptists." When Blue got off work at four, they grabbed a six-pack, walked to the Market, got some pretzels, and partied some more in the stall of a vendor who'd left for the day. Tammy was glowing; it was good to be in the company of someone nice and friendly, especially after feeling for so long that no one could be trusted. They drank and sang too loud and laughed a lot until the light began to wane and the Market Master appeared, telling them firmly, yet politely, it was time to leave.

"I wish every day could be this good," said Tammy.

"You just keep coming in to see me, you hear?"

"Long as I got legs," she said, grinning. "Did I tell you? I made a deal with myself that everyday things would get better and so far, so good."

"Yeah, every thing's gonna work out. You believe that and it'll happen."

She saw it in the corner of her eye—gangly, ribs poking out of its patchy, brown coat, distended belly, tail between its legs, cowering in uncertainty yet pleading with its eyes. It was only a pup, maybe four months old, a true Heinz 57, the only obvious trait being the black tongue of a Chow. That tongue was sticking out, panting, rib cage heaving. Tammy spoke to it, "You must've been running from something, dog-catcher maybe. C'mere you," she called. The dog stood there, sizing her up. "It's alright, I ain't gonna hurt you. I see you got no collar, you're on your own just like me."

The dog cocked its head as if trying to catch her words, and Tammy jumped on that. "You hungry? Look here, I got some Doritos. You like Doritos? They're crunchy and just a little spicy." She held out the orange-red chips and the dog jumped back a foot. "Oh," she said, "you're not used to any kindness. I see. Well, how's about I just sprinkle these on the ground and then you come get it when you're ready?"

She did that and went back to her roadside solicitations, keeping watch on the dog, pretending she didn't really care if it stayed or left, putting more chips on the ground and when those were gone she put down some raisins. The dog inched closer and closer and, after eating all the little snacks she had stashed in her coat pockets, it felt comfortable enough that she was able to stroke its neck and talk to it like a confidant. "You wanna team up?" she asked. "Maybe I'll do better with a pretty pooch like you, people'll see I'm not just in it for myself. I got a dependent, another mouth to feed. It could work. I'm willing to try. All you gotta do is stand by me and look cute."

The dog wagged its tail ever so slightly. "Good, it's a deal then.

Now we introduce ourselves. I'm Tammy, Tammy Johnson, and you are … hmm, I think I'll call you Ruby after my mom."

That morning, on yet another whim, she'd made a new sign which read WILL WORK FOR TAMPONS. However, this one wasn't doing much for her cause. After she got a few more bucks, she walked to the liquor store, Ruby trailing ten feet behind. It was a cold day and she wanted to get a half-pint of peach schnapps. It was something that Blue turned her onto, a sweet liquor with a nice kick, and it was just a few bucks. They walked in and instead of Blue behind the counter, there stood a cigar-chomping, old white guy, nose like a purple pickle and disdain in his eyes. The old guy eyed them up and down; he'd seen every variety of person in his day, and he made a snap judgment about Tammy and Ruby.

"What you want?" he asked, ice-cold.

"Is Blue around?"

"No, he ain't," snapped the old man.

Come to think of it, she hadn't seen Blue for a week. She thought to ask him to elaborate, because she was suddenly dread-worried that Blue might've got fired or got hurt somehow, but the guy's demeanor was so bristly, she decided to leave it be.

He looked down at the dog. "We don't tolerate no fleabags in here."

"*Grrrrrr*," snarled Ruby.

He grabbed a pipe from under the counter, threatening to hurt her, saying, "Get that cur outta here and don't come back anytime soon."

They left, walking down Broadway toward the Market. It was Friday afternoon and the place would be bustling. On the main entrance to the Market, along the east side, there was a big band-stand, concrete floor with a wooden canopy. It was a gathering place for street people and citizens alike, anyone, really, in need of a place to simply pass the time. There were milk crates to sit on and smokes to be had. Often there was live music, crude but spirited, someone playing a mouth harp with a couple bad notes or banging on an empty pail with a stick, hoping for some pocket change. Tammy didn't frequent the place too much, not wanting to socialize, but today she was drawn to it. Maybe she wanted to show off Ruby.

Some of the guys milling about she knew from the shelter. "Nice dog," they said. "You better watch out, somebody'll steal that dog, roast it on a spit," they laughed. One guy had a spool of twine and he braided a collar for Ruby. Another guy she knew only as Slick tried to get Ruby to eat an apple. "You dope," chided the twineman, "dogs don't like fruit. They like meat and eggs and fries, but mainly meat."

Slick shot the guy a look and said to Tammy, "So how you gonna care for that dog, living in a shelter? You think they're gonna let it come in with you?" Tammy said she'd think of something.

That evening when it came time to check in, she put Ruby in her shirt, buttoned it to the top, and tucked it in beneath her bulky coat. She got past Big Al the doorman without consequence and made haste to the female dorm. It wasn't unusual to have three or four bunkmates, but this evening there was only one other, a skinny old hag with long, crazy hair who muttered to herself and never even acknowledged Tammy. She took Ruby to the lavatory, where she washed up and gave the dog a drink from cupped hands. "We gotta get you a regular dog dish," she told Ruby. Next, she went to her cot and settled in, Ruby snug against her bosom. After a while, Big Al came in, switched off the lights and said, "Goodnight, ladies." It was around eleven when Ruby began howling, Tammy frantically trying to calm her down. Too late. The lights came on and suddenly Big Al stood over her, asking what the Sam Hill was going on. The old hag sat bolt upright, her ragged nightie falling of her shoulder, presenting what looked like a deflated balloon.

"Oh, jeez!" said Big Al, averting his gaze. "Cover yourself up, Jessie, you're gonna give me nightmares."

The woman scowled in Tammy's direction. "Get that damn dog outta here," she croaked. "I can't sleep with a dog in here. What kinda hotel is this anyway?"

Big Al ignored her. He hunkered down and gave Ruby a friendly scratch behind the ears. "That's a pretty dog," he told Tammy, "but you can't have no dog in here. So, you've got to make a decision: Either you stay and the dog goes, or you both go. What'll it be?" She knew the answer, although she didn't like it.

They slept that night under a viaduct huddled together in a ratty old sleeping bag that was too thin for the weather, Tammy holding Ruby close and trying not to be too hard on herself, the words of her mother bubbling up: You do what's right and damn the consequences. At first light, she arose and stretched, rolled the sleeping bag tightly, put it in her pack, and headed to the Moto-Mart for coffee and donuts. At least it was a sunny day and from the radio at the store she heard a DJ say the temperature would reach a high of forty-three.

She took her place at the foot of the off-ramp; Ruby found her spot in the weeds nearby. With Ruby there, the time went faster. She found herself talking it up, percolating thoughts about anything and everything, Ruby being a good listener. "Maybe we'll make enough to sleep indoors tonight. There's a hotel downtown, twenty bucks a room, least that's what I heard. Yeah, I'll get a shower and we'll watch TV. What shows do you like? Give me a good sitcom. You ever see *The Dukes of Hazzard?* You'd like that, they got a basset hound named Flash. Gee, I hope there's a TV in the room." The morning went by and she did well in the handout department—sixteen bucks, a tangerine, a spatula from a dinette salesman, a pink superball, and a free pass to The Shrine Circus "Featuring The World Famous Lipizzaner Stallions."

They took a break and walked back to the MotoMart, Ruby parked outside near the door while Tammy went in and bought dollar hot dogs. For a buck it was a good deal, because the dog came with a nice soft bun along with all sorts of condiments including this runny cheese that came out of a dispenser when you pressed the button. They sat at the curb on the side of the building eating their lunch, when a couple of young kids came along. They stopped to look at the woman and her dog and then they began to point and talk. After a minute they approached, a bit shy yet determined to speak.

"Hey, lady," the short, pudgy one called, "is that your dog?"

Tammy looked to Ruby and said, "How 'bout it? Are you my dog or am I your human?"

"That dog got a name?"

"Yeah, Ruby."

"Oh. It looks just like our dog, Nubby. We stay right over there," he pointed to a cluster of gray high-rises off in the distance, "and Nubby ran off four days ago."

Tammy stiffened a little. She looked them both in the eye and said, "This can't be your dog, I've had her longer'n four days."

"Hi, Nubby!" called the other kid, slapping his pantleg for the dog to come. Tammy put her arm around Ruby, drew her close.

"Nubby, you want a biscuit?" asked the short, pudgy one and Ruby's ears pricked up.

"Lady, I think you got our dog. Nubby even has that same white paw on her front leg."

"I think you're mistaken," said Tammy, "and now I've got to go." The two kids stood there and watched them walk off, shaking their heads in disbelief.

When they got out of earshot, Tammy addressed Ruby. "Well, maybe you were their dog, but I can tell you weren't too happy 'bout it. You're mine now and I'll treat you a damn sight better than they ever would." They walked along, Tammy quiet for a minute, thinking of the ramifications. "Still, this isn't good, not good at all. What if they have big brothers, dads, uncles who might come around, try to take you from me? Look at my situation. I'm out there everyday, in the open. If they want you back bad enough, well, we're easy to find. So, given the turn of events, it pretty much seems like there's only one thing to do and that is we've got to go to another part of town." She bent down to scratch Ruby behind the ears—Ruby loved that, she knew—and she tilted the dog's head upward slightly so they made eye contact. "I hope you appreciate what I'm doing for you. My life was simple enough before you came along, just eat, sleep, panhandle." She chuckled at the thought of this. "Now it's getting so complicated, it's making my head spin!"

She and the dog walked south on Broadway going nowhere in particular. She had decided to take the day off. "Maybe we'll hitchhike down South," said Tammy. "See where we land. I've always been intrigued by Alabama—don't know why, really. I saw a picture of it once, they've got flowers everywhere. Hummingbirds, too. Anyway, we make it to Alabama, we won't have to worry about freezin' to death. Course, it'll be warm enough here in just a few weeks. We could tough it out, you know? That ain't so hard. Main thing is, we got to have an income stream, no matter how small. Hey! Can you do any tricks?"

But relocating was easier considered than done. For one thing, any other good panhandling spot would already be taken by someone and that someone wasn't likely to give it up without a fuss. Tammy could be assertive but she wasn't bellicose, wasn't going to come to blows over turf. Then, there was the convenience of Soulard Market where a buck would buy fresh fruit or veggies to last the day. Was she really so willing to give up her coveted situation over a dog? What was she—stupid? Didn't she want to improve her lot, get off the dole, get back to productive society, have her own shower again? This animal had done nothing but sandbag her. She stopped and said to Ruby, "Give me one good reason not to ditch you right now," and Ruby looked at Tammy, head tilted, one ear up and the other down, as if to say I can't believe you're even thinking something like that. Tammy busted a big grin and said, "Oh, it just kills me the way you cock your little head like that. Let's just stick together, see what tomorrow brings, and the next day, and the next. It'll get better, probably."

They came to an industrial Dumpster resting on the side of a mattress factory. It was filled with planks and lathe and torn-out electrical equipment, but there was also an Imo's Pizza box laying on top of it all. Tammy peeked inside. "Bingo! Leftovers, anyone for pepperoni?"

They kept walking while they ate the pizza, stale and brittle, taking in the sights, exploring the environment. Tammy didn't have to leash Ruby, who never strayed far from her side. They kept on Broadway until they got to Cherokee where they turned west and, coming down the hill toward the old Lemp Hall, she saw a guy who looked like a bulldog actually lead a bulldog into a corner tavern.

"Just like that, huh?" said Tammy to Ruby. "Don't see no sign 'Dogs welcome here,' but let's see for ourselves." They went in. It was early afternoon, a dozen faces looked up from their potato soup and meat loaf—special of the day—and then went back to eating. The guy with the bulldog was sitting at a table in the far corner near the jukebox. Tammy walked up to the bar. Bartender came over. Big guy, friendly, flat cap pushed down over his brow.

"What'll it be?"

"How much for a beer?"

"Right now, two-fifty a pint, any domestic. You wait a couple hours, it's a buck-fifty."

"That's a good deal alright, but can I just have a water for now?"

"You bet. How 'bout one for your dog, too?"

Beside her, on the counter of the bar, a video game was in play by an older guy, stocky, gray goatee, looked like Burl Ives. The game was displayed on a screen the shape and size of a computer monitor and what it did, it brought up the same two pictures, side by side, but at closer look one picture was different, certain details having been slightly altered. She watched him play a couple games. Apparently, you had only so much time to find the differences and this was done by touching the screen where something was amiss. Seeing this was a revelation to her, since up until now she had thought of a bar as a place where people just drank and blabbered and frittered away their time, not a place where you could challenge your mind with clever games.

She and Burl Ives struck up a conversation, idle chit-chat. Before long, she was talking to several guys at the bar and they started buying her drinks. First, she had a beer and then another and then she had a sloe gin fizz, something the guy with the red, plaid Elmer Fudd hunting cap on her left said she had to try. Her new pals seemed to be friends, not like they walked in together, but that they hung out there—a lot, probably. She explained she couldn't pay them back, not now anyway. They said it was alright, they'd all been there. They asked about Ruby, and one of them picked her up and put her on his lap so she could join the party. He held her for a while and then, inexplicably, he started to French kiss Ruby and Ruby responded by licking him profusely on the mouth.

"Haw!" said Elmer Fudd, "don't go thinkin' your pooch is smitten. Howie here just had himself a cheeseburger."

Still, Howie let Ruby lick his face, dog slobber on his chin, and he was talking to her in some weird affected accent he may have picked up from watching Maurice Chevalier movies. Or Pepe LePew cartoons.

"Ah, Rub-ee, *mon cheri*, come fly weez me to Pair-ee. We'll stroll ze *Champs-Élysées* all day and make ze beautiful love all night. Ah, Rub-ee, *Je t'aime! Je t'aime!*" The place roaring with laughter. Then Howie put Ruby on the bar. He poured some Guinness in an ashtray and Ruby lapped it eagerly. The sight of a dog drinking stout added to the merriment. What zany thing would happen next? Then Ruby burped or was it a dry heave? And then another, more pronounced, and someone said, "Uh–oh!" Ruby's chest began to heave and she was making a sound like a sump pump.

"That's enough, give her here," said Tammy, reaching for the dog, but it was a second too late for Ruby was now barfing. But instead of garden-variety dog barf, this barf was white and frothy and teeming with live, squirming tapeworms. They were on the bar, they were on Howie's shirt, they were on the floor. The raucous laughter had suddenly stopped and all the barflies looked on in horror. "Ewwww!" screamed Howie, sounding like a teenage girl. He flung his arm out violently several times and centrifugal force sent a sickening glop of tapeworms flying off his shirt sleeve. Now other guys had tapeworms on their clothes and in their drinks or food. Some began to retch and some began to wail and a few began to vomit.

The bartender was urging everyone to stay calm, the mess would be cleaned up. "We'll freak out if we like," said Burl Ives at the bar, turning his pint glass, checking for anything slimy, "but meantime you got tapeworms on your cap, brother."

Howie, now standing, picking tapeworms off his shirt, had thrown Ruby down in disgust and she splayed on the floor with a small yelp, no inkling of what she'd done to deserve this treatment. Tammy started yelling at Howie for hurting her dog and Howie was about to clock her for even having the dog, bringing it in here, when the bulldog suddenly slipped away from his upright, two-legged counterpart, skittered across the floor, got in between them and began lapping up tapeworm stew.

"Get outta here, the both of yas!" called the barkeep, and when Tammy merely acknowledged the command, nodding yes in his direction, he added, "*Now!*"

Tammy grabbed her pack from the barstool, picked up Ruby, and made for the door. "Don't worry," she told every pot-licking son of a bitch in the place who cared to listen, "we won't be back here any time soon!" She heard their applause as the door shut. They hurried down Cherokee, just trying to put the experience behind them. "How was I to know?" she asked in exasperation. "How long you had them nasty things? You're hardly more'n a pup and you got worms, a whole belly full. Reckon that's what happens when you're living on the streets eating garbage, huh? You don't think I got 'em, too, do you?" Ruby just kept trotting, nose straight ahead, like she didn't care. Tammy wagged her head in denial. "Well, we can't have that. No dog of mine's going to be sickly. We got to take action. We got to get you to a vet and get some worm pills, no way around it."

They spent the night in an unlocked car on Osage Street, Tammy in the back seat holding Ruby close but apprehensive about more tapeworms spilling out. It wasn't the coldest night on record, but cold enough that she didn't want to leave the small comfort of her sleeping bag in the middle of the night to go out and pee. Instead, she held it until morning and because of that hardly got any sleep.

The next day they hoofed it back to the 7ᵗʰ Street off-ramp and took up the position. Tammy was decidedly demonstrative that morning, hailing drivers with an enthusiasm never before equaled, smiling, waving, moving her cardboard sign up and down and sideways. By two o' clock, she'd collected a bus pass, a stogie in a wrapper that said IT'S A BOY!, a toy racecar, a brochure on the attractions of New Harmony, Indiana, a wooden coin that read GOOD FOR ONE FREE LOAD AT WISHY-WASHY LAUNDROMAT, and nineteen dollars and seventy-six cents. She walked off with Ruby at her side.

She'd heard about a place on the Southside, Dr. Hogan's Animal Medical Hospital and Gift Shop, where she could get some help for Ruby. "They're real nice people there, treat your dog like royalty," said a helpful motorist. It was a good hike, one that took an hour of walking through residential neighborhoods and industrial areas, down Gravois with its radiator shops and Bosnian markets, past Bevo Mill with its slowly-turning windmill, and finally to the place. They walked in. The clock said four-twenty, the receptionist looked up from her book. Tammy told her the problem. She handed Tammy a form and went back to her book.

In the space that asked for an address, she put the address of St. Labre. Same for the phone number. For Emergency Contact, she put down the name Blue. For phone number of her Emergency Contact, she wrote Stadium Liquors—look it up in the phone book. For insurance, she wrote Working On It. For method of payment, she put Cash On Hand. Besides the nineteen bucks and change, she already had seven dollars and forty-four cents. Surely that would be enough. She returned the form and sat back down.

There were no magazines, nothing to do but look at the heartworm posters on the walls.

Finally, a woman in a print smock came out to say that Dr. Hogan would see her now. The assistant led them to an exam room, where they waited some more. Like most dogs in a veterinary clinic, Ruby was nervous, sensing with her acute canine ESP the various procedures, from toenail clipping to euthanasia, that had occurred in this room and wanting none of it. The dog began to shiver and Tammy held her close. The door opened and in shuffled Dr. Hogan, a benevolent-looking old gent with a jowly face and longish silver hair to match a silver mustache that twirled at the ends. "Well, well, what have we here?" he wondered.

"My dog has worms," said Tammy.

"Oh? Is that anything like 'My Dog Has Fleas'? You know? Scales. On the guitar." He took in her blank expression and saw she didn't get it. "Okay, well, let's have a look. Put her on the table." Tammy placed Ruby on the examining table and the vet checked her all over.

"How long have you had this dog?" he asked.

"About a month," she lied, not knowing why.

"I only ask because she appears to have been living out in the elements. Her paws are cracked. Her teeth, some of them, are broken, and she's likely been eating garbage. That's how she got worms. Is she a stray then?"

"Well, yeah, but not anymore."

"I saw the form you filled out. I happen to know that address you put down, it's St. Labre Shelter. I take it that you're homeless, both you and your dog."

She raised an eyebrow in mild surprise. "I've got to hand it to you, doc, you're a good guesser, but I don't see what that has to do

with—"

"Do you know what it costs to cure a dog of worms?"

"I'm hoping twenty-seven dollars or less."

"You can't just give the dog medicine willy-nilly to clear up the infestation. You saw tapeworms, but there could also be round-worms, pinworms and more. We've got to get a stool sample and do a series of lab tests to see what Ruby's hosting. That alone runs about eighty dollars. Then, and only then, when we have a diagnosis, you add the cost of the medicine and the visit to this clinic—my time is money—it comes to around one-hundred and fifty dollars. Do you have one-hundred and fifty dollars to spend on this animal?" He patted Ruby for emphasis, just to show there was nothing personal in his delivery.

"Whoa! I didn't think it would be that steep. I'll get the money somehow."

"I could start treating Ruby today. I could take what you have as down payment and bill you for the rest, but we both know that money would be a long time coming, if ever. I've been through this a thousand times, picking up the cost of veterinary care for indi-gents like yourself—no offense, but it is a drain on my resources."

"You've done good deeds in the past then, why not just this once more?"

"Because it never stops. It's always 'just this once, promise.' The next person to ask for charity will be even more pitiable than you are."

She put her head down in such a way, cradling her skull with the palm of her right hand, that he could see she was greatly vexed. Grudgingly, he relented. "Okay," he said, "tell you what. I might be able to help you out, but you have to do something for me."

She looked at him in amazement. Appearances could be so

misleading. "Okay, but you have to wash it first," she said.

"What're you talking about? I'm saying that if you answer a simple question correctly, my services are pro bono—you know, free to the poor. Are you ready? What's the state fish of Hawaii?"

"Huh? What kind of question is that?"

"Just answer it correctly and you win." He was getting kind of excited.

"I don't know, a bass?"

"Acchh!" he sputtered. "What a ninny. It's the *humuhumunuku-nukuapuaa*, they call it the 'fish with a pig-like nose.'"

"How'm I supposed to know this?"

"Let's try again. What's the state capital of New Mexico?"

"Listen doc, I flunked geometry in seventh grade. These questions aren't for me. Can we try baseball or something?"

He laughed heartily. "I think you mean geography—oh, that's rich. The answer is no, we can't try something else. Now give it a shot. State capital of New Mexico."

"Denver."

"Oh, no. No, no, that won't do. It's Albuquerque. Albuquerque! Say it."

"I never heard of it."

"Say it, will you."

"Alber-kirkee. What the hell."

"I'll give you one more chance," he said rather sternly. "If you want the worms out of that dog you'll answer this one right."

"No pressure at all, huh? Go ahead, fire away."

"Which major city sits at the confluence of the Missouri and Mississippi Rivers?"

She ruminated on this, feeling like the answer was in her brain and if she thought hard enough it would somehow rise to the top.

"It's very close," he prompted. She could see he wanted her to get it right.

She thought some more, drumming her fingers on the counter. She knew the Mississippi ran through St. Louis, but where was the Missouri? Out West?

"It's got both a professional baseball team and a football team." He stood before her, pining to hear the the proper answer.

That did it. The answer flashed in her mind. "Oh! Kansas City!"

Dr. Hogan slumped, all the hope gone out of him, dejected. "I tried," he said, "at least I tried."

"You mean we don't get—"

"That's right, no free veterinary care for Ruby here. This is the price you pay for sloughing off in that seventh grade class, talking to your neighbor probably, instead of paying attention to the lesson at hand. It's tragic, that's what it is, a tragic case of squandered opportunity. No wonder you're out on the streets today, a rudderless vagabond, grasping at any straw of a chance." He pressed the intercom and called the assistant. "Cynthia, would you please escort the patient in room three back out. Thank you."

The room seemed larger, more cavernous than before. There were several people sitting with their pets, waiting to be called. Enveloped in a cloud of self-pity, she barely sensed their scrutiny. Still, it was a long walk through that waiting room. She had her hand on the doorknob when she heard a "Hey!" It was one of the most compelling heys she'd ever heard and it sounded like it was meant for her. She turned and from a corner of the room, sitting on a bench with a dog at his feet, the man called, "Where you going so fast?"

She and Ruby walked over. The man stood up. He smiled through a row of even, white teeth. "Oh, it's you," she said.

"Yeah, it's me. How you been? I've been thinking about you."

"I've been thinking of you, too," and she felt herself flush, knowing she was blushing like a fool. She looked up at him, a good head taller than she. "I didn't know you were so tall," she said. "I mean, the last time we were together you never stood." And she blushed even more.

"Yeah, it runs in the family. All of us Jacksons are big boys. We clean our plates, too," he laughed. He glanced at Ruby, stooped down and put his hand near her snout for her to sniff. "Nice dog," he said, looking up, "but I don't remember you having her when I met you."

"She's a new addition. She found me, same place that we met, just two days ago. Changed my life, that's for sure." She rolled her eyes for effect.

"Dogs'll do that. I know, I've got a mess of 'em. This here's Toby. Toby say hi to—"

"Ruby," said Tammy, her hand on Ruby's collar. Toby, a handsome Airedale, began to wag his tail.

"What's up with Ruby? Did the doc take care of you?"

"The doc? I never in my life met anyone like him, silly bastard. Ruby's got a case of the worms and when he found out I didn't have enough to pay for her treatment, he tried to—"

"Take advantage of you?"

"No! Well … yeah, kinda. He made me take this stupid geometry quiz and when I couldn't answer the questions, he told us get out." She was getting worked up just thinking about it. He saw the tear welling in the corner of her eye. "What kind of person does that?"

"Don't worry, we'll fix it. Come on," he said, and he led her by the hand over to the reception area, Toby and Ruby trailing. He stood over the girl, so engrossed in her Harlequin novel she didn't look up. He cleared his throat to get her attention. "Please tell Doctor Hogan that I will cover the cost of any treatment this young lady requires for her dog. Just add it to my account and bill me."

"Sure thing, Mister Jackson. I'll tell him." She went back to her book.

"No, I mean would you tell him now?"

At that moment, Hogan walked through a door behind the receptionist, a miniature Schnauzer cradled in his arms. He seemed startled to see Tammy with possibly his best customer these last twenty years. Tom Jackson looked amused. "Perfect timing!" he said. "Doc, I want you to meet a dear friend of mine, Tammy. Tammy, meet Doc Hogan, the best vet in St. Louis." Tammy and the vet nodded hello. The Schnauzer was trying to squirm free.

Tom Jackson said to Hogan, "Listen doc, I don't what happened between you two, but I'm thinking we should all just start over. No one pass any judgments, no games of any kind, but we simply practice the best medicine we can and get her dog taken care of. Any problem with that?"

Hogan pursed his lips and wagged his head in a sort of shudder. "Oh, no, Mister Jackson, no problem with that at all. In fact, I was just coming out to find Miss Johnson, hoping she hadn't left already, to tell her not to forget the stool sample."

"Okay then, we're all set," said Tom. "And by the way, doc, that Schnauzer looks good on you."

They turned and went back to the waiting area, Toby and Ruby trailing. He told her how he loved animals, kept a house full of them, and when he wasn't working as a finishing carpenter he loved romping with his dogs. "We play Frisbee and fetch and tree-the-squirrel," he told her. "Sometimes it's eat-the-squirrel."

"How many dogs you got?"

"Well, you see Toby here. Toby has three live-in buddies—Barnie, Butch and Misha, the first two being cocker spaniels, brothers from the same litter, and Misha being a lovable bitch of no particular pedigree." He chuckled at his own words. "If that weren't enough, I also have two black gerbils, Mike and Ike."

"That fruity movie theater candy we got as kids?"

He beamed at this. "The very same, but that's not all. I have a tabby cat, Miss Kitty, a ferret named Sam, a green anole—you know, a chameleon—named Harpo, and a mess of guinea fowl in the backyard, fourteen at last count."

Is this guy for real? she wondered.

They sat there for a while talking, Ruby and Toby getting acquainted, too. When he and Toby were called, he asked her to wait for him. When they finished their business with the doc, they all climbed into the Dodge Ram and Tom drove to his place, a sprawling red brick home off Broadway near Bellerive Park, where you could look out the picture window and see the river, the barge tows chugging past. He said that he wanted to show her his menagerie, but she sensed in his voice that Tom, affable and, yes, handsome as could be, was starved for human companionship. She felt immediately comfortable in his home, adoring the furniture, liking all the pictures on the walls, appreciating his collection of African-American kitsch items, pickaninny salt-and-pepper shakers and such. Tom made drinks and they sat in the backyard, watching the dogs romp, Ruby seeming to find her place in the social order, the guinea fowl huddled at the fence eying the new dog warily.

Tammy stayed for dinner and, as the evening wore on, she knew she would spend the night. She took a long shower, brushed her teeth, combed her hair, looked at herself in the mirror and said, "Girl, you clean up pretty good." She switched off the light, went to the adjoining room, a Marvin Gaye album already playing, and slipped in bed with Tom. As they lay there nude, caressing each other, on the brink of something good, she said, "It feels pretty wonderful to be here, just so you know, and I really do appreciate how you've treated me today. Not like some random person who you once paid for sex, but like someone who you care about. That means a lot to me."

He stroked her cheek lightly and replied, "The minute I saw you standing there with your hand out and that crazy smile on your face I knew that you weren't a hooker, just someone going through a bad patch, and someone who I wanted to get to know, deeply." And then he put it in her.

She still marveled at the series of events that had led her here, away from that dead-end existence at the shelter. Well, it wasn't so terrible bad back there, there were some good days. But here in this big old house on a bluff overlooking the Mississippi, every day was a good day. It was a year later and Tom had taken her in just as she had taken in Ruby. They were now a couple, quite compatible as it turned out, and she flourished in this house, truly feeling that he loved her with all the sweet little things he did, like leaving lovey-dovey notes, half-hidden around the house, for her to find. She still went down to the old neighborhood, shopping at Soulard Market with Tom on Saturdays, saying hi to some of the familiar faces, wishing Stumpy Joe was one of them, then catching herself smiling, thinking of him trying to reel in a marlin with one arm. Just as good, though, she'd found Blue, who informed that he'd gone missing due to being picked up on an old warrant. He had a stall at the market now, selling fresh buffalo and catfish, and always gave them the best price. As for Ruby, she had disappeared within the first week. Dug a hole beneath the fence and absconded, never to be seen again despite exhaustive attempts at recovery—daily checks of animal shelters, wanted posters offering a REWARD! on every telephone pole within a three-mile radius, she and Tom canvassing the neighborhoods. Some dogs you just couldn't figure out. Eventually, Tammy got over it, what with all the other animals to care about. She had a particular fondness for Sam, the ferret, who would actually fetch a ball and loved to be scratched on his belly. And that's how she spent her days while Tom was at work—tending to the animals, beautifying the house and the yard, watching the river flow. She didn't mind at all, it was something to do.

Roark Manning
FIELD HERPER

"IF YOU SEE WHAT LOOKS LIKE A STICK IN THE ROAD and it moves, it's a snake—okay?"

I looked at Roark with his pleated khaki hiking shorts, binoculars strung round his neck, and Aussie bush hat. Six-foot-two, he looked like a big Boy Scout striding along with purpose. I said, "And if it doesn't move, it might be just be a stick?"

"There's a bright girl," he said. Roark could be pretty facetious when he wanted to be, but of course I tended to egg him on. Since we were kids it had been that way, Roark the charming but annoying know-it-all, and me, the little sister, playing dumb. Kind of like Rowan and Martin on *Laugh-In*, a really funny show that came on Monday nights.

We'd been walking on this dirt road—the snake road—for nearly a half-hour now and we still hadn't seen any moving sticks, a bit disappointing since Roark had played it up so much during the two-hour drive down here from St. Louis. The snake road was a three-mile stretch in the Shawnee National Forest. Roark explained that each year, between mid-March and mid-May, the Forest Service closed off the road to traffic in order to let the snakes migrate without getting squished. The Forest Service people do the same thing in the fall, close the road when the snakes return. Roark said that was very considerate of them, since most people go out of their way to harm a snake when they see one.

I had my nose in the road map, studying the whole of Southern Illinois. I saw where we were going, just off Route 3, at the edge of an area called Little Grand Canyon. "Just wondering aloud here, the Shawnee Forest looks to be the size of the entire country of Lichtenstein. Why close off the road in that particular spot?"

Roark tapped the ash from his Marlboro into the ashtray. "Because it's the perfect habitat. Two-hundred-foot bluffs on one side of the road, two thousand acres of spring-fed swamp on the other. The snakes overwinter in the bluffs—that's hibernate to you. All these niches and crevices in the limestone make nice dens out of the harsh weather. A couple dozen snakes might gather into a particularly roomy crevice and cluster there for months. And not just copperheads in one den and blue racers in another, but different species in the same space, nice and cozy, all coiled up in one big snake ball. Togetherness. Springtime they make their way down to the base of the bluffs. They hang out there until their instincts tell them it's time to leave. Temperature and light conditions set off their alarm, that's what I've heard, something like seventy-two degrees or more at least three days in a row and boom! they're off to find their territory. You get there on the right day, it's a mass migration, the road like snake spaghetti. A truly amazing sight, nothing like it anywhere else in the country."

"And they can't sneak up on us, right?"

"That's the beauty of it. They're on the road, exposed, we see them before they see us. We intercept them and identify them and, if I need one for my collection, we put it in the bag. You'll see."

"It sounds like the National Geographic special I saw on the Serengeti Plain, all those wildebeests and zebras thundering along, going who-knows-where in a big hurry."

Roark smiled that not-so-secret smile that told me I was basically a dolt. "Yeah, Luce, like that. Only these critters don't thunder, they slither."

We parked the car, got our gear, and set out on the road. After a while we came to a place where a small lagoon on the bluff side had spilled over the road to meet the swamp. It was about 18 inches deep and I started to take off my Keds to wade through it. "No need for that," said Roark, "I'll carry you on my back." So I climbed on his back and we sloshed through the high water.

"Oh, wow, look at that, down there," I said in Roark's ear. The water was crystal clear and, as we moved along, we disturbed the peace of jillions of polliwogs settled in along the shallows. Black dots with tiny tails undulating every which way. "Can you believe how many? What will they be when they grow up?"

"Probably toads, maybe frogs. Either way, they'll be snake food." Just then, he bent over so fast that I flipped off his back and landed in the water. Took me completely by surprise and I sat there among the polliwogs, stunned, muck on my face. Roark was still hunkered down, splashing and thrashing, and then he stood up holding a four-footer by the tail. The thing was really struggling, alternately showing gray on the top side and buff on the other. "Yellowbelly water snake," he said, grinning hugely. "*Nerodia erythrogaster flavigaster*, if I'm not mistaken." The snake lunged for him and he moved his arm out even further, arching his torso away from the pissed-off creature.

"'That's the last time I play horsie with you," I said, getting up, wiping off my clothes. "Thanks a lot, bro."

"Jeez, I'm sorry, but I saw him getting away and there was no time to say, 'Would you mind climbing off my back so I can catch him?' Now do me a favor and get the field guide from my pack and go to the water snake section. The camera, too. Hurry, please."

I caught his excitement and so I did it, just like he asked. And it was a yellowbelly, the scientific name flabbergaster—whatever he'd said. "This species is pugnacious and will strike or bite viciously when captured," I read aloud as the snake went for Roark again. "But that ain't all, mister herpetologist. Listen up: A foul-smelling musk is also excreted from glands at the base of the tail. It's often mixed with feces and smeared on the captor. Sounds lovely. Just don't be handling *my* baloney sandwich."

"Just get the picture, will you?"

"Oh, you're not going to keep him?"

"Nah, too big and too crazy. These guys don't do well in captivity. I'd have to build a major aquatic habitat." I pulled out the Pentax, squeezed off a few frames, Roark holding the snake fore and aft, grinning like a fool. He set it down and it took off like an arrow shot from a bow. It swam along the surface for a while and then submerged into the swamp, our first encounter with the serpentine tribe.

We kept walking under a canopy of green, may apples and trilliums dotting the roadside. On our left the bluffs towered, chalk-colored, small trees cropping out here and there, ferns abounding. This was possibly the most beautiful place I'd ever seen, magical, but then I hadn't been to Hawaii or Europe. And I had Roark to thank for it; he'd been bugging me for weeks now: "You've got to see this place. Soon as the weather warms up, we'll go." A field herper's paradise, he called it. Roark had been coming here for five years now, ever since he got his license, usually alone, although he would meet others on the road and walk along with them, sharing stories. Roark heard about this place from Charlie Hoessle, Curator of Reptiles at the St. Louis Zoo. Charlie had been coming here for years and years and Charlie, in turn, had been introduced to the snake road by his predecessor at the zoo, the famous Marlin

Perkins, who had walked this road starting in the '40s. So there was a long history of snake-catching to live up to.

Back then, in the days of Charlie and Marlin, if you saw a pretty snake and wanted to take it home, you could. There was no one to stop you. Now it's all restricted. There was a sign at the start of the road, in the little clearing where we parked, that collecting was strictly prohibited. Snake tongs okay, snake bags not okay. Roark had both, a golf putter to handle any snakes he came across and a cotton pillowcase to hold the ones he wanted to keep. The putter was from the Tommy Armour line of clubs; it bore Tommy's signature and that's how Roark referred to it, as in "Hand me my Tommy Armour." As if he were a surgeon asking an OR Tech for a special scalpel. But Roark didn't care about any rules posted on a bulletin board in the middle of the forest. His only rules were be thorough, look sharply, leave no rock or log unturned in the quest to add a new species to his growing collection. His snakes, by the way, had recently been relocated, after that fricking black rat snake got out and scared the crap out of me. It could have been an embarrassing visit to the ER. I mean, when I lifted the toilet seat there it was, coiled up in there like a lariat. I had my pants down, ready to go, and I almost sat without looking! After that, I insisted he find a new place for his animals. By then he had something like 22 snakes in 17 homemade cages, mostly in the basement of our apartment, but some in his room, the feeding of them on the way to becoming a full-time job. Then, too, the place was starting to smell pretty weird.

Roark found a warehouse a few blocks over and rented a corner of the third floor, the space coming with a long, wooden work-bench and big opaque, industrial windows that cranked open to let in the air. He tended to his pets each morning and sometimes if it rained and I didn't have to work—I'm a landscaper—I'd go with him. Okay, I like snakes, but I'm not obsessed with them like my brother. Roark thought of himself as the Austin Stevens of the Midwest, Austin Stevens being this South African wild man who started collecting at the age of 12 and, by the time he finished high school, his reptile collection included some of the most exotic and venomous snakes in the world. Roark had a well-thumbed copy of Austin's book, *Snakes In My Bed*, and he liked to read to me from it. He had dog-eared certain pages with hair-raising accounts of close calls with snakes so dangerous you may as well jump into a volcano instead of try to capture them. Just about all the pages were dog-eared.

Anyway, they'd all be there in their little boxes, his scaly darlings, waiting for the lid to open and the pinkies dropped in like manna from heaven, pinkies being newborn mice about the size of a fingertip. Kind of sad, for the baby mice, I mean. But Roark was serious in his mission and from his frequent day trips he'd brought back many snakes, each one with its own story. The red milk snake he'd found under a rock in Audrain County. The gorgeous speckled king snake he'd caught sunning on a steaming pile of manure out near Defiance. The fat black cottonmouth that'd dropped from a tree branch into his canoe during a float trip on the Meramec— "Ker-plop, there it was right in front of me, showing his fangs, both of us equally surprised. I quick emptied the cooler and tossed him in." Back at the apartment he kept only one, the two-headed bull-snake mutation aptly named Freakazoid, Roark insisting that one needed special attention. At feeding time, he had to place a piece of cardboard between the heads so they wouldn't fight over dinner.

Off in the distance a couple guys appeared on the road. "Her-pers," said Roark, and sure enough, when they got closer we saw they had the tale-tell articles—tongs, cameras, field guides poking out of their packs. We stopped to compare notes, and so far their experience was much more interesting than ours since all we had to offer was a single encounter with a common water snake. These guys had come all the way from Ohio; zoology profs at Antioch College, they'd heard about this place at some symposium they'd attended. It was spring break for them and they were spending the week here, trekking this road back and forth. They'd seen and documented all kinds of snakes, lizards, salamanders, turtles, and even some rare blind crayfish found in a stream that ran out from the base of the bluffs. When Roark asked them if they had anything in their packs they were aghast, saying how they would never do such a thing, that photographing them was good enough, and how the animals would never be happy if removed from their native habitat. "That would just be cruel and it would serve no good purpose," said the one with the bushy red beard.

Roark wasn't one to be chided, but then they didn't know that he was the snake-collecting king of St. Louis, caught his first snake, an Eastern garter, sunning on a greenhouse windowsill, when he was only seven years old. Ran three blocks home, holding it just below its neck, like you're supposed to. He kept that snake for four years, cared for it meticulously, tamed it, exercised it, and it grew into a healthy three-foot long beauty that would have won first prize at the snake show if they had snake shows. Roark looked red beard in the eye and said, "Yeah, well, sometimes an animal is better off in captivity. I'll just leave it at that."

They shrugged and started to walk off, but not before suggesting that we check out the bank near the large willow up ahead about a quarter-mile. Not 15 minutes ago they'd seen a sizable specimen of *Crotalus horridus* there. Roark's ears pricked up. I knew he was salivating over this, because he told me in the car on the way down that'd he never seen a timber rattler before and he hoped today would be the day.

"Where'd you go?" wondered Roark, parting a green curtain of willow branches. He scanned the immediate area, the banks of the swamp, looking for that rattler. Then, with binoculars, he looked out onto the swamp itself. There was duckweed covering the surface and you could plainly see the trails left by snakes in their comings and goings. Elongated S-shapes defined against a field of living green. "It can't have gone far," he said. "Let's just hang here for a while. We can have lunch."

We ate our sandwiches on a fallen oak, not wanting to sit on the ground where we might get chiggers. Roark was in high spirits and he wondered if I was having a good time, too. I said I was and even if we didn't see a lot of snakes, it was worth the trip down, just for the walk. Roark reached for the nape of his neck, felt around, and after some investigating, he plucked out a seed tick. He held it between thumb and forefinger, pondering, its tiny legs pedaling some imaginary tick bicycle. I thought he was going to crush it, I mean, that's what you do with a tick, right? But he set it down on the oak and it disappeared under the bark. I just looked at him.

"What?" he said.

"You let it go to suck our blood another day?"

"What the hell, everything's got a right to live."

"Okay, Gandhi, I'll remember that the next time you treat your carnivorous pals to a pinkie dinner."

"Oh—well, touché. I never said I wasn't a hypocrite."

Then he jumped up, knocking over his Dr. Pepper, pointing at the swamp. "Look there, look who's back." We went over. It was on a log on a small earthen island about ten feet out from the bank, its plump body half-in, half-out of the water.

"It looks to be deep in thought," I said.

"It's waiting for movement," said Roark, "something to come by, a little lunch. It's got all the patience in the world."

"It's probably meditating on its place in the cosmos," I offered, thinking Roark would pick up on the sarcasm. He moved closer. I stayed where I was. I watched him take off his pack and put his billfold and smokes on the ground. The golf putter in hand, he began edging up to the water line.

"No, don't even think of doing that," I called.

"It's alright, I just need to get closer."

"Can't you just look at it? We'll photograph it. You don't need to handle it!"

"It's alright, don't worry." By then his legs below his knees had disappeared under the duckweed. The rattler was about six feet away. If it was aware of his approach, you couldn't tell for that far-off stare. He inched closer, the water now up to mid-thigh.

"Roark! You're fearless, everyone knows it, but this is reckless. Please, please, turn around!" Just then he slipped on something and the sudden movement of catching his balance startled the snake. But instead of going away from Roark further out into the swamp, the snake went after him. It happened so fast, in a blink, the big snake cutting through the duckweed, Roark reacting, Tommy Armour now a weapon, frantically smacking the water around him again and again. Then quiet. Roark stood there, his back to me. He dipped the putter into the pea soup and lifted up the snake, dangling by its midsection. It wriggled just a little.

"No! *No—oooo!!*" Roark howled and everything stopped. The frogs stopped croaking, bugs quit their tittering. The bluffs reverberated his anguish. He brought that rattler back on land and he laid it out, shaking and crying. It wasn't dead, but it wasn't ever going to catch a swamp rabbit again. "Oh shit! Oh shit! This is exactly what I *didn't* want to happen," he said, not even trying to choke back emotion. You would have thought that was his own stricken child laying there on the ground.

I put my arm around his shoulder. "It's a shame," I said, "but you had to. Self-defense, no question. What do we do now? The snake, I mean. I really think we should move on."

"Do you know how many timber rattlers live in this conservation area?" The voice came from behind us. We freaked. There, like a magician who suddenly appears on stage, was a man in the uniform of the Fish and Wildlife Service, standing straight, arms folded, a Smoky The Bear hat shading his eyes. We didn't say a word, just kind of cringed and moved away from the snake. A half-minute passed; we were definitely not at ease.

"I'm waiting for an answer," he said, finally.

Roark complied. "How many? No sir, I don't know, never took a count."

"Well, I'll tell you then. As far as timber rattlers? There's not a hell of a lot and you just destroyed one of them. You're in a national forest, that's a federal crime. You're both under arrest."

Funny, I had always harbored a feeling that snakes would be Roark's undoing. I never thought I would go down with him.

You might think it queer that a brother and sister would choose to live together as grown-ups, if that's what we were now. But looking back on it I can see we were destined to stick together, what with our family life in constant turmoil. Starting early on, there had been this attitude we shared: Me and You Against the World. That's the full of it; I know Roark felt the same. We grew up in a modest three-bedroom bungalow in Kirkwood—fireplace in the living room, glider on the front porch, big backyard to play in. Dad was in construction. He left early, we saw him only at dinner, and then he turned in early. Mom was the social one. She belonged to every club, organization, and society in a 20-mile radius. If she wasn't organizing a walkathon for a cure to cancer, then she was attending a Junior League luncheon, sucking down sherbet as the guest speaker went on about her goodwill mission to Sumatra. The one group she didn't get involved with was the Girl Scouts, and that's a shame.

All that hobnobbing with socialites gave her pretensions and she would make these outlandish purchases on the family credit card, often without telling dad. He would come home and find a surround-sound stereo system in the middle of the living room, waiting for him to assemble, and he would blow his stack. Mom would be on her fifth martini by then and she would blithely dismiss his rants, saying, "What good is money if you can't spend it?" Dad dealt with this by self-exile. Weekends, he would sit in the Chrysler Newport parked in the driveway, smoking, listening to the radio with our terrier, Barney, at his side. He started referring to mom as "the monster." Roark and I tried not to take sides, we just needed one of them to fix us dinner, maybe help us with homework. As time went on, they were too busy sniping at each other to do anything but take a five-minute breather and go at it again. Kids naturally find an escape from unpleasant situations. Roark had his snakes and I had my flower garden in the backyard.

After high school—Roark graduated a year before me—we both got jobs and decided to get an apartment together. By then, for all we cared, mom and dad could feud and fuss in that bungalow until the termites ate the rafters. We found a great old place on one of the state streets on the deep Southside, taverns and markets all within walking, and there we settled in. Even now, we don't seem to need the company of others. I mean, we've got friends, just a few, and even though we are not unattractive people, neither of us has ever had a paramour—you know, a main squeeze. Maybe that will come later, love and all that, but meanwhile we're in it together, really enjoying this new chapter in our lives, even if we do have to scrape to come up with the rent.

Tell you this, though. Going to court over the incident on the snake road didn't help our financial situation. Not a bit.

Petty Offense Court in East St. Louis, Illinois, held twice a month in the federal courthouse, isn't quite as hilarious as *Laugh-In*, but it could make a decent sitcom. All of us were there because our offenses, however trivial, had occurred on federal property. We didn't have a lawyer; we planned to plead guilty and face the music. So we sat in the front pew and listened to the bailiff read the offenses as U.S. Magistrate Walter Kilgore looked on. There were some hardened cases, alright. The pregnant doctor who failed to heed a NO PARKING sign at the VA Hospital where she worked, and a teenage couple who'd been caught in the act among the headstones in a national cemetery.

Roark leaned over and whispered, "You ask me, the collective misdeeds of these desperadoes wouldn't even earn the respect of a hubcap thief." The bailiff, a huge black man with a shaved head, looked like the Buddha, caught this murmur and shot a warning look in our direction. He stopped what he was doing, walked over and stood in front of us, meaning business. "You got something to say," he directed, "you wait your turn and say it to the judge. Otherwise, put a lid on it."

"We had nowhere else to do it," explained the girl to the judge.

"And the place is so well-kept, so inviting," added the pimple-faced boy.

The judge was not sympathetic. He gave them a finger-wagging lecture like they were bad children. "It is well-kept and inviting," he said sternly, "but for those family members to visit the graves of their loved ones who have served their country. It is a hallowed place that demands respect. It is not a place for the fulfillment of base, carnal desires."

"But then where can we do it?" asked the boy. "The woods are full of chicks and tiggers."

"He means ticks and chiggers," said the girl, snickering.

"Have you ever thought of holding off until marriage?" asked the judge, arching an eyebrow that looked like a caterpillar from where I sat. "No one's ever done *that* before—sheesh! Now, how do you plead?"

They both pleaded guilty, but insisted they weren't ashamed and that they would likely do it again. Apparently, they really enjoyed screwing outdoors. Judge Kilgore put them on probation for a year and fined them $250 each.

"Ouch," whispered Roark in my ear.

Then it was our turn. We stood as the bailiff read the charges: "The United States of America versus Roark Manning and Lucy Manning." The effect was alarming. It sounded as if we were being tried for treason. The judge motioned us to come before the bench. He said, "You two are charged with destruction of wildlife in a national forest, a Class B Misdemeanor, punishable by one year in jail and up to a one thousand dollar fine. What's the story here? Can't you just enjoy the scenery of our beautiful parks and forests without having to kill something that lives there? You may even have seen one of those signs posted at the entrance to some of these places: 'Take nothing but pictures, leave nothing but footprints.' Wise words, don't you think?"

The judge looked at Roark then at me, expecting an answer. I'm a much better writer than I am a talker—I tend to stammer in front of strangers—and I had told Roark earlier that when it came to the crunch I would appreciate him speaking for both of us. Roark cleared his throat and replied. "Yes sir, Your Honor, sir, those are wise words and I wish we had followed them. Killing that snake was unintended, the result of an instinctual reaction—it was about to bite me—and, believe me, causing its death, even inadvertently, has brought great remorse to both myself and my sister here. We have a hard time living with ourselves over this."

Bravo, brother.

"I see," said the judge, "but I'm not quite hearing a sincere tone of contrition. It sounds as though you rehearsed your comment. Just what sort of snake was this?"

"A timber rattler, sir, Your Honor."

"Hmm. I know a bit about snakes and it's my understanding there aren't any rattlesnakes in our state. Cottonmouths, yes. Copperheads, yes, in spades."

Roark saw his chance to mitigate the situation. "Well, it sure looked like a timber rattler, but maybe it wasn't after all. You may be right there, sir, a case of mistaken identity."

"Did you get a look at its pupils? Vertical pupils, it's venomous —round pupils, it's harmless or at least non-venomous."

"I'm afraid I didn't get that close to it, Your Honor, sir."

The judge flashed annoyance. "What do you mean? You were close enough to whack it to death, weren't you?" The judge reflected a moment and continued. "You know, I have a place down near Benton, not so far from the Shawnee National Forest, and in the ponds around there is the diamondback water snake, big stout fellow, mean as a welt. He could easily be mistaken for a rattlesnake."

"Your Honor, sir, for all I know about snakes, which isn't much, it could have been a diamondback water snake. I'm just sorry it's gone."

"Oh, you're merely sorry now? Before you were remorseful. That seems like a step in the wrong direction. You were bothering *it*, I assume. Not the other way around. And even if it were a common water snake instead of this non-existent rattlesnake, do you think that should make a difference in the magnitude of your offense?"

I could see Roark mulling this. It must've been killing him to pretend he didn't know his snakes. "No sir, Your Honor," he replied. "But compared to some offenses, it is a rather small magnitude, like maybe a four-point-three that just rattles the windows and sends the cat up a tree."

"Enough of this back talk!" boomed the judge. "How do you plead?"

"Guilty as charged," said Roark.

"And you, young lady?"

"Yes, sir."

"Yes, sir, what?"

"Like he said, Your Honor."

The judge seemed pleased, at least he stopped glowering at us. Then he admonished us some more and fined each of us $150 plus court costs. Snake killing, it appears, is not as great a slight to society as wanton copulation in a cemetery.

You might think that after the snake road incident my brother would have cooled his jets over the discovery, collecting, and curating of elongate, legless, carnivorous reptiles of the suborder *Serpentes*. In fact, he got into it even deeper, spending virtually every waking moment either caring for the snakes he had, finding food for them, building new cages, or going on field expeditions to acquire new ones. Some of these Missouri counties were so distant that I'd never even heard of them. He'd be gone three-four days, collecting by day, camping in State Parks. During one week in August alone, he returned with a Northern scarlet snake, a Great Plains rat snake, and a flathead snake, pale and rubbery-looking, hardly bigger than a night crawler.

If that weren't enough, Roark began buying non-native snakes over the phone. He did business with a place in Florida called General Exotics. Usually, three days after ordering, a boxy brown truck would roll up in front. The UPS guy knew what he had. Walking up, he carried the delivery—a sturdy cardboard enclosure, partly screened, with a handle on top—held out at arm's length, as far away as possible. Roark would be waiting for it and upon receipt he'd immediately open the box, excited as a kid on Christmas morning. "Look at this," he'd say, fondling his newest acquisition, a caramel motley corn snake priced at $39.95. "Isn't she a beauty!" At this time, Roark had only a part-time job at a convenience store down the street, so he had to pinch pennies and choose his purchases wisely. Then he got international. One month it was an emerald tree boa from Brazil and three months later it was a Dahl's whipsnake native to the Balkans. The snakes came with a lavishly illustrated booklet that covered their natural history to include care and feeding.

This thing was getting out of hand. I could see that, but Roark couldn't. Every now and then, I would suggest that maybe he had enough snakes, that outside of the zoo his menagerie was the most extensive in the metro area. I even tried to get him to think about collecting a single specimen to represent the genus instead of one for every species. Roark would grudgingly admit that he probably was spending too much time on snakes, that what had been a mere hobby had become a passion and that passion was now a way of life. But despite that frank self-assessment, we both knew there was always one more rock to turn over, one more species to acquire. It would continue until something else came along. That something was the Gaboon viper.

I can understand why Roark wanted this thing. It was absolutely

stunning with its intricate light brown on dark brown pattern that would make it perfectly camouflaged on an expensive Oriental carpet. Roark saw it in the General Exotics catalog and had to have one. The St. Louis Zoo had one as well, and Roark had been coveting it. This particular snake marked a new level of collecting for Roark. Not only was it the most expensive purchase to date, but it was far and away the most venomous animal he would ever own. The guy in the snake store in Florida had even warned him. "Are you sure you want to have this in your home? When it decides to bite, it's with fangs that reach up to two inches. On top of that, the Gaboon viper has a huge amount of venom to deliver and that venom is one of the most toxic anywhere in the world. I would rather be bit by three rattlesnakes at once than a single Gaboon viper," the snake salesman concluded.

"I would rather take precautions and avoid getting bitten altogether," said Roark. "I'll take it."

The Gaboon viper was late in coming and finally on the day it did arrive, Roark and I were both out somewhere. The tenant in the other first floor apartment, a retired machinist named Stanko Dobrinic, signed for it. I got home a bit before Roark, and Stan was in the foyer waiting, the familiar container with the handle on top beside him on the floor. "Hallo, Missy," he said in his slight European accent. "The delivery man dropped this off. You and your brother were out, so I take it."

I began to thank him, but he waved it off. "Ach, a favor. What are neighbors for? You would do same, I know. But what is in here—something alive, yes? There is a little window with a screen. I look in there, something throw itself at me. Is it a monkey? I think it is a small monkey."

"No, it's a snake that my brother ordered. He's crazy about snakes, and this one is a real—I don't know too much about it except it's best to keep away from it."

"Oh," he said, knowingly, "we have many snakes in Croatia. The poskok, for one. Very pretty and very dangerous. Is called in English 'horn-nose viper', but they are almost gone now. So many stupid people kill them, they say the only good snake is a dead one."

Roark rolled in minutes later and we immediately went to the warehouse. Though it was early September and still sweltering, Roark put on a jacket and heavy gloves. Carefully, he went to work with a boxcutter as I stood on a chair watching. Finally the cardboard lid bent back and Roark stood there for a minute, taking it in. "Wow! This guy is amazing, just amazing! The colors. Take a look."

"I'll see him when he gets in his cage," I said.

Roark had a new putter for handling snakes, Tommy Armour having been confiscated by Smoky The Bear. This one was a Gary Player, a pretty good name for a golfer. Roark dipped into the box. I tiptoed an inch higher. The snake came out dangling from the putter and in one swift, sure motion Roark grabbed him near the tail, lifted him up, and with the other hand grasped him just below the triangular-shaped head. Of course the snake didn't like being manhandled, it was struggling to break free, four feet of scale and muscle, everything between the hand-holds twisting, striving. Arms outstretched, Roark went to the long workbench where a new cage, built large especially for this guy, awaited. It was the last cage in a long line of cages on that workbench.

Once he had the snake in there, the top clamped down on its hasp, I took a look. It was exploring its new digs, raising itself to the ceiling, nosing into the corners, checking out the big porcelain water bowl. It came right up to the screen, making a sound like a high pressure air hose leaking, and I backed away. It *was* pretty. Pretty scary.

"You look in those eyes, you wonder what it might be thinking," said Roark.

"It's like looking into something primeval, something that doesn't think beyond hunt-kill-eat-sleep."

"The perfect predator."

"Is it a boy or a girl?"

"I'll have to look at the anal glands."

"Oh, please don't do that," I said. "I don't really want to know the gender. But I see it's got that flat head, hard to believe it has two-inch fangs in there."

"They're there alright," he assured, "but they're retracted."

"Just do me a favor, will you? Put a padlock on that cage."

The days went by and Roark tended to his snakes while I worked my landscaping and gardening business. Whenever I got a big job, some estate out in Chesterfield, three acres or more, I'd ask Roark to help. He could prune shrubs or plant a rock garden as well as anyone, and it gave him some decent walking around money. One day in September, we were planting boxwoods around a Tudor-style mansion when he reached in his back pocket and handed me an envelope, folded in half.

"Something life-changing?"

"Just read it," he said.

I unfolded the envelope and saw the return address in the upper left corner: SELECTIVE SERVICE. I didn't need to see any more. "Oh, Roark!"

He shrugged what-the-hell. "My number came up. It's no surprise, really, not when you're twenty-two, unemployed, able-bodied, and no plans for college."

"What is your draft number?" I wondered. In fact, I was

perversely fascinated by the lottery system the government had set up for the draft. They took your birthday, wrote it on a piece of paper or something, put all the birthdays in a big pot and drew them out one by one until they reached 365, the number of days in the year. Say they drew July 16 first, everyone with that birthday would be number one on the draft pick. They drew November 2 on the 300th draw, all those November 2 birthdays would be number 300. What they did with those Leap Year Day birthdays I don't know, maybe assigned them another day. The lower the number, the greater your chances of being drafted. However, if you were number 12, but you were in college, you got a deferment. It was very much like a game, poker or Lotto maybe, but at least with those you could win something tangible. Here, with a war going on, you stood to win a trip to Southeast Asia and take your chances of coming back in a body bag. Luck of the draw, that's all it boiled down to.

"My number's twenty-three," said Roark, "so actually the only surprise is that it didn't happen before now."

This eventuality had been bumping around in my head for a long time, but I would never bring it up for fear of jinxing the situation. Now here it was, all too real, causing a lump in my throat. "How can you be a soldier? The Boy Scouts wouldn't even have you. You won't look good in olive drab. Those uniforms make you look frumpy. Besides, I'm not done with you. You can't just go off."

He lit a cigarette, took a drag, and acted nonchalant about the whole thing. "I've been reading up on Vietnam," he said, "and you know, there's some very interesting snakes over there. The Asian cobra for one."

"There's another reason you can't go off and play Army, your snakes need you."

"I've already decided to sell them, give them away, or let them go. This is bigger than field herping. This is huge."

Roark got very busy after that. In the run-up to his induction, he either found homes for all his snakes or he released them into the wild. To his credit, the ones he released, he tried to release precisely where he found them, even if it meant driving halfway across the state or over into Illinois. Finally, he was down to two: Freakazoid, the two-headed bullsnake, and the Gaboon viper. Stan had agreed to take the bullsnake, saying that an oddity like that might bring him luck. That left the viper which had been worrying Roark, because it wasn't eating well and seemed more lethargic than normal. Still, he was determined to place it, hoping a new environment would cause it to perk up. Through a pet store connection he found a buyer, and before long the guy was driving up from Evansville to get it.

It was a Tuesday morning in mid-December, I will never forget it. An inch of snow had fallen and snowflakes were still wafting down, perfectly light, taking their time, the kind you can easily catch on your tongue. We were in the warehouse waiting on the buyer to arrive. I looked down the long wooden workbench, bare now except for some gloves, crushed soda cans and whatnot, but once a thriving hamlet. Snakeville. "You seem to be taking it pretty well," I remarked.

He knew what I meant. "Yeah, it was fun while it lasted. They're all hibernating by now."

"You mean overwintering."

He laughed lightly. "You know the lingo. It was good having you along on some of those trips even if you did chatter most of the time—oh, hell!"

"What?" He was lifting the lid of the cage and starting to reach in.

"There's a piece of lint or something on its eye."

Roark always was a bit on the OCD side. "Let it be! C'mon, it's not important."

"I can get it, don't—ahh!" He jerked his arm out and looked dumbly at the twin punctures just above the wrist, leaking blood and venom. "This is not good," he said fairly matter-of-factly, shutting the lid and locking it. Of course I knew what just happened, but my brain was struggling to wrap itself around the grim reality that my brother had just been bitten by one of the most venomous creatures on earth, that he could well die if we didn't act quickly. Already, the color had drained from his face and he was starting to shake. "I'll probably go into shock before long," he said, "so I need you to go to the market on the corner and call nine-one-one."

"I am so incredibly worried," I said. "I won't let you out of my sight. You come with me, as far as you can."

He shook his head. "That won't work, Luce. Walking will step up my heart rate, send the poison through my body faster. Go now, please." And he sat on the floor.

"Okay, okay, I'll go." I put on a tourniquet up above the elbow— we knew that much first aid—tightened it good, and then I dashed out.

As I burst out the door of the building there stood a guy on the sidewalk, looking up at the broad, red brick facade, just studying the building. He said, "Is this Manning's Snake Emporium? I don't see an address," and I skidded to a halt like one of those cartoon characters you see.

"You're the buyer from Evansville!"

"Well, actually Poseyville, it's just outside Evansville."

"Doesn't matter," I told him, "we need your car. Now!" He looked at me, unglued, demanding, and probably wondered what had he gotten himself into here. I made toward him, he backed off. I think I was gesticulating like a crazy person. "Look," I urged,

" it's an emergency. Roark got bit by the Gaboon viper, the one you came to get."

The guy's jaw dropped. "Oh crap! He's a goner then—uh, I mean, get me to him."

Roark was sitting where I'd left him, propped up against the workbench. His head was down, his arms wrapped over his torso strait-jacket style, and he was rocking slightly. He looked at the two of us, his rescuers, and smiled through a face dripping sweat. "Oh, jeez," said the buyer, whose name was Kurt Earhardt. He put his hand on Roark's shoulder like a coach talking game plan to a quarterback. "Okay, man, here's what we're doing: I'm going to pick you up, carry you to the car, and we're going to the ER, okay? We're going to get you some help. Right now." Fortunately, he was a big guy. He slung Roark over his shoulders in a fireman's carry and down three flights of stairs we went.

Alexian Brothers is not the first choice hospital having the best equipped ER with the most highly trained doctors on staff, not as preferable as, say, Saint Louis University Hospital or Missouri Baptist out in West County, but it sure as hell was the closest. It took us all of five minutes to get there, Roark sprawled out in the back of the Skylark, his head on my lap. Kurt Earhardt, driving as fast as road conditions would allow—it was still snowing—kept saying, "Hold on, buddy, don't pass out on us." Over and over, like a mantra. And what luck it was, him being there at that moment, me not having to run for help, wait for an ambulance; it saved at least 30 minutes.

We pulled into the circular drive at Alexian, Kurt Earhardt giving several emphatic blasts on his horn, jumping out, not waiting for the attendants to run out with a gurney but doing the fireman's carry again, hustling Roark right into the hospital.

Inside, they saw he was bad off. They asked some specific

questions, got the gist of the thing, put him into a wheelchair, and rolled him into a draped-off cubicle with a bed and all sorts of machines and equipment. Roark was shaking even worse, convulsing, looking wide-eyed, panicky, at the people gathered around him, and saying things like "No, not there, you can't put it there," and "Do we have enough mustard?" That was when the doctor pulled me out of the room.

"Are you sure it was this viper snake?" he asked. "It's very important, the antidote is species specific."

I glanced at the name plate on his white lab coat. DEV PRADESH, D.O. "Yes, yes," I told him, impatient to get back to Roark, "a Gaboon viper. African snake, very poisonous. You want me to write it down?"

"I got it, but we're going to have to find the antidote and that may be difficult."

"Well, start phoning," I said. "You might try the zoo first, they've got a Gaboon viper."

It turned out the zoo didn't have the antidote. Years later, zoos were mandated to carry antidotes for every venomous snake in their possession, but this was 1971. When informed of the situation, Charlie Hoessle, the reptile curator, jumped in. I don't even think he knew he was helping Roark, a personal acquaintance. Charlie got on the horn, called around and found the antidote. It was at the Brookfield Zoo, maintained by the Chicago Zoological Society. Chicago is 300 miles away, four-and-a-half hours by speeding car, so what did they do? They put that antidote on a private plane, operated by a medical transport company, and flew it to Lambert Field. From the airport it went to a waiting ambulance and ran lights flashing to Alexian Brothers, twenty-some miles away. Still, the whole trip start to finish took almost three hours. The venom had pretty much done its damage by then.

Just before the antidote got there, Dr. Pradesh took me aside again. "We have done what can be done," he said somewhat apologetically. "He is experiencing severe hypotension, dangerously low blood pressure that can lead to cardiac arrhythmia. We have tried to stabilize that with intravenous infusion—IV—which also stimulates urine output, the more the better. We have given medication to calm him down. You and others have reassured him, and that is important. As you can imagine, we don't get much of this injury here so we have been on the phone with experts on snakebites, Regional Poison Control Centers. We found a man in North Carolina, at the university there, who is knowledgeable on the bite of this particular snake and he has informed that this venom is a hemotoxin, that is, the coagulation profile is deteriorating to the point where he could have circulatory failure. Already, he has had several seizures. So it is touch and go, as they say. Also, this man informed that the affected area is almost always subject to amputation. You saw his arm, so you know what I am saying."

I had seen his arm alright. It was swollen as big as a horse haunch, the bite area by now a large open wound, ugly blisters around the perimeter which seemed to be spreading, the flesh just eaten away, almost to the bone. I nodded yes, I knew what he was saying.

"Well then, you understand that tissue necrosis will eventually take that arm. We must act sooner than later."

"If you have to, you have to. Do you need me to sign something?"

"The paperwork is being prepared," Pradesh remarked, and then gave a sort of conspiratorial wink, adding, "You know, there is one piece of luck in all this."

"Oh really? What could be lucky about this?"

"Amputation. He could have been bitten on the face or head."

As for luck or providence or fate, however you may think of happenstance and its repercussions, Roark couldn't decide if losing an arm was a good thing or a bad thing. It did give him a certain notoriety in general and, in particular, elevated him to celebrity status in the loose-knit society of field herpers. It pleased mom and dad, who put aside their acrimony to come visit Roark during his recuperation at home. Why did the loss of that limb please them? Because he was no longer draft material. The Army was out of the picture and so was the possibility of getting killed in Vietnam. Roark didn't share their sentiment. He never actually said this outright, but I sensed that he really wanted to be a soldier. He hadn't done much with his young adult life except catch snakes and I think he saw the military as a ticket out of town, a path to some worthwhile calling. Besides snakes, I mean.

Unarguably, the bad thing about losing his right arm was the inability to do simple everyday things like cut his pork chop or tie his boots. It brought him down, you could see that. Even so, he wasn't sure if he wanted to go with a prosthetic.

"You could be Captain Hook when they do *Peter Pan* at The Muny," I said.

"The stump is not so bad," he'd say. "Maybe I'd rather be the one-armed man on *The Fugitive*." *The Fugitive* was another TV show we watched in reruns, the wrongly convicted Dr. Richard Kimble on the loose, perpetually searching for his wife's killer, the elusive one-armed man.

Another thing he had trouble with was writing letters. One day he handed me a tape recorder, a pocket Sony that ran on batteries. "Do me a favor, Luce. Play this out and transcribe it, will you? Write it as a letter—salutation, body, complimentary close. I'll sign it."

I went ahead and did it after dinner. It didn't take long. It was directed to Roark's personal hero on the other side of the planet.

To Austin Stevens, Snakemaster

Hartebeespoort Dam Snake and Animal Park, Pretoria, South Africa

Dear Austin Stevens,   10 April 1972

I have followed your career and exploits for several years now and must say I am quite impressed. As a lifelong collector and curator of snakes native to this region, I feel a solidarity toward herpetologists worldwide, but you, sir, take the prize. I cannot fathom undertaking a challenge such as you took, spending more than three months in a cage with 36 of the deadliest snakes in Africa. What nerve! I read that on day 96 you were bitten by a cobra and yet you refused to leave, instead asking to be treated inside the cage. What determination! Finally, on the 107th day you emerged from that den of death. Let them call you bonkers all they want, but you succeeded in besting the existing Guinness World Record, a feat that stands to this day. Bravo! I myself survived a bite from a Gaboon viper, a snake you are likely familiar with, and I can say from experience there is no horror to compare with seeing a deadly strike find its mark on your flesh. Still, we remain undaunted, our mission to collect, curate, and safeguard these animals as strong as ever. I know you agree. I hope that you get a feel for my outlook, because now I cut to the chase. My question to you is this: In your capacity as Curator of Reptiles at the Snake and Animal Park, could you see fit to hire an assistant? A one-armed assistant, but nonetheless an assistant who is willing to learn from and co-operate with a true master. Please respond at your earliest convenience.

p.s. I can pay my way over.

Fraternally yours,

Roark Manning

St. Louis, Missouri USA

So I was wrong about Roark. Not only was he uninterested in turning a new leaf, leaving the snakes behind, he wanted to take it to a new level and apprentice with a superstar in the field. We sealed that letter in an envelope, slapped a mess of stamps on it, and dropped it in the nearest mailbox. It was probably the best thing we ever did.

Each November, just after Thanksgiving, I head to the airport. I have saved all year for this trip and it never disappoints. It's amazing, really, how you can simply walk out your door in St. Louis, take a twenty-minute taxi ride, board a plane and, after one refueling stop, two TV dinners, and one trashy novel, emerge in an exotic location. Discombobbled, yes, but excited as hell. And South Africa is so different from the Midwest! Just looking out the window on the bus ride from Johannesburg to Pretoria is a National Geographic special in itself. And Pretoria—Church Square, Atterbury Value Mart, the Van Wouw Museum, there is so much to see and do. I wouldn't be surprised if I was walking ten miles a day, leaving Roark's place in Weavind Park after breakfast and covering ground, conversing, snapping pictures, sampling local fruits, doing fun stuff until noon or so, and then making my way to Hartebeespoort Dam where Roark is a tour guide at the Snake and Animal Park. I'll buy a ticket and join the others, both tourists and locals, as Roark, in his matching khaki shirt and slacks, pith helmet at a rakish tilt, leads us from habitat to habitat, expounding on this or that deadly species. The delivery is quite informative, but it's also laced with wry humor. Then as an added feature, he handles the snake—expertly, carefully, perhaps lovingly, showing it off to the audience standing safely behind an enclosure. He doesn't handle every snake, of course, and he uses tongs, but the serpent at hand could be a puff-adder, a boomslang, or a swampjack, which is a cousin of the Gaboon viper. You hear the crowd *oohing* and *aah-ing* as Roark risks his life for their edification and, at some point during each presentation, I find myself nudging the person next to me and saying, "That's my brother."

Bertie Dubois
ON THE **IVORIES**

IT WAS COLD EVEN FOR JANUARY IN ST. LOUIS, the streets of Soulard practically deserted. Here and there, the occasional figure might be glimpsed, bundled, hunched against the cold, darting from a gangway to the corner tavern—and there was a tavern on every corner. The old Reed Hotel at 9th and Barton stood out, a beacon in an otherwise bleak landscape. A street lamp shone into the entryway, illuminating a flurry of snow there. The windows, opaque with condensation, emanated a warm, rosy glow, hinting at the comforts within. A large, red door with a brass knocker led into the bar, which took up the back-half of the spacious lobby. Each opening of the door allowed the escape of lilting piano strains, overlaid with a buzz of conversation, to the cold world outside.

The Reed had fallen on hard times. Since the shipyard had closed and, a year later, the iron foundry, the hotel had gone from a mainstay of working Joes paying month by month to what some now considered a flophouse. There were three floors with eight rooms each and only half of them taken, occupied by pensioners, hucksters, and salesmen, bachelors all, eking out their existence in the shadow of the world's largest brewery looming off to the south. Yet the hotel bar was still a popular spot, and this evening two score customers crowded round the piano and its player, the music loud and lively. Tradesmen, still wearing the day's work clothes, stood at the bar regaling one another, guffawing, back-slapping. On the floor, an older couple swayed in mild delirium. Some drank beer and some drank cheap booze; it warmed their insides the same as the expensive stuff.

Situated off in a corner, beneath a mounted stag, once majestic, now a hat rack, the piano player gave them ragtime, honky-tonk, some new jazz. Those who knew the songs sang along, and those who did not bluffed their way through. After each number, and sometimes during, he would pause for a sip and a drag. Two Naturals was his whiskey; Lucky Strikes his smoke. Drinks and smokes were important to the fat, balding, blind piano player.

"Hey Bertie, play 'Stormy Weather,' will ya?" The request came from nearby. Another voice, more emphatic, called for a different tune. "'Barney Google,' Bertie. C'mon, play 'Barney Google.' That cracks me up!" This opened the floodgates for requests; everyone had his favorite.

He dabbed below one eye with a hankie and said, "What'm I, your personal jukebox?"

"Yeah, as a matter a fact, you are," answered a voice known to Bertie as a regular named Jinx.

"Well then, why don't you put a quarter in me and watch me light up?"

Bertie heard the coin hit his jar. "Jukebox gives three songs for a quarter," said Jinx. "'Smoke Gets In Your Eyes'—you know it?"

He laughed wryly. "Know it? Hell, I'm *livin'* it."

"Then play it, pallie, play it for me."

Bertie nodded, took a drag from his Lucky, and banged away at the old Story and Clark which had seen better days. Bertie disdained dark glasses. His eyelids had been shut for so long —eleven

years since the accident—that by now they were glued down and would not open even through his own will. And for some damn reason his eyes produced tears, not constantly, but enough that it gave Bertie the appearance of crying. It irritated him that he had to keep a hankie nearby to dab away the tears just before they rolled down his cheek. Some of the customers, seeing that, might think that Bertie was choking up on his own music, a real sentimental sap. *Let them think what they damn well please. Nothing's further from the truth.*

Bertie finished the tune, called out for another drink and the barman obliged. All Bertie's drinks were on the house. He was a fixture at the Reed, playing the week nights for drinks and tips. It was a swell job for a man pushing fifty who liked to entertain and drink good house liquor. Bertie launched into a Bix Beiderbecke number, a request from another regular who said it reminded her of her first husband. Meanwhile, the snow piled up on the windowsills outside.

After midnight, the crowd thinned out considerably; Bertie kept right on playing and drinking. A few remaining diehards were ushered out at quarter of two and Bertie, rising stiffly from his stool, made ready to leave. Now there were only two of them left in the bar. Jerry, the barman, spoke to his employee. "Cold as a banker's heart out there. You wanna lift home?"

Bertie considered the offer then wagged his head from side to side, his jowls quivering slightly. "Nah, I been on my ass all night long, walk'll do me good."

"Suit yourself," said Jerry. "One for the ditch?"

"Does a horse drink water?" Bertie steered for the bar, side-stepping the maze of chairs like a man with built-in radar.

Jerry was more generous with his drinks after closing time. Into a pair of smudged glasses he poured double shots and added a little ice. Jerry clinked Bertie's glass as he handed it to him. "Cheers," said Jerry. Bertie echoed the salutation.

Bertie lived only three blocks away, in a run-down flat over Mayer's Sign Shop. Once they had been friends, he and Emil Mayer, but now the old Kraut, crotchety to begin with, had become nearly intolerable, given to frothing rants. "Dose dunderheads at city hall!" he'd spout, irked by the latest muckraking headline in the *Globe-Democrat.* If it wasn't dunderheads, it was shitbums, a choice word he'd picked up from McGlynn, the resident beat cop. "Ya, dees shitbums moving into za neighborhood, dey respect noth-ing!"—only Mayer said it as "nussink." In Mayer's world, practically everyone was a shitbum or a dunderhead or worse. The man lived to carp and bitch and too often Bertie was his unwilling sounding board. And there was no escaping him, because Mayer lived below in a large room at the rear of the shop, practically walled-in by all manner of clutter. Bertie suspected that his landlord was in the onset of some sort of mental illness, prompting Bertie to consider giving notice after all these years. A damn shame, too, because the place was convenient and easy. But right now he just wanted to climb under the covers. Walking home, he had trouble staying on the sidewalk. The mounting snow muffled the sound of his cane as it struck the concrete, throwing him slightly off course. But that was not the sole reason he weaved and wobbled.

Hearing the crunch of his own footsteps on the snow was pleasant. It reminded him of winters as a kid and how he used to love watching the big flakes float down, turning the city into a magical, white wonderland. *And the snowmen we would make!* If the world beyond his nose was perpetually black now, well, at least he had his memories, each one like a scene from a movie playing in his head. Bertie lit a smoke. He had no gloves and felt stupid for leaving home without them. The cold froze the tears to his cheeks. Bertie kept his head down and picked up his pace.

He entered the side gate, passed through a narrow gangway, and went up the back stairs. Atop the landing, he put up his cane and dug into the pockets of his overcoat. Discerning the house key from the rest on the key ring, Bertie tried the door. For some reason, the key failed to insert. Again he tried, and again the maneuver failed. He probed the keyhole with nimble fingers. Seemed right. He felt the key to make certain it was correct. It was. This had never happened before. The problem baffled him and, further, he was getting colder and wearier by the minute.

At last, Bertie managed to get the key half-way in the lock; it now refused to budge, in or out. *What the hell is going on?* Bertie gave the obstinate door a good kick. *This is the worst possible time.* He pulled hard on the key ring and finally yanked them free. The keys fumbled in his hands, a slippery fish, and then, *Oh shit!* Bertie felt them glance off his shoe and hit the boards at his feet. A second later he knew they had fallen through the slats to the ground below.

"My friggin' luck," he muttered. Bertie took his cane and started down the steps, one hand on the railing. He estimated the location, and on his hands and knees started the search. He soon realized there were at least three inches of snow on the ground. Without gloves it was tough.

Bertie's hands were neither delicate nor without callous, yet they weren't prepared for an exploration of the backyard terrain. It wasn't long before his left palm tore when he passed over some-thing in the snow, broken glass or maybe the lid of an old can— Bertie did not know.

His hands, his fingers had become raw and chafed. *My poor mitts, it's a good thing I can't see them.* For a while there they tingled, but that sensation had left and now they were simply numb. He imagined himself in his nice warm bed, the radio on WIL, listening to Ray Manning and the Dawn Patrol, drifting off to sleep. It was times like this he wished he had a dog or even a wife, someone he could rely on.

Bertie blew on his fingers then placed them in his mouth; the taste of blood and grit turned his stomach and he retched. It took extra effort to light a smoke, his coordination a bit off. He was not giving up, no sir, just taking a break. But meanwhile there was something he had to know. He held the lit-end of his Lucky to the tip of an index finger. The hot ash made contact and he heard a faint *tsstt* but felt no pain whatsoever.

He went to rise and bumped his head hard on the underside of the steps. It brought him back down to the ground. Gingerly, he felt the knot on his crown, his fingers coming away sticky and wet. *Why is this happening? There can't be any good reason. It's just bad luck piled on bad luck.* He began flailing in desperation, assaulting the frozen turf with his body.

"Oof!" he grunted. "Unhh! Oh!" Teaching himself a lesson, by god. Snow filled his ears and mouth, went up his sleeves and down his collar. Panting, he sat up. How long had it been since he left the Reed? One hour? Two? The city was in a deep freeze and Bertie sat on the ground, cursing and whimpering.

He was tired, tired. Huddled beneath the stairs, arms folded over his chest, he pondered his options. He might rouse Mayer, but they'd had a row the day before, the rent only five days overdue, yet the Kraut scolding him like a naughty schoolboy. It was just more evidence that the man was losing his faculties and Bertie had even told him to his face that if he didn't start controlling himself he was going to get a stroke and die on the spot. At this, Mayer bristled—the malevolence palpable—and in that menacing Peter Lorre accent said, "Ya, mein herr, we see. We see who lives longer and who laughs last."

Bertie decided he'd be damned if he'd ask that son of a bitch for anything. *Leave him to his old piss-and-vinegar self.* He was only yards from Mayer's door. He imagined the Kraut standing at the kitchen window that very moment, a cup of tea in his hand, staring at him in his misery. He put his mind on something else. The aroma of hops and malt in the air, the brewery going full-tilt even at this hour, putting out bottle after bottle of the King of Beers, and he could use one right about now. But to the matter at hand. The Third District Lock-Up was only a few blocks away, over on 13th and Lynch. The cops. *Ah, screw that. No, wait. Okay, alright, I'll go for help—why the hell not?* He went to get up and felt woozy. He sat back down. He'd go in a few minutes, after he rested.

On the Street
OLIVER AND **PORTIA** HEDGEPATH

"Tell us again why we must get out in this awful part of town."

The driver sighed impatiently. "Son, I've already explained. It's a test. Your mother and I want to see how well you two can fend for yourselves. If you show ingenuity and resource, then you should be home by nightfall. If not—well, let's just wait and see."

"But father," cried Oliver, "it's the day before Christmas!"

"That's right," pleaded little Portia, her blond bangs falling over worried blue eyes. "This is no time to be out and about. It's cold and it smells funny here."

Always the optimist, mother said, "That's true, darling, but I'm sure you'll get used to it in no time at all."

The Lincoln Continental had stopped in a mean part of the city. It was early morning and frost was on the ground. Red brick houses loomed on either side of the littered street, their chimneys spewing thin, gray smoke. Every other house, it seemed, was derelict in some way—boarded-up, falling down, busted windows and missing doors. Shells of former homes. Three mongrels, no collars, skulked along, keeping their distance from the big black car, searching for some garbage-breakfast. Father turned to his offspring in the back seat. "Okay, this is it," he said. "Oliver, do you have any money?" Oliver said that he had a couple quarters. Father held out his hand, palm outstretched. "Give it to me," he declared. "You know the rules. No money for bus fare, phone calls, or toothsome treats."

"Aw, gee!"

"No ifs, ands or buts, you two. Now, do you have your survival gear?"

Oliver dug into his jacket and produced a compass, a sextant, and a pocket-sized street guide. He held them out for father to see. "Outstanding," said father, approvingly. "Now hit the pavement."

Mother clasped their hands and smiled. "And remember," she said with a wink, "if you make it home by midnight, there'll be eggnog and gingersnaps waiting by the fire."

Portia expressed her delight. Oliver turned up his nose and said he hated eggnog.

"Oh, you hate eggnog, eh? Well, maybe eggnog hates you as well," said father, rather annoyed. "Life is tough. Now move it!"

The two stood at the curb and watched the Lincoln drive off. "Can you beat that?" said Oliver, shaking his head in dismay. The day was bleak; ash-gray clouds hung over the city like a dingy bedsheet. Oliver zipped his jacket as high as it would go and he fastened the hood of his sister's coat. In the distance, a pole with street signs. They went to it. Portia read aloud, "North Twentieth and East Prairie. Okay, now what?"

Oliver contemplated his little sister in all her doe-eyed naiveté. He could see that he would be the captain on this expedition. "Simple. I'll find it on the street guide and then we'll know where we are." But after several minutes, Oliver shrugged his shoulders and said he was baffled.

"Give it here," said Portia, snatching it from his hand. And before Oliver could say, "See, I told you so," Portia had her finger on the very intersection where they stood. Earnestly, they studied the street guide, turning pages back and forth, consulting the compass, trying to plot a course. Finally, Oliver pointed to what he thought was due west. "We head that way," he announced, "twenty miles, maybe more. Lucky it's still early. We'll be there in time for dinner."

They began the journey, walking the cracked and uneven sidewalks, careful not to tread on the occasional pile of dog dirt. Before long, dark-complected people appeared on porches and at bus stops. They said very little, merely staring with blank expressions as the youngsters passed. Portia gripped Oliver's hand tightly. She said in her best grown up voice, quite matter-of-fact, "This is Darktown, isn't it? I heard mother in the car say, 'We're really going to Darktown?' It's all so strange, so unfamiliar." Oliver squeezed her hand in response. "We'll get through it," he assured. "We're Hedgepaths."

They came to a store marked CONFECTIONARY over the door. A small bell tinkled as they entered. A bare light bulb hung over a large glass case of brightly packaged candies, but there was no one minding the place. Elsewhere, displays of cigarettes, cough drops, mousetraps, coloring books, religious candles, picture frames, small toys, school supplies, and sundry items of practical use. The children were exploring the place when the big woman walked in from a back room.

Seeing them standing there, she did an exaggerated double-take, her jaw dropping in mock surprise. "What you childrens want?" she asked, her tone quite skeptical-sounding. Oliver politely asked for directions to Town and Country. "Town and Country! Town and Country!" the woman whooped, clutching her bulging belly and laughing as though she'd heard the funniest thing in the world.

"Oh my, you poor li'l lambs is a *long* way from home. Town and Country! My momma cleaned houses there when I was a girl, used to take the bus out and back. Ain't never been there myself, 'fraid I can't tell you the first thing about gettin' to no rich white folks' neighborhood."

As the woman spoke, Portia seemed mesmerized by the contents of the candy case. She pressed her face against the glass and a rivulet of drool started down her chin. Oliver saw this and was moved. "Please ma'am, if you can't tell us how to get to Town and Country then could we have some candy?"

"Pretty please?" echoed Portia.

The big woman asked whether they had money to pay and when they said no, she wondered what they had to trade. Oliver showed her the sextant and she examined it by the light, squinting, turning it slowly like a jeweler considering a diamond. "It's for finding your position at sea," Oliver remarked. The woman harrumphed at this, showing a bright gold tooth. Finally, she agreed to swap the sextant for two handfuls of candy, a pencil, and a small notepad. Remembering their manners, the children thanked her kindly. Then, a light went on in Portia's head.

"Would you like to come to our house for Christmas dinner tomorrow?"

"That's a swell idea!" Oliver agreed. "We always have roast duck with all the trimmings and cranberry sauce and au gratin potatoes and oh! there's several wonderful desserts! Mother and father won't mind. You could even bring your friends. We always have plenty. It's one-one-four-five-three Larkspur Lane."

The big woman beamed at them. "Well, that's mighty nice of you childrens," she said, jotting down the address. "I'm Vi—that's short for Violet. My friends and me'll be happy to come eat y'all's food."

"About twoish then?"

"Wouldn't miss it," said Vi.

"Merry Christmas!" called Oliver and Portia on the way out.

"Merry!" returned Vi.

Outside, they gobbled down their candy and immediately felt energized. "Let's skip," said Portia. So they skipped along the sidewalk, sidestepping broken chairs and mattresses and various household items, the forlorn aftermath of tenant evictions. Hand in hand, they skipped along until they came to a neighborhood even worse than the one they had left.

As they rounded a corner, they came face to face with a shabbily dressed man standing at a blazing barrel. He did not acknowledge them, but continued feeding the fire with pieces of furniture that lay on the ground around him. Oliver and Portia stopped and stared. Squat and hunched with skin the color of coal, the man reminded Oliver of an aborigine, Oliver having just turned in a report on the Australian outback for geography class. His gray hair was long and wooly, totally unkempt, specked with burrs and bits of lint; his nostrils so cavernous they could have concealed chestnuts.

At length they ventured a hello.

"Wha' zah," he answered, his speech visible in the frosty air.

"Nice fire," tried Oliver.

"Are you a real bum?" asked Portia innocently.

The man scrutinized them with suspicious yellow eyes. He scratched himself and dabbed at the snot running down his nose, yet he made no reply.

"Aren't your feet cold?" wondered Portia. The man took an interest in this question. He looked down at the plum-colored nubs poking out of his shoes—his poor toes, cracked and filthy.

He thought to wiggle them, but they were stuck in place.

Oliver took the initiative and volunteered that they were trying to reach their home in Town and Country. At this the man suddenly grew animated, shouting a string of vile epithets against Town and Country and all who lived there. Shocked, Portia responded by plugging her ears.

Now the man began to shuffle his feet and do a little dance around the fire barrel. A second before he'd been raging, but now he seemed happy in a world of his own. He pulled a pint bottle from his tattered coat, uncapped it, and began to drink. After several swigs, he made a vulgar smacking sound and belched. He then took a drawer from what had been a chest of drawers and tossed it into the fire.

"Please sir," ventured Oliver. "May we stand by your fire?"

The man looked hurt by this request. He said, "Don't ask, little man, jus' do it. Do the thing."

They gathered round the fire barrel, but not so close that their eyebrows would be singed, and they kept warm. But not in silence. The man was humming, then mumbling, then talking lowly, barely audible, to himself apparently. At one point, he leaned over and sniffed Oliver, made a show of sniffing his hair. "What you got on your head, little man?" he asked. "Smells good, flowers or somethin.'"

"It could be the shampoo," returned Oliver. "Mother buys Herbal Essence in several fragrances. This morning I used Wild Strawberry."

The man spat on the ground and said something unintelligible. What he said next was perfectly clear. "Hey, little man, you got any squares?" Oliver did not know how to answer. The man brought two fingers to his lips in pantomime.

"I think he means cigarettes," offered Portia. "No sir, we don't have anything like that. We're too young to smoke."

Hearing this, the man laughed raucously. He laughed so hard he began to cough and collapsed in a fit. The pair rushed over and helped him sit up. He hacked up a bolus of green phlegm, spat it out, and wiped his mouth with his coat sleeve. Portia patted him on the shoulder and asked him his name. He told her: "Rucker."

"Mister Rucker," she said, "you've been so kind to let us get warm by your fire, we'd like to return the favor. How would you like to come to our house tomorrow for Christmas dinner with all the trimmings?"

"And after dinner, if you like," said Oliver, "father is a physician, he could examine you for emphysema. Or tuberculosis. You likely have one or the other."

"Would he really do that? On Christmas?" asked Portia.

"Of course he would, and free of charge. Any friend of ours is a friend of mother and father."

Rucker looked at them with mouth agape. He said, "I got a cousin with an ol' Dodge Maverick. On its last legs, you know? We get that wheel banged on, we'll be out tomorrow. Tha's a promise, little man. Shoot, I ain't had me a good meal in twenny Sundays."

Oliver wrote the address on his notepad, tore off the page and gave it to Rucker who tucked it away. They asked if they could help him up and he said no, he'd rather lie on the ground for a while. Wishing him a Merry Christmas, they walked on.

A long time later, and without incident, they reached a wide and busy street. North Grand Avenue was bustling. People everywhere carrying bags, going in and out of stores, gathering round an open-air barbecue stand or makeshift kiosks where sweatshirts and caps and gloves were sold. People hailing one another, laughing, shouting, gesticulating, and just being part of humanity.

Oliver said to Portia, "If there's a North Grand, then there must be a South Grand as well, but I believe we need to be in between the two—you know, the starting point of both, that's probably the median north-south line for the city. Once there, we'll head west according to the compass." Portia was impressed. Oliver said that his geographic sense, keen as it might be, stemmed from that one year in Boy Scouts where the troop had collected canned food in the city and he'd been able to get the lay of the land, as it were. That was before father decided to pull him out of the organization—too much riffraff, father said.

Portia said she had seen a TV show where two kids lost in the woods found their way home when one of them spit into an open palm and then smacked the spit with the other hand made into a fist. Whichever way most of the spit went was the direction they should travel.

"That doesn't sound very scientific," said Oliver. "Street signs, numbers, and a sense of reckoning are what's going to get us home." He pointed to a dilapidated building with a sign out front: JOBE'S TONSORIAL PARLOR. "Look at the number on that building, what does it say?"

"Fifty-five thirty-eight," she answered.

"What that means," said Oliver, "is that we are fifty-five blocks from the starting point of North Grand. Each block is a hundred, but sometimes the numbers skip a couple hundred. Like, one block may be the twenty-five hundred block and the next block may jump to twenty-eight hundred. What happened to the twenty-six and twenty-seven hundred blocks? Who knows, but the good thing is we probably won't have to walk fifty-five blocks to get to the next station."

"How many stations are there?" wondered Portia.

"I don't know," Oliver told her, "and we're not going to find out until we start walking. How are your legs?"

"Tired and sore. What time is it?"

"It's a little after two."

"Oh, boo-hoo. I'm missing my favorite TV show." Suddenly, Portia flushed and stamped her feet. "This is so ... oh, so dumb! My Laura Ashley dress smells like smoke and my loafers are getting ruined. I can't believe mother and father would do this to us. I think they're mean!"

Oliver put his arm around her and pressed his head to hers. "Courage and fortitude, we've definitely got it and that's what will see us through. As for mother and father, I think they mean well, but—you know, Portia, you're right! I'm not going to defend them, this *is* dumb!"

"Good for you," said Portia, giving him a little squeeze. "Alright, I'm ready if you are."

At that moment, in the third floor bedroom of a Georgian-style mansion on Larkspur Lane, mother and father were dressing for four o' clock services at the Third Presbyterian Church on Warson Road. Mother was in the walk-in closet, deciding whether to wear her black Halston dress with the gold brocade trim or go with the more ostentatious Betsey Johnson frock, a definite eye-grabber that had the runway crowd in Milan all abuzz this past summer. She came out and held up both for father, who was standing before the mirror, deftly knotting his candy-striped bowtie. "Choose one," she told him.

"Easy," he replied. "The Halston is more elegant and it will better show off your pearls."

"Then when shall I wear the other?" she pouted.

"We've got that fundraiser coming up," he said. "Dinner,

cocktails, dancing at the top of the Chase. Moonlit veranda. It would be appropriate for that."

"*Au contraire*, it would be perfect for that. After all, it is not a conservative dress. It is a dress that speaks of love and desire. Which fundraiser is this?"

"It's for some malady, child leukemia or lupus. Perhaps irritable bowel syndrome," he chuckled.

"The disease *du jour*," she retorted. "I can't keep track of them either." She let her clothing fall to the floor and began to don the Halston. Father glanced at her, standing there in her black bra and panties, and decided he felt amorous. Later on, after church, he would make his move.

"I wonder where the children are by now," she said, liberally spraying her neck and shoulders with Givenchy *Ange ou Demon Eau de Parfum*.

"Probably having hot chocolate in some quaint cafe in the Central West End, having talked the waiter into coming back tomorrow and paying the bill—with an added bonus."

Mother chuckled at the thought. "They're so cute. I know I'd give them hot chocolate *gratis* if they asked."

"I suspect they'll do the same thing with their transportation," said father. "Hail a taxi and tell the driver he'll be paid handsomely at the drop-off. At any rate, that's what *I* would do."

"Yes, Mister Clever, I can very well see *you* doing such a thing— but will they think of that?"

Meanwhile, the young Hedgepaths trudged on, always careful not to cross against the light. Their eyes were wide open and they saw things which they had never seen before—a fierce and bloody dogfight, a street corner evangelist proclaiming through a bullhorn, and a bedraggled woman in the middle of the street haranguing traffic.

"This is like another country or something," said Oliver, walking along with his hands in his pockets. "You don't know what's going to happen next. I feel a bit scared and excited all at once."

Portia bobbed her head in assent. "Do you really think mother and father will be there when we get home? What if they've moved away? Or what if they've adopted another boy and girl to take our places?"

"Oh, don't be silly. Mother and father wouldn't do that. They love us, it's just that they have a weird way of showing it. Like the time they—unhh!" Suddenly Oliver tumbled and fell flat on the pavement."

"Hey, watch it!" an annoyed voice called from the shadowy recess of a beauty parlor entrance.

"Who's that?" Oliver called to the silhouette.

"It's Mazie, you clod. Who else would it be? You tripped over my leg."

Oliver said he was sorry. "Well," said Mazie, still unseen, "no real harm done. My skin's too tough to bruise anyway. Come closer. Who's that with you?"

"This is my sister, Portia, and I'm Oliver."

"Let me get a better look," was the reply and from the vestibule came a rustling and a stirring. Then, like a mountain out of a mist, Mazie appeared. A big woman to be sure, but Oliver wondered just how much of her was dressed for the weather, layer upon layer of clothing. Her eyes dark and squinty and her long gray hair set in a ponytail, she had the rough-and-tumble look of a hod-carrier at the end of a long day. She wasn't young, but she wasn't old either. "Well, well, well," she said in a sing-song voice, stepping near. The children shrank back. Mazie ignored their concern and began to stroke their shoulders affectionately. She ran the back of her rough hand down their cheeks. She tousled their hair. "Very nice," she crooned. "Too nice for street urchins, I'll say."

Oliver and Portia protested the label and explained that they lived in an affluent suburb and that they were taking the long way home.

"I never heard such nonsense," said Mazie, her lips fluttering over an enormous set of yellow teeth. "I think you're lost, tired and hungry."

As the children watched, Mazie reached into the the dark vestibule and grabbed two large shopping bags, both brimming with stuff. She began clomping up the street. "Well, c'mon," she called without looking back, "it's just around the corner."

"What is?"

"The diner, what else?" So the children scurried after her and in a minute they were in an alley, standing at the loading dock of a grocery store. Mazie stood beside a big green Dumpster. "Welcome to Mazie's Diner!" she announced, slapping the side of the Dumpster, causing a startled rat to leap out.

Portia asked Mazie if she expected them to eat garbage. Mazie gave her a hurt look. "First, it's not garbage, it's good, delicious, nutritious food that's just a little past fresh. Second, don't knock it 'til you've tried it." Mazie found a plastic milk crate laying nearby, set it near the Dumpster, stood on it, and leaned into the bin, her legs sticking almost straight up. Oliver and Portia watched with great curiosity. "Let's see what's on the menu," she said, her voice a bit muffled. "Hey, we're in luck. Lots of good stuff here. Tomatoes, slightly mooshy. Lettuce, a bit brown around the edges, and—what is this thing?—oh! an onion, just a bit soft. Here, take this box— catch!"

She tossed down the produce and before long Mazie had whipped up a salad, slicing the items with a hefty jackknife that had once lived in a tackle box and had gutted and scaled hundreds of catfish caught from the river. She arranged the contents just so in the cardboard box. "Alright, dig in," she said.

"We need a bowl," said Oliver.

"Do you have silverware?" from Portia.

"Ingrates! This box is a bowl. Can't you see that? And who needs silverware when you've got fingers?" With her thumb and forefinger she dug in and with a flourish pulled out a tomato wedge and a sliver of carrot. "See?" she said, popping it in her maw. "Not bad, not bad at all, especially for the price."

Oliver and Portia were reluctant, their hunger pangs not strong enough to overcome years of good breeding. Yet Mazie exhorted them, browbeat them, actually, so unmercifully that they gave in. Picking out the less disagreeable items from the rancid concoction, they chewed.

"Ick!" said Oliver, retching. "It tastes like dirt—not that I really know what dirt tastes like."

"Yuk!" said Portia, making a sour face. "It's no use," she told Mazie, fighting back tears. "We just can't eat this. We're used to finer things."

"Chicken Kiev," said Oliver, licking his lips.

"Almond tortes," countered Portia, wistfully. "Oh, Oliver, let's hurry home. Mother and father are waiting for us. The good life, Oliver, the good life is waiting for us."

They thanked Mazie for her kindness and in turn invited her and her friends to their home in Town and Country the following day for a nice Christmas dinner with all the trimmings. "Why, bless your sweet little hearts!" she exclaimed. "Mazie don't travel, but I know a raft of people who'd love to go. Street people, sure, but salt of the earth. Give you their last swig of hooch, they would."

"Any friend of yours is a friend of ours," said Oliver, "and we've plenty to go around."

Gathering her bags, Mazie insisted that she accompany them for the next leg of their journey, at least as far as the Hodiamont Tracks.

"We were going to find the starting point of Grand Avenue then head west," said Oliver.

"This way's quicker, believe me, your dogs will thank me. C'mon, I'm your Indian guide, follow me."

They walked through the night, zig-zagging through neighborhoods, stepping briskly to ward off the chill. Many of the big brick homes were illuminated and if the blinds or curtains were open they could see activity within. "Probably stringing popcorn or baking cookies for Santa," said Portia.

"More likely going to the fridge for another beer," said Mazie.

At length they came to a bleak-looking stretch of emptiness, what was left of the railway where the streetcars once ran. Mazie stopped them just short of the gravel bed that held the iron rails and wooden ties. "This is where I turn back. Mazie don't go past these tracks. That's a whole nother world out there," she said, "and those folks is welcome to it."

"There's no lights," observed Oliver.

"Don't need lights," sniffed Mazie, "just follow the tracks thata-way until yous come to Martin Luther King Drive then turn west—or right, however you look at it. After that, well, one foot in front of the other 'til you get to where you're goin.'"

"Do you have a dollar?" asked Portia. "Maybe we could ride the bus home."

"Yeah," said Oliver, "our dogs are thanking you, but they really need a break."

"C'mere yous," said Mazie, but instead she advanced to them and put her big arms around both of them, giving them a bear hug so exuberant that they grunted from the pressure on their rib cages. "If I had a hunnerd dollars I'd be tickled to give it, but Mazie don't carry no money. Don't have use for it. What I do have, let's see …" And she rummaged in her many pockets and came out with a whistle on a lanyard. "This here's an Acme Thunderer," she told them. "It's small, but it makes a big sound. Listen." The resounding blast from the little whistle made them cover their ears.

"Wake the dead," said Mazie, grinning. "Take it, may come in handy, you never know. Now, skedaddle down them tracks and be careful. Keep to yourselves and don't talk to nobody, hear? I'll be thinking of yous. Now, git."

Meanwhile, in the second-floor study on Larkspur Lane, mother and father lay nude on the plush carpet in a tangle of discarded clothing. Father was trying to catch his breath, feeling quite chipper over his virile performance; mother was staring at the ceiling wondering if she had put enough sugar in the gingersnap cookies. The recipe called for one cup of white sugar, but she was so distracted by the absence of her children, not knowing where the heck they were, that she may have inadvertently put in one tablespoon. She was pretty sure she had added all the other ingredients correctly—the flour, the baking soda, the cinnamon, the shortening, the molasses and, of course, the ginger. Wait, did she remember the egg? Her train of thought suddenly snapped—*Oh, good god, what's he doing now? Nibbling my ear, putting his icky, wet tongue in there! Mister Lothario wants to have another go. Please!*

They'd come home from services fortified with goodwill toward their fellow man and, true to his erstwhile spasm of lust, father began the process of seduction. First, he poured Frangelico into a pair of ice-filled snifters. Then, he invited mother into his study, dimmed the lights, and put Mel Tormé on the stereo. He asked her to dance, dance with him slow. She complied. With both hands he grasped her fanny and pressed into her pelvis. There! He felt a stirring. He asked her if she knew Mel Tormé's nickname. She did not. The Velvet Fog, he told her.

"I can see why," she said.

Slyly, he said, "Do you know what they call me?"

"Who is they?" she wondered.

"Women," he said, "women call me the bodice-ripper."

She laughed, but not derisively. She said, "Men are silly if they think women enjoy having their fifty-dollar brassieres rudely torn from their torsos. There are better ways to thrill a woman."

Said father, "You mean like this?" And with a savage gleam in his eye, he lowered her to the carpet and ravished her then and there.

It was late when they reached Martin Luther King Drive, heading right—west by the compass—as Mazie had told them. They hadn't gone two blocks before they saw a sign that said WELCOME TO WELLSTON, POP. 4,460. They kept on, hardly believing their eyes, for, if possible, this place was even worse than the miserable environs they had already trekked through. Apparently, this was the main thoroughfare and yet the buildings were crumbling, evidenced by their having to step around loose bricks and architectural ornament fallen from the parapets to the sidewalk below. Here and there, yellow plastic tape stretched from perhaps a tree to a fence to a light post, telling pedestrians DO NOT ENTER – CRIME SCENE. Sad cars lined the curb. Some were burned out, fire having ravaged the interior. Others had been picked clean, the tires gone and hood yawning open to reveal everything except the engine block. It was a dreary, scary place, especially on Christmas Eve when their own cozy world beckoned some twelve daunting miles hither.

"I know," said Portia, "let's sing Christmas carols."

Oliver led off with "Silent Night," Portia complementing his tenor baritone with her mezzo soprano, their voice lessons at La Academie paying off. They walked on, time passing less grudgingly now with renditions of beloved yuletide carols, both secular and non-secular. It was while singing "Frosty the Snowman" that they heard a separate and, decidedly, ominous chorus behind them.

"De-mar-co, the homeboy, had a crack pipe for a soul—haw, haw!" They turned to see five young men, teens, a little older than they, striding briskly, almost upon them. They wore their hair long and poofed up, a style that Portia knew from her magazines as a 'fro. Not only that, they all sported similar outfits—baggy blue jeans rolled up to show the tops of black army boots, and sleeveless denim jackets that spelled out, in fiery letters, PHARAOH'S ARMY. At ten steps away, the encounter imminent, Oliver and Portia saw their accessories: rococo rings and gaudy necklaces and dollar store earrings, all glinting in the filtered light of an illuminated pawn shop sign.

They came upon the two, not saying a word, some grinning and some leering. The intruders formed a circle around them and simply stood there, arms folded, silent, as if waiting for a command. Portia was the first to speak. "That's not how the song goes, and you know it," addressing the tallest one wearing the most jewelry. They all snickered at this assertion, bold as it was.

"That's right, Ba-Pharaoh," smirked a punk with a wonky eye, "you don't know your Christmas songs. You gonna get a lumpa coal in your stocking."

"Okay, Whitney Houston," egged Ba-Pharaoh to Portia, "why don't you show us how to sing it?"

Portia did just that. She sang "Frosty the Snowman" for Pharaoh's Army and they liked it so much they even joined in on the parts they knew: "There must've been some magic in that old silk hat we found, 'cause when we put it on his head he began to dance around ..."

Then they wanted more songs, because Christmas carols were not sung where they came from. But Oliver and Portia explained that they had to get home by midnight.

"Oh," said Ba-Pharaoh, "and I suppose your highnesses want us to chauffeur you?"

"Oh, no, sir," said Oliver. "We have strict orders never to take rides with strangers."

The gang laughed at this and one of them quipped, "You can't get any stranger than us."

Then Ba-Pharaoh said, "We ain't got no wheels anyway on account of a certain traffic court judge. And he's gonna pay for that, 'cause we know where he lives." He stooped over to be in Portia's face. Eyeball to eyeball, he said, "What do you think of that?"

She did not blanch or look away. "I think you should accept the consequences of your actions and not entertain thoughts of revenge upon authority figures, that's what I think."

Ba-Pharaoh jumped back in mock alarm, arms akimbo, his mouth agape. "Well, that's so, um, *mature* of you to think that, but I bet you'd think differently if you were in our boots. Street's our home. No one gives us a break—no one! And we fight back any way we can. We take what we need whether we need it or not."

"That's right," said a husky voice behind Portia, "and I think I need them pretty things attached to her ears. More bling for King

Tut." Then Portia felt a hand on her shoulder and another hand stroking her ear. She tried to squirm away, but the hands tightened.

"Hode on there, Tut," said Ba-Pharaoh. "Whyn't you just ax the girl for her earrings? No need to get physical ... yet."

Tut, still restraining Portia, replied, "Look man, you said it yourself: We take what we need and I am in the process of taking, so back the hell off."

Instantaneously, Ba-Pharoah whapped Tut upside the head. Tut released his hold on Portia and lunged at Ba-Pharaoh, going for his throat. They hit the pavement hard, a flurry of pounding fists and guttural sounds. They kept on fighting, punching and gouging, despite the series of shrill, clarion blasts from the Acme Thunderer.

"Gimme that thing!" demanded the one with the wonky eye. But Oliver dodged the attempted grab and blew the whistle yet again. Mazie was right, it had to be the loudest whistle in the world. Finally, three soldiers corralled Oliver and wrested the whistle from his grip. But it was too late, for the whistle had summoned help in the form of a big orange truck, PUBLIC WORKS written on the side panel. The truck pulled up to the curb, scant feet away, yellow lights flashing, and a man jumped out. With a wild yell he ran straight to the melee, pulled out a baton, and began beating the two on the pavement. When he was done with that, he turned to the rest and said, "Who else needs a tune-up?" A few of them backed off, but the one with the wonky eye stood his ground. "I see you wearing a City of Wellston patch on your uniform," he said, "but that don't make you no cop. You nothin' but a janitor."

"You're right," said the man, flashing a grin, "a janitor who loves nothing better than to screw with punks like you." And from a flap in his overalls, he brought out a cannister of pepper spray and spritzed wonky eye square on his startled face. He screamed in anguish. Then the man whirled about, spraying Ba-Pharaoh and

King Tut just starting to get to their feet, and while they were yowling and rubbing their eyes, he hit them some more with the baton.

"Beat it!" he roared. "Get on back to your cracks and crevices, you cockroaches. Stay there until you learn some respect." When the members of Pharaoh's Army didn't immediately turn tail, he raised the baton, threatening to bludgeon them "until you cry for your mommas." That did the trick.

He turned to Oliver and Portia and took an exaggerated bow. "Calvin Rhodes, public servant, at your service," he said. The man listened with great interest as the intrepid pair told their tale, concluding with the passionate appeal that they really had to get home sooner than later.

"Well, this must be your lucky day, I mean, night," said Calvin Rhodes, "because I just now got done with my street sweeping and Elsie—that's my truck—is ready to roll in any direction you say."

"Oh, Mister Rhodes," said Portia, "you are just the nicest man ever. It can't be that far and, when we get there, I'm sure father will see that you're rewarded."

"I like that idea, yes ma'am, sounds good to me."

"And there's eggnog and gingersnaps waiting," said Oliver.

Calvin Rhodes shuddered as if a bad memory had been dredged up. "I hate eggnog," he confessed.

Mother happened to be looking out the window toward the street when the big orange truck pulled up, lights flashing. She saw the door open, saw her children clamber down from the cockpit or cab or whatever you called it, saw a dark figure come round from the other side, put his arms around them, and walk toward the house. It was precisely four minutes to midnight, Christmas Eve.

Calvin Rhodes took note of the splendid display of Santa and his reindeer on the lawn; the illuminated, animated Frosty the Snowman repeatedly taking a bow; and the multi-colored, blinking Christmas lights that outlined the windows, doors, and eaves of the handsome house. "Guess your people is really into this Christmas thing," Calvin Rhodes remarked, and by his tone it was evident that he did not share the same enthusiasm.

"Oh, yes, father prides himself in his presentation," answered Oliver.

"Each year it gets more elaborate," said Portia.

Mother answered the door. Seeing the children, her face lit up. "My, what a pleasant surprise!" she exclaimed as Oliver and Portia hugged her waist.

"Who the heck is it?" called father from somewhere.

"It's the children, dear, with their friend—"

"Calvin Rhodes, ma'am, public works, City of Wellston."

"Well, ask him in," shouted father, emerging from a hallway. "Oh, he is in." Father stopped in his tracks. He wasn't expecting an escort as black as a frying skillet and built like a tank.

"Father! Father!" Oliver and Portia ran to his side. Father stroked them about the head and shoulders much like someone would pet a dog. "You two smell like smoke," he said. Then he looked to Calvin Rhodes and forced a smile. "Where did you find them?"

"Martin Luther King Drive," replied the street sweeper, "caught up in a scuffle."

"It was a miracle he came along when he did," said Portia. "Otherwise Pharaoh's Army might have had their way with me."

"Oh, my god!" cried mother, clutching her breast.

"You should have seen the way he repelled them," added Oliver, "just like an action hero. Those guys are going to have some serious bruises."

"Well, I can't thank you enough," said father, holding out his hand.

Calvin Rhodes engaged the handshake, pumping a bit too vigorously, father thought. But when the handshake was done, the man torqued his calloused hand a quarter-turn and now the palm was outstretched, open in the time-honored attitude of someone about to receive alms.

"What's this?" asked father, knowing darn well what it was.

"You can't thank me enough," answered Calvin Rhodes, his deportment serious now, "but you haven't really tried yet, have you?"

"I see," said father, nodding. "Yes, I do think remuneration is in order." He took out his wallet, removed a bill, snapped it smartly for effect, and handed it over.

Calvin Rhodes took the bill and examined it critically. "I bring your children home, save them from a vicious street gang, and that's worth ten dollars to you?"

"Oh, alright," conceded father, thinking anything to get this fellow out of here.

Father put another bill in the man's outstretched hand. Again, Calvin Rhodes examined the currency and shook his head in an exasperated manner. With thumb and forefinger he held the note out as far as his arm would stretch, like it stunk, and said to father, "This here is Andrew Jackson, the seventh president of the United States, but I prefer the eighteenth president of the United States."

"And who would that be?" inquired father.

"General U.S. Grant!" from Oliver.

"You are a smart boy," said Calvin Rhodes. "Daddy here should be so smart. Now, how 'bout a couple General Grants, Daddy?"

"Now, see here," sputtered father, "you can't just waltz in here and start demanding money. I could call the police and have you removed."

"Oh, I like that idea!" said Calvin Rhodes, rubbing his hands together. "And when they come, I can tell them how you abandoned your children."

"Oh, fiddlesticks! They were no more abandoned than the man in the moon. They're participating in a church-sponsored urban Outward Bound program. Besides, my parents did the same thing to me forty years ago, and I had to get home from East St. Louis— a harrowing undertaking, believe me."

"Yeah? I grew up in East St. Louis, finest town in Illinois. But you know what I believe? I believe you owe me more'n thirty bucks."

"Oh, father," cried Portia, "please be generous. He's worth it. We could still be walking, our poor toes on the verge of frostbite. Or worse, lying dead in a gutter, our vacant eyes staring into oblivion."

Calvin Rhodes gazed upon her admiringly. "Girl, you was born for a poet."

Father harrumphed and again took out his wallet, but before he could produce the next payment Calvin Rhodes snatched it out of his hand. "Enough of this ten bucks here, twenty bucks there," Calvin Rhodes told him. "You think I'm some Steppin Fetchit who's gonna be thrilled with your pissant tip? Screw you, I'm taking what's right."

Horrified, father watched Calvin Rhodes thumb through his wallet, remove every bill, fold them in half and put them in a side pocket. He then thought twice, took the wad back out, and made a show of placing a single dollar bill back in the wallet, which he then handed to father. "I leave you with George," he said, "the *first* president of the United States, case you didn't know."

Calvin Rhodes turned about and made for the door. His hand on the doorknob, he looked to mother and father, wagged his forefinger in admonishment. "Don't even *think* about mistreating these li'l darlings again, hear? I got eyes and ears all over this city. I hear of any foolishness, I'm coming back, hear? And next time I won't be so nice. Anyway, y'all have a good holiday."

With that, he was out out the door, but a second later the door opened, just his round face poking through, speaking to them. "Oh, by the way, I'm taking your Frosty Snowman. Not for me—I can't stand the sight of it, spooks me—but I know some kids who'll like it."

In the kitchen, over eggnog and gingersnap cookies—considerately, Oliver's eggnog cut with orange-pineapple juice—the youngsters recounted their adventures. "And then Mister Rucker almost fell into the fire. But we saved him—didn't we, Portia?"

"Yes, we saved him, purple toes and all," she chuckled. "And then Mazie tried to make us dinner from slop she found in the back of a market, but we couldn't stomach it."

"I was worried about contracting worms," said Oliver.

"Who, pray tell, is Mazie?" wondered father.

"She's this homeless person," answered Oliver, "a big old thing who seems to do quite well living by her wits and on her own. She walked with us to the Hodiamont Tracks."

"Our Indian guide," reminded Portia. "She may be here tomorrow, along with some of the others we've invited. I do hope they come."

"That's nice," said mother, popping a gingersnap into her mouth.

Portia continued, "Shall we buy more food? I worry there may not be enough. And wine, Mister Rucker likes—"

"Who could that be at this hour?" said father, mulling the portent of the sound of a doorbell.

Before mother or father could get up, Oliver ran to the door and opened it. And before anyone could leave their seats, Oliver was back in the kitchen with three others in tow.

"Look who it is!" said Oliver to Portia.

"Vi!" cried Portia. "You made it. How wonderful!"

"Yeah, we took a few wrong turns, got stopped by the po-lice for a missing bumper, but we made it. I know we a bit early, and I hope you don't mind, but—"

Uncharacteristically, Portia interrupted. "Introductions first, if you please. Mother, father, let me introduce Vi, that's short for Violet, who owns a confectionary in the city near where you abandoned us. She was nice enough to give us candy and other useful things."

Mother and father, utterly shocked at the sudden turn of events—three Negroes in their kitchen, acting way too familiar—could only nod in dumb recognition.

"Oh, I'm so happy to see you made it home safe n' sound," said Vi, giving Portia a hug. "But like you say, innerductions. This my sister, Rose—mom named all us girls after flowers. And this my cousin, Theophilus. We call him Tee." Rose and Tee beamed at the mention, extending enthusiastic greetings to mother and father. Eyeing the cookie platter and the pitcher of eggnog, Vi went on. "So, I was sayin', I know we early, but, see, we snuck Tee here outta the rehab center and we gotta get him back before eight tomorrow, 'cause that's when they give the methadone shots."

That was when mother choked on her gingersnap.

Mike Shotwell
ZOO TRAIN CONDUCTOR

WE WERE STANDING IN THE MIDDLE OF BELLERIVE CEMETERY, a beautiful nature preserve in tony West County, which also happens to be a resting place for the dead. And we were gathered there around the casket of my pal Bud Wilkinson, the open grave yawning, the forklift on standby, and we were waiting for the minister to say his final words so that Bud could properly go into the ground for a nice long nap when somebody farted. It was a deep, rumbling sort of fart like a tuba in an echo chamber, and I am sure the responsible party felt much better having passed it. But the mourners were many, gathered in a group off to the side of the casket, and the culprit chose to remain anonymous. Didn't matter, I knew who blasted. The beet-red face of George Pawlik a dead give-away, the guy shuffling around, edging away from the others, trying to move away from ground zero before the stench got really bad. Figures. Oh, more than a few folks were snickering. Certain infantile people will always find amusement in a fart, but Bud wouldn't have found it funny. Bud was a straight-shooter, real sincere, he didn't appreciate buffoonery. I'm not saying he didn't enjoy a hearty laugh from time to time; Laughter is good for the soul, he used to say. Sometimes, early on, in the Safari Grill, before we went to our trains, all the conductors would be sitting around drinking coffee and having bagels, just shooting the breeze before the zoo opened, and Bud would come up with the funniest stuff. Real knee-slappers, like, Why does a bald man not need a key? And we'd scratch our heads for a while and finally say, Don't know, Bud, why? And Bud would get this twinkle in his eye and he'd say, Because he doesn't have any locks! George Pawlik would scoff and act disgusted, saying, That's just a corny riddle, old as Methuselah. Can't you do better than that? George was always a bit hard on Bud, but Bud was too gracious to ever let it get to him. He'd just smile and say, Well, George, we can't all be Henny Youngmans. For those of you too young to remember Henny Youngman was the king of the one-liners, a great guy to have at your party if you could get him to come. Henny Youngman was old school, and so was Bud Wilkinson. And now Bud was dead as dead can be. In death, he holds the distinction of being the only employee of the St. Louis Zoo, founded in 1910, who has died in the line of duty. That counts for something in my book.

I looked over and saw Ruth, newly widowed, and she was blubbering something awful, poor gal. Ruth had her arm around Hope, the only child of their longtime marriage, and Hope was bearing up better than mom. Not exactly stoic, but at least not watering the sod at her feet. All around, in fact, the handkerchiefs were out. And why not? It was a funeral and you're supposed to weep, right? Not only for the deceased, but for your own miserable self and the mortal coil that is just too damn short. I mean, one day you're gumming your pablum and, before you know it, you're all crotchety, watching daytime TV and yelling at kids to get off your lawn. Well, that's my take on the matter, but it was Bud's show now. He was in the box, the center of attention, the cause of much sorrow and, as of today, never to be seen again. Tell you this, though: Bud's final appearance back there at the funeral parlor we'd just left was pretty memorable, him being decked out in his conductor outfit. The blue denim bib overalls, the engineer's cap, the red kerchief around his neck, and the watch fob trailing from a buttonhole on the overalls to a solid sterling silver, Swiss-made pocket watch held in his lifeless hand. I almost expected him to spring up from his casket and shout, "All aboard!" It was a very nice touch, but not too surprising. The man's entire life was wrapped up in scale model trains and I'm glad the family had the good sense to send him off in style.

I got home around five, having had a few snorts with some of the guys at a bar near the cemetery. The wife was in the kitchen tossing a tomato-mozzarella-basil salad. I walked up behind her and gave her a big hug. I kissed the back of her neck and told her how I loved her and if she loved me, she would never dress me up in a silly train conductor costume when it came to my funeral. She laughed at this and asked me how it'd gone that afternoon.

"It was a great day for a funeral," I said. "Lots of teary eyes, quivering lips, and smeared makeup. Several people got up and gave testimony about how Bud was a bona fide hero, staying on the train until it crashed."

Mary looked astounded. "Hero? That's rich! The man didn't have enough sense to leap from a runaway train and save his own life. A toy train at that! What good did he think he was doing by sticking around until the end? There were no lives to save. All he had to do was step off, maybe do a tuck-and-roll, and then he'd be here today. I'd say old Bud was a bona fide fool, not a hero."

"I hear you," I nodded. "Almost anyone else would've jumped and just let the damn thing crash, but Bud was really dedicated to the job, took it very seriously. He probably thought he could stop it in time. He was probably working the controls, pumping the brakes, until the last second."

"Idiot."

"He did what he did and he paid."

"Now the zoo's going to pay through the nose for his dedication."

"Nah, the family won't sue. They know that Bud wouldn't like that."

"Are you really that naive?"

"Yeah, I think so."

"Well, that's why you're my lovin' man. Now get ready for dinner, will you? Oh, a reporter called, wanted to speak to the Mike Shotwell who works at the zoo. The number's on the cork board."

His name was Steve MacArthur and he worked for that fishwrap, the *Post-Dispatch*. Big beefy guy in a sports jacket, no tie, a nuts-and-bolts news writer who aspired to feature writing. So he said at the get-go of our meet. His editor had told him to go to town on Bud, find out what made him tick. Steve agreed to meet at The Village Bar, not far from my place, the following Tuesday around five. The Village Bar is all that's left of the old commercial landscape around Manchester and I-270, just an old-time tavern surrounded by monstrous steel-and-glass office buildings. We took a booth in the corner and ordered Budweisers from Kelly the barmaid. Steve had his notepad out, ready to go. I said I wasn't sure if I wanted my words on record.

"I mean, the whole thing is still pretty fresh," I said. "Bud's been buried three days. The family is still in mourning. I don't want to cause them more grief."

"I've never been accused of misquoting anyone," he countered.

"I'm not so concerned about that," I told him. "It's me and my big mouth. I have a habit of putting my foot in it."

"Alright then, let's just talk and see what comes of it," said Steve, closing the notepad, and I shrugged what-the-hell.

"I can give you some general background on the guy, and you may already know some of this if you've done your homework. Okay, here goes: Bud—God rest his soul—was a retired chemical engineer, worked at Monsanto his entire adult life. He married late, mid-thirties, and he loved Ruth, his wife, and Hope their daughter, an analyst with Stifel Nicolaus. Loved them with all his heart until the day he died." I paused to glimpse at Steve, leaning forward, his elbow resting on the table, arm upright, right hand supporting his chin like that famous deep-in-thought statue by the French guy. Was he intending to memorize all this? He motioned for me to continue.

"Yeah, so Bud retired three-four years ago, must've been about sixty-three. Now, with all this time on his hands, he had to find something new to do. He tried gardening, tried volunteering at the Red Cross, he joined the Shriners and wore a fez, but none of this did it for him. For Bud, time was precious and he didn't want to squander what time he had left. He was looking for something meaningful, a pastime or part-time job that he could relate to when a neighbor told him about an opening at the zoo for a scale-train operator. He was immediately intrigued and he applied the very next day. And he was pretty confident he'd get the job, if only because he looked the part of a zoo train conductor."

"He told you all this?" asked Steve.

"We talked, yeah, talked a lot. I'm the youngest conductor and Bud was the oldest, but we got along. Some of the other guys ribbed him for being such a … oh, I don't know, a Dudley Do-Right, maybe. You know, the cartoon character."

"The Canadian Mountie? Dumb as a box of rocks, but a heart of gold."

"Yeah, only Bud wasn't dumb. Anyway, that first day they showed him the train he'd operate, the *Pierre Laclede*, he absolutely fell in love with her. He loved the route, the scenery, loved the passengers, loved the uniform, loved shouting 'All Aboard!' and 'Hold on to your hats, folks. Here we go!' But most of all, he loved the train. He'd had model trains as a kid and in his twenties he got back into it. With the job at Monsanto, he had the money to go all out and buy some really nifty model trains and accessories. In fact, that hobby was what kept him from dating and marriage for so long."

Steve lit a smoke and nodded knowingly. "Now I see what you mean by Dudley Do-Right. A grown man playing with trains, kind of weird. Arrested development, maybe."

"I don't try to analyze it," I said. "I mean, everybody's into something, right? Most guys are into baseball, football, hockey, whatever. I thought it was kind of touching that a guy would nurture a pastime that he really liked, even though others might think he's a dork. I saw it like he was in touch with the boy inside him. And it didn't stop when he got married. Ruth was very supportive, whatever he wanted to do, and he had turned their basement into a miniature town with model trains running on tracks and little dioramas of people doing things in this town. I was over there once, he showed it to me, the whole thing built on a couple of ping-pong tables. His own little world, everything just perfect."

"That's really bizarre. I mean, interesting. Did he have a name for this town?"

"Yeah, he had a little sign at the train station—'Pleasantville' or 'Happy Valley'. Nothing original."

"You say he drove the *Pierre Laclede*. I know that name as one of the founders of St. Louis. Are all the trains named after historic figures?"

"I drive the *Lewis and Clark*. Then there's the *Auguste Chouteau*, the other founder and the stepson of Pierre Laclede.

George Pawlik drives that. Melvin Bobo drives the *Mark Twain* and Pete Newsome drives the *Heinie Manush*. Five trains in all ... well, four now."

Steve just fell out at this, laughing uncontrollably, spitting beer all over the table. After he came up for air, he said, "Heinie Manush, you've got to be kidding! Left fielder for the old St. Louis Browns. There's a train named after him?"

"Hall of Famer, too, don't forget. It used to be the *T.S. Eliot,* but he got the boot when the new zoo director took over a few years back. His wife was somehow related to Heinie and she talked him into changing the name."

We called Kelly over for another round, and then we gabbed some more. This wasn't half as bad as I thought it'd be. I told Steve to go ahead and use the notepad if he wanted.

"Try and describe the social environment of the job," said Steve. "What was it like working with these guys? Good camaraderie? Petty feuds?"

"Well, there were only five of us, so I'd say we were all pretty thick. Up to a point. I mean, just to compare, my last job was as a union carpenter. You talk about camaraderie, we were flush with it. The engineers—the train operators—we don't fraternize outside the job, but we do have fun with each other while we're there. There's a fair amount of kidding, the occasional practical joke. We generally start the day together, meet in the Safari Grill before the zoo opens, right? And we sit around having coffee before the first run. Some of the guys are so much hot air, quick with the smart-ass remark, but Bud was very sincere. Oh, he'd joke around, but never anything that had to do with the trains. The job was too important to joke about. I think he even wanted to take it to the next level. He once told me that he imagined himself as the engineer of a real train, one of those luxury jobs from the fifties—

the *Super Chief* or the *El Capitan*—running from Chicago to LA. That would be Nirvana for a guy like Bud."

"What kind of practical jokes?" wondered Steve.

"Ouch, there's that foot in my mouth. Couldn't we just forget about that? Your readers wouldn't be interested in our hijinks."

"Oh, they might. Anecdotes can really make a feature article. C'mon now, Mike, spill the beans."

"Nah, I can't. Confidentiality."

"*Please.*"

"Oh, alright. It's just stupid stuff like the time they caught a mouse and put it in Bud's lunch pail. No one got to see his reaction when he saw the mouse, but wow! You can imagine."

"That's a good one," said Steve. "What else?"

"They put some super-glue on his seat so when he sat down his pants were stuck to the seat."

"The seat on his train, where he sat up front?"

"Oh, no! That would be vandalism of zoo property. This was his customary chair in the Safari Grill. That place is not owned by the zoo."

"Well, I'm glad to hear that," said Steve. "So, were these practical jokes played only on Bud?"

"You know, come to think of it, mostly they were. He was the new guy, after all. Back in my carpenter days, new guys got the same treatment. It's sort of an initiation, all good fun."

"But Bud had been on the job for two years when the accident occurred. Were the practical jokes still happening to him up to the end?"

"Oh, I don't know, maybe. But if they were, he took it good-naturedly. You know, I never saw him raise his voice or show anger. He was liked by everyone, he knew that. Hell, he could've played practical jokes on the rest of us—a little payback, right? But that wasn't his style."

"You say 'they' played jokes on Bud."

"How do you like this place, nice atmosphere, huh?"

"Mike, focus. Who is 'they'?"

Jesus, this guy was persistent and I hated to play him, but the line had to be drawn somewhere. "How do you think the Cards'll do this year? They got a good bullpen."

"Yeah, hmm. Well, let's go to the day of the accident. What do you recall about that? Same old routine? Anything different, out of the ordinary?"

"That day he was feeling his oats and he looked great, too. I mean, his outfit: perfection. The overalls were spotless and the pant legs *creased* for crissake! Ruth must've done that for him. He had his engineer cap tilted slightly back on his head and he'd added several pins to it. Some of the guys like to wear little souvenir pins on their hats. You get 'em at the model train store—names of railroads, famous trains, and whatnot. Bud was into it, every aspect of training, no doubt about that. Anyway, no one really knows what happened in those final minutes because he was alone, but as best as we can tell, it was some kind of mechanical failure."

"That makes sense," said Steve, getting excited, "it happened first thing."

"Right. He had just left the train shed and was heading out on the route, but instead of stopping at Discovery Corner Station to pick up passengers, he kept going. Not like Bud at all to disregard protocol. And he kept on going, past the next station and there some folks saw him frantically working the controls. It seems the train was accelerating and yet, for some reason, Bud couldn't stop it. Top speed on these four-cylinder jobs is around twenty-five, but we rarely press it. I think Bud was going that fast when coming

into the African exhibit. At that point, the *Pierre Laclede* was heading for the South Terminal, a set of steel beams sunk into concrete.
But of course you'd normally stop well before reaching those steel
beams. So Bud was on a runaway train, he had to be aware of the
danger. He had to know he had precious little time to take action,
to save his own self. He had to have thought to jump but, no, he
couldn't abandon ship. But this was a train, not a ship. And he
was an engineer, not a captain—so that rule doesn't apply, right?
I would have jumped, believe me. Any of the other guys would
have jumped, but Bud, for some reason we'll never know, he stayed
with it and the impact sent him flying some twenty feet right over
a fence and he landed in the hippo pond. Hippos are very curious
by nature, did you know that? By the time they had got to Bud, the
hippos had nibbled his body."

"You're kidding!" said Steve. "No, you're not, but that's just too
much! Nibbled by hippos, here, in the middle of a large Midwest-
ern city. You couldn't make this stuff up if you tried."

"Well, they weren't eating him," I emphasized, "just sort of
mouthing him." And at the thought of it I chuckled, a tiny little
thing under my breath, like *hee-hee-hee*. Then Steve started to
laugh, which was contagious, making me laugh full bore.

"This doesn't happen to people in real life," said Steve, not even
trying to keep a straight face.

"But it did," I said, and we ordered another round.

I got home around six-thirty and Mary was in the kitchen at
the island counter making something good. Scallions and parsley
were chopped and placed in neat little piles and paprika was pretty
much everywhere. I walked up behind, gave her a big hug, and
snatched a piece of sautéed meat from the frying pan. I popped it
in my mouth.

"What is this—raccoon?"

"Lamb. I'm making Bulgarian sour lamb soup. I saw it on *Anthony Bourdain*. He was in the Balkans or the Caucasus or somewhere. It's ready for the pot and then it needs about an hour, so fix yourself a drink and tell me how the interview went."

Great idea. I fixed a rum and tonic with lime, my favorite summer drink, and then I moved to a stool across from Mary. I love watching her play with food.

"Well?" she said, while dicing one last thing.

"He's a good guy, we got along great. We talked about Bud, the trains, the way it is at the zoo. I told him some personal stuff about Bud that I now wish I hadn't."

"Let me guess, he plied you with liquor and then seduced you into being a gossip queen."

"Something like that. You know what a pushover I can be."

"I know how clever some of those reporters can be."

"Yeah, well, the only thing that really bothered me is that I laughed when talking about them finding Bud in the hippo habitat. I couldn't help it, it just came out like a sneeze or something. And it's not funny, that's the thing. It is tragic ... isn't it?"

She looked up from her work. She had that look in her eye, somewhere between *Alright, listen up, stupid* and *You don't really want to hear this.* "You're wondering if it was tragic, what happened? In my opinion, for what it's worth—and it's worth a lot—the Cards getting swept in a three-game series by the Cubs, that's tragic. Gas at four bucks a gallon, tragic. But that's not life-and-death, you say? Well, how about a polar bear at the zoo dying, because he ate some plastic trash that someone threw in his area and it got caught up in his intestines? That's tragic. But Bud, old Buddy Boy, sticking it out to the bitter end and paying for it with his life when he didn't have to, that's not tragic. That's something else. Colossal bad judgment? Oh, I don't know—misguided sense of duty? false pride? Do any of those work for you?"

"You're right, as usual, and thank you for putting it in perspective. I mean that. I just hope that session with Steve is the end of this whole mess. I just want to go to work and have things be normal again."

"Don't fret. Things will be normal again," she said. "As normal as they can be at the zoo."

The next day I walked in to work only to be told to go home. "I'm sorry, Mike," said Dale Danzig, one of the administrators in HR, "but these NTSB guys showed up unannounced and they're more or less commandeering our scale train operation for the day. In other words, there's no train for you to drive. You'll still be paid for the day, in case you're wondering."

I just looked at Dale somewhat dumbfounded, trying to make sense of his words. "NTSB?" I puzzled.

"Oh, sorry. National Transportation Safety Board. They're investigating Bud's accident."

"You mean the people who investigate airplane crashes and bridge collapses? They're here to investigate a model train mishap?"

"Any time there's a fatality involving a public conveyance they have to conduct a thorough investigation into the cause of it. That's what the guy told me."

"Okay, well, I guess I'll take the day off then."

"You do that," said Dale, exasperated. "Wish I was taking the day off. I've got to escort these guys from morning to night, as long as it takes."

It was only eight and suddenly I had the whole day to goof

off. I decided to walk through the zoo just like any other schmoe come to visit our animals. It's a pretty good zoo as far as zoos go. I mean, I've been to the San Diego Zoo and the Cincinnati Zoo and they're as good as ours, but you've got to pay to go in. Ours is free, which blows me away, because they could easily charge ten bucks and the public would still flock here thinking it's a good deal. I walked over to the Jungle of the Apes, past the bronze statue of Phil the Gorilla, who was famous for being Phil, but that was before my time. A couple years back, they put in that big outdoor habitat for the orangutans and the gorillas, must be at least two acres, and you can watch them through Plexiglas windows doing stuff. There was one not more than twenty feet away, the big male silverback, and he was taking his morning dump, trying not to look silly. Ha, ha, I thought, caught you. I tapped on the Plexiglas and the big lout looked up, sort of annoyed, and you know what he did? Took his steaming pile and flung it at me. Missed altogether, but can you imagine?

I kept on going and found myself in the Reptile House, which was a bit scary, because I'm secretly afraid of slithering things with long sharp fangs like needles. But I went in there because, I don't know, maybe I wanted to feel my skin crawl at the sight of deadly black mambas and fourteen-foot-long Indian cobras that stand up and sway in this weird hypnotic motion. That really creeps me out. And it just killed me to hear about that time years ago when the tic polonga escaped and they had to close down the zoo. That night, Charlie Hoessle and Ron Goellner rode around in the golf cart with their flashlights and snake-catching gear until they found that bad boy and bagged him. Not bagged him like you would a buck— I mean, put him in a canvas bag and tied it off. So here I am in this place with lots and lots of scary snakes, fairly empty this early, and I'm standing at the fer-de-lance, evil-looking bastard, and I'm counting the number of times it flicks its tongue in a minute when someone tapped me on the shoulder, scared the shit out of me.

"Hey Mike, what're you doing here? Why ain't you on the train?"

It was Paul McCandless, the old codger who runs the cotton candy kiosk over by the Insectarium. Nice guy. "Oh, hey there. We got the day off, because they're investigating the train crash that killed Bud."

"Oh Jesus, that was horrible," he said crossing himself. "How can something like that happen here? This ain't no Grand Central Station. Some kind of skulduggery going round, you ask me."

"Okay, I'm asking. Why skulduggery, why can't it be an accident?"

"Because I saw Bud on that train just before he crashed. I was probably the last one to see him alive." He closed his eyes and shuddered like the memory chilled him.

"Yeah, really?" I said. "What did you see?"

"I saw a man going to his death," said Paul dramatically. "I was standing at the kiosk making my first batch of cotton candy for the day and I'll be go-to-hell, here comes the *Pierre Laclede* lickety-split down the tracks with only Bud on board and he didn't even sound the horn as he approached the pedestrian walk. Of course the gates lowered as he passed, but failure to sound the horn, that, as you know, is a violation that can cost a guy his job. My guess is that he didn't sound the horn because he was distracted by something gone wrong with the train."

"Yeah, right, we all think that, too. But why do *you* think that?"

"Because he was waving his arms like a crazy man and he was shouting 'Vazleen! Vazleen!'"

"Vazleen? What the hell does that mean?"

"You know, I've thought about it since that day," said Paul, "and

I've come to believe it's a woman's name like Darlene or Earlene."

"No way! Bud was married to Ruth, he loved her. He's not going to be shouting some strange woman's name while at the controls. It means something else."

Paul shrugged at this, his theory shot to hell. "Well, anyway, I waved to him as he passed and that's the last I saw of him, poor guy."

"He was a good man," I offered.

"One of the best," said Paul. "He always had a joke to tell, not dirty or sick like the ones some other guys like to tell, but clean and funny. Like just a few days before he passed, we were shootin' the breeze and he says out of the blue, 'Hey Paul, do you know where otters keep their money?' And I said, 'I don't know, Bud, where do otters keep their money?' And he says with a wink, 'In river banks.' I laughed so hard I about pissed myself."

I gave him a nudge and said, "It wouldn't surprise me if you had."

"Had what?"

"Pissed yourself, like you said. What are you doing here anyway?"

"Oh, I've got a few minutes before the kiosk opens and, well, truth be told, I'm trying to overcome my fear of these guys," he said, pointing to the fer-de-lance. "All my life I've been fascinated by snakes, yet they scare me. I mean, really scare me. You might call it a phobia. But I don't want to be held back by a phobia, an irrational fear, so I come here and little by little—you know what I'm saying?"

"More than you realize."

The next morning when we showed up for work as usual, Dale Danzig was there in the change room and so were a couple of the

NTSB guys, standing at attention over in the corner and looking pretty damn serious. The operators filed in one by one a few minutes apart. I was first and then George followed by Pete. Melvin came in last, and as soon as he got to his locker Dale took him aside and we heard Dale ask Melvin to accompany him to the main office. Melvin demanded to know right then and there what this was about, Dale explaining that these guys just want to ask some questions in private. Melvin got pretty defensive and started saying how his brother-in-law was a bigshot civil rights lawyer and him being the only black guy in this room, they had better not mess with him or else. Dale was Mister Understanding now, talking real sweet to Melvin, saying, "Yeah, yeah, don't worry, no one's in any trouble. No one's trying to trick you. We simply want to talk to you away from your co-workers." Finally, Melvin calmed down and they all paraded out. Whoa!

Well, that little episode kind of dampened our mood. George Pawlik tried to make light of it, saying, "I told that spear-chucker to stop eating them poppy seed bagels. Now he's tested positive for heroin. See ya, Melvin. Nice knowin' you." In fact, we did have to undergo random drug tests, never knowing when Dale or somebody in his office would give us a clear plastic cup and tell us to fill it, so George's snide comments were not totally out of whack. Still, what a son of a bitch.

So we went to our trains and we did our routes, 1.5 miles of track covering 18 acres, and we put on our happy faces and we picked up passengers and we made informative comments over the loudspeaker and we sounded the horn at every crossing and we waved to the pedestrians as we passed. By ten-thirty, I was happy to see the *Mark Twain* back in commission with Melvin behind the wheel. At noon, the four of us had lunch at the Safari Grill and naturally all eyes were on Melvin.

"Well?" said George, at last.

"You talking to me?" said Melvin, somewhat perturbed. He didn't like George much anyway.

"Yeah, I'm talking to you. Are you going to keep us in suspense all day or what?"

Melvin was busy chewing his chicken quesadilla. He took his own sweet time to answer. "You want to know what went down, right? You want to know what those assholes wanted with me? Alright, I'll tell you. They found something in my locker, but it wasn't mine."

George held out his arms, palms open, in exasperation. "Yeah, and—"

"Yeah, and that's all I'm saying. I guess y'all will see the big picture as time goes on."

The next day was Friday and that went without incident. Then the weekend when the regular operators were relieved by a back-up crew—"understudies" we called them. The following Monday, though, it was frigging déjà vu all over again. I walk in with Pete and there's Dale and the same two NTSB guys standing in the corner, silent, watchful. Next to them and looking like slobs in comparison were two of our own, Zoo Rangers Al Bigelow and Rick Dengler. Not good. In comes Melvin and he doesn't say a word, just goes to his locker and starts changing. Normally, we'd joke it up at this time, a little friendly banter, and in fact Dale was trying to make small talk asking how did our weekend go and blah-blah-blah, but the presence of these creeps was a real conversation-killer. Then George comes in and the NTSB guys perk up.

George stopped in his tracks, sized up the situation, and said, "I brought the cheese curls and potato chips, but did you guys remember to bring the dip?" Just classic, and the rest of us—well, me and Pete anyway—we started snickering, hoping to egg him on because, hey, any silly comments would postpone whatever ugly thing that was about to happen. But the tension was still heavy in the room when, a few seconds later, the government guys made their move.

They walked over to George and George kind of muscled up as if bracing for an attack. They stood on either side of him and pointed to the sink where we washed up. One of them said, "You see that container of Royal Crown Hair Dressing? Does that look familiar to you?" On the ledge above the sink was a bright red-and-yellow metal container, fairly big, with a picture of a crown on the front, little jagged bolts of light coming off the crown. I had never seen it before.

George shook his head in denial. "I don't use the stuff," he told them. "I've got a beautiful young stylist who does my hair, makes me look like a movie star. So buzz off."

One of the agents, the taller of the two, walked over and got the container. He went back to George as we all watched. He pried off the lid, tilted the container toward George and said, "You see this? Most of it's gone. It's a fourteen-ounce container and most of it's gone. The average guy who uses this stuff—pomade they call it— needs just a little, a dab here, a dab there. So where did it go? That's what we wondered when we found this in Mister Bobo's locker. Where did it go? Hmm."

George was acting nonchalant, like, Big deal, what's this have to do with me? But I could tell he was freaking out inside. Then the agent dipped his fingers into the pomade and he made a big show of rubbing the stuff between his thumb and the two fingers next to his thumb and he said, "If there's anything greasier than this I don't know what it is. Know what's in it? Lots of good stuff. Lard, Vaseline, oils, beeswax, and more lard. You've got to have some pretty unruly hair to need this stuff. Look at your co-worker over there. Does Melvin's hair look in need of this product?"

It was a trick question—I think it's called rhetorical, meaning that you don't need to reply because the answer is obvious. In other words, Melvin's hair was cut close. His noggin looked like a fuzzy billiard ball. George didn't like being the center of attention, not on these terms. Little beads of sweat forming on his jowly puss said as much. Then he tried to blow the whole thing off, telling the agents let him be, they were making him late for his route.

"Oh, you won't be driving today," said the other agent, the not-as-tall one who looked Greek or Italian. "You'll be coming with us. You see, we found a good deal of this pomade on the manual controls of the *Pierre Laclede* including the brakes and the accelerator, so much that an operator would have a hard time grasping those controls. It's ridiculous to think that Bud Wilkinson would smear pomade on his own train, so who did?"

George laughed—no, guffawed. It was definitely a guffaw. "You guys are federal investigators and you're asking me? Ha! That's perfect, just perfect."

"Come on, let's go have a little talk," said the agent. "We've got a room reserved for you downtown. Let's go."

"No way, I've got my rights. You can't take me against my will."

"You're correct, you do have rights. Joe, read him his rights, will you?"

Joe, the taller agent, didn't need a script. He knew by heart the rights of a guy who was being arrested and so he recited George's rights to him—in a kind of snotty tone, I thought—and I swear it seemed as though George deflated right before my eyes, all the bluster gone out of him. Then Dale called for our Zoo Rangers and, sure enough, they walked over to George and put the cuffs on him. George was bitching like hell, saying they had no proof and telling Dale to hurry and call the legal department, he was being shanghaied. They started marching him out, Al and Rick, but when he got to the door he tried to shake loose.

"Wait!" he called really emphatically, and they stopped. Turning to us, and I mean us, his co-workers, he said his piece. "You guys know I didn't do what they're saying, you *know* that. Bud was my pal. Once, when I forgot my lunch, he gave me half of his tuna sandwich. That's right, he did that for me, and it was the best damn tuna I ever had, albacore with real mayo and diced celery, a touch of Grey Poupon. That's the kind of guy he was, a prince—you hear? A prince! Why would I think to hurt him?" George paused a moment and you could just see his brain working, trying to come up with something convincing, something that would make him seem like an alright guy after all. He went on some more. "But even if I did do it, and I most certainly did not—even if I did do it, it was just a joke. We're all jokesters around here, right? Just a joke, remember that."

"Get this asshole out of here," said Melvin Bobo, and they took him away for good.

"Pomade," I said as I walked in the kitchen where Mary was cooking something good. She turned and gave me a quizzical look. I said it again. "Pomade!"

"You say pomade, I say marmalade. Let's call the whole thing off."

I laughed and she smiled. "You are not going to believe this," I told her. "Federal investigators arrested George Pawlik for sabotaging Bud's train. He put this pomade, this really oily, greasy stuff all over Bud's controls, which made it so Bud couldn't grab hold of anything and that's why the train crashed."

"The hair gunk preferred by primping pompadours—there's a mouthful. *That* pomade?"

"You got it, and the best part is that George tried to frame Melvin Bobo by putting this pomade in Melvin's locker. But the ruse was so obvious the investigators caught on right away and they zeroed in on George. You should've been there, it was like an episode of *Columbo* where Peter Falk assembles all the suspects, presents his evidence, and the bad guy gets singled out. It was beautiful, and actually exciting as hell, George shitting bricks toward the end."

"Mike, please don't use the brown word in my kitchen. So how did they know it was George? He just looked guilty or what?"

"They checked his credit card purchases. That's what Dale said after they took George away. In fact, they checked all of our purchases going back two months, but with George they saw that he'd been to LaWanda's House of Beauty earlier this month where he'd bought just one thing and it wasn't an Afro wig."

"He was planning it out. That takes it up a notch from some silly spur-of-the-moment prank."

"He said it was a joke, but the joke backfired and now Bud's gone and George is ruined."

"So then, case closed. That's a relief, yeah?"

"Yeah, except now there's two openings for scale train operators. Know anyone who might be interested?"

She moved in to me and wrapped her arms around my ribcage, making a purring sound in my left ear. "I might be interested in driving your train," she whispered, "right after dinner if you like."

"I'll wear my engineer's cap," I said.

"And I'll toot your horn," she said.

Charlie Shaw
FOR THE **DEFENSE**

AT FIRST BURNHAM CLAIMED IT WAS NO PROBLEM. He could handle it himself, he didn't need Charlie Shaw to defend him even if Shaw had tried hundreds of murder cases and held a record of acquittals that Perry Mason himself would envy. What rocked Burnham's self-assuredness was when the chief detective for St. Louis County sat him down in his office and told him straight out that the State wasn't interested in Manslaughter or even Second Degree.

"No, don't say a thing," he told Burnham with a wave of his hand. "You've invoked your right to silence, but I'm just thinking out loud here and your goose is cooked. The County is going for Murder One. The prosecutor said he feels pretty damn sure he can get a conviction." The detective paused, shuffled a bit, took a step in, got up in Burnham's face, and pretty much summed it up: "You can flip a coin," he said, "to see if you're looking at a death sentence or life without parole." It was then that Tom Burnham called Charlie Shaw.

It was a Friday afternoon in early September and Charlie had taken off early. He wanted to get some work done at his ranch. The Shaw ranch was in Pacific, just 27 miles from Charlie's law office in St. Louis. But for the rustic look of it, horse trails and pine stands and pastures, it might as well have been in the middle of nowhere. The original spread was 280 acres. Charlie kept adding to it, the less-than-well-off neighbors only too happy to sell. Over time, it became 500 acres. More land meant more fencing, and today he was hoping to add a hundred yards of barbwire before sunset. He and a helper named Raymond Bess had been at it for two hours when Charlie's wife, Joyce, came riding into view on a blue roan gelding. Joyce dismounted and stood there a minute, not saying a word, just surveying their work. Then she walked over to Charlie and handed him a pair of gloves.

Charlie smiled as he held up a torn work glove for her to see. "How'd you know?" he wondered.

"Barbwire's bound to bite the hand that strings it," she answered. "Let's see it get through these. Ordered them from Cabela's, just came yesterday."

Charlie started to slip the new gloves on, but Joyce stopped him. She took a hand and ran her own hand over it, a caress that carried admonition. "Charlie, they look horrible. When will you take care of them?"

Charlie gazed at his hands, turning them over, palm to weathered back. They were gnarled, no doubt about it, the fingers crooked and the knuckles swollen. "I don't know the answer," he said. "Fencing's got to be done. There's no machine can do it."

"The help could do it while you supervise," she said.

Charlie shrugged. He wasn't keen on supervising a job like this. Ray could work the post-hole digger, sure, but he had to do the wincing and fastening of the wire to the posts. These guys, the so-called hired hands who bunked on his ranch for weeks at a time, were in actuality mendicant clients who agreed to barter labor for Charlie's services. Ray Bess, for instance. Charlie pled Ray from a Class B felony down to a misdemeanor for receiving stolen goods.

Ray got a month in the Workhouse. The day he was released, Charlie picked him up, took him to the ranch to start his "second sentence." Ray Bess and the others did what they were asked and sometimes more. They didn't all have their hearts in the work.

Joyce was back on her horse, pulling the reins to point her back home. Then she remembered. "Oh, J.R. called. Tom Burnham's out on bond and he wants you to take his case. He's already given J.R. the retainer. Try to call him today or tomorrow. The number's by the phone."

Charlie twisted his mouth into a kind of a what-the-hell expression. He was well aware of Tom Burnham, a character almost as colorful as himself—not that Charlie thought of himself as colorful, but he knew that was the general consensus. He said to Joyce, "The gun-toting bar owner who thinks he's living in the Wild West. Cops say he shot an unarmed man in the back. This'll be a good one."

Charlie Shaw was already famous when he started his law career in 1949. As a captain and navigator in the US Army Air Force with many missions to his credit, his B17 was shot down over enemy territory in October, 1943. Charlie and the others who bailed out were soon captured and interned in a POW camp in northeastern Germany. And even though he was treated in decent fashion, relatively speaking, by his captors, Charlie was restless. And determined. He made seven attempts at escape and was captured six times. Like young Winston Churchill, who some 45 years before managed to escape from a Boer prison camp during the Boer War in South Africa, Charlie spent weeks hiding in enemy territory only to emerge safely in the arms of the allies. Also like Churchill, he later learned that his exploits had been splashed over the front pages of newspapers back home, millions of papers snapped up by a public hungry for a bona fide war hero. Years later, when Charlie had made his bones as a criminal defense lawyer, *The Great Escape* came out. It was well-known, at least in St. Louis, that Charlie's exploits had inspired the screenplay. The high-security prisoner of war camp depicted in the movie and the prison from which Charlie escaped were one and the same: Stalagluft III. And when his family and friends would boast about Charlie's connection to the film, they would make a small distinction. "In the movie," they would say, "Steve McQueen gets away on a motorcycle. Charlie stole a bicycle!"

Charlie didn't mind the notoriety. Notoriety fit right in with his flamboyant personality. Flamboyant and at times shameless. He once won an insanity acquittal in a murder case. He then tried to free his client from the mental hospital by citing, in his habeas corpus motion for release, the prosecution's testimony at the trial that the man was sane. Yes, Charlie Shaw was considered the best, the first choice if you were charged with murder—if you could afford him.

Charlie met with Tom Burnham in his office on Monday morning. Oddly enough, the hour coincided with a funeral happening across town, that of Paul Cassise, the young man shot dead by Burnham. Charlie extended his hand to Burnham and they shook, sizing each other up. Charlie saw a man-boy, muscular build, with wavy, brown hair a bit too long, sky-blue eyes, and a mustache. The eyes had a certain devilish twinkle that Charlie had seen before in certain other clients, bad-asses, many of whom were now doing time. There was a third man in the room, tall, full head of white hair, serious face. "This is J.R. Moore, my investigator," said Charlie. "He'll sit in with us." Burnham nodded at J.R. and they all sat down.

For the next ninety minutes, they hashed out the facts of the case, the nuances of the case, and possible strategies. The killing happened at Burnham's bar, the St. Louis Opera House, on Olive Street Road out in West County. Actually, it was a saloon—peanut shells on the floor, antique light fixtures, beer served in frosty, fishbowl mugs. It was just after ten on a weekday night, the place filled with jubilant Cardinal fans fresh from Busch Stadium, having seen their team best the Phillies six-two. Maybe they'd make the play-offs after all. The place was slammed and the servers had no time for chit-chat, yet this kid, Cassise, was intent on talking to Stacey Hammond, who had the biggest section in the house. Yeah, they might've been going out, said Burnham, but that didn't matter, because any way you looked at it, he was interfering with her doing her job. Burnham said he warned the kid once, not being a prick about it.

"Just drink your beer," I told him. "Relax, wait for her to clock out and then have your conversation." But the kid wouldn't listen, recounted Burnham, and he kept on corralling Stacey, talking, gesturing, looking like he was imploring her about something. Burnham went over again and told the kid to mind himself, he wasn't going to tell him a third time. "There won't be a third time," Burnham had the kid saying, "because in two seconds I am going to place my right foot on your left ear and there won't be a thing you can do about it."

"And he did just that," said Burnham. "He kicked me hard, so hard that I would've fallen had I not grabbed the back of a chair. I saw stars and while I was seeing stars I had a nagging thought that there was something I should have known about this kid. Turns out he was a karate expert, a fucking black belt, and that line about placing my right foot on your left ear and nothing you can do about it? That's from the movie *Billy Jack*, said by Tom Laughlin just before he kicks the shit out of some redneck."

"So the kid lacked originality," said Charlie. "What happened next? This is key."

"What happened next is I went to my office in the back to pull myself together—I'm still woozy from the kick—and not two minutes later there's a pounding at the door which I had the good sense to lock. 'Let me in, motherfucker. I'm gonna finish the job.' It's him, so I get my gun out of the drawer, the one I have a permit for, and I tell him to leave, the cops are on the way. He starts kicking the door, making threats. I can see daylight with every kick. I am seriously thinking about shooting him through the door when I hear voices outside saying stuff like 'Leave it alone' and 'Get out of here now' and then it's quiet. I sit there for maybe five minutes, listening, and when I feel it's safe, I go out. Now I'd seen this kid in my place before and I knew he drove a blue Toyota Corolla, so I went out back to look in the parking lot, see if his car was still there. I'm standing there by myself and guess what? The kid is thirty feet away walking to his car. He turns, sees me, lets out a weird laugh, and charges me. He's gonna finish the job, so what choice do I have? I shot him once, aimed for the torso, and that's where I hit him. Stopped that little prick dead in his tracks."

Charlie looked at J.R. J.R. looked back at Charlie. They were quite accustomed to accused murderers fabricating details, changing or deleting altogether incriminating aspects of the story to suit themselves, especially if there were no witnesses to contradict. "Any witnesses?" asked Charlie.

"No, not that I know of. Plenty of gawkers afterward, though."

Charlie pursed his lips a bit, thought for a second and said, "Well, if what you're telling us is true, it seems to be a clear-cut case of self-defense. Only problem is the prosecutor's office doesn't see it that way. They say you shot Cassise without compunction, in the back, as he was walking to his car."

"Only a punk would do that," said Burnham, "and I'm no punk."

"Forensics will give us a good idea of what happened," said Charlie, "and, really, it could make or break our case. But those findings aren't yet available."

"Make or break the case. How's that?"

Now J.R. weighed in. "Angle of projectile entry, entrance wound, exit wound—if there is one—blood splatters on the ground, they all provide certain information. They all tell a story."

"Toxicology," added Charlie, "that's going to tell us whether this kid was coked up or whatever at the time of death. Could be very helpful, but those results are still out, too."

Burnham, annoyed, said, "You mean I've got to wait for some lab tests to come back to find out if I'm going to get my life back?"

"That's about the size of it," said Charlie. "Meanwhile, J.R. here will do his thing. He'll be checking out the background of the deceased, interviewing those witnesses we know of, the ones who saw the initial altercation, and he'll be canvassing for new witnesses. Don't be surprised if you see him in your place."

Then Charlie and J.R. had an aside, talking specifics, leaving the accused to sit and mull for a minute, when Burnham interrupted. "Listen," he said, looking straight at Charlie, "I understand it's difficult, maybe impossible, to predict an outcome here, but I need to know if you think I'm going to do time on this thing. Because, during the trial, if I even think I'm going to be convicted I am gone, man, gone to parts unknown, never to be seen again. I've got the means and the resources. No way in hell am I looking at four walls day-in, day-out. Just so you know."

"I don't think your bondsman would much like that," said J.R., stone-faced.

Charlie heard those words coming out of Burnham's mouth, he

got this look, like, Don't insult me in my own office. "Try to have a little faith," he told him. "There's more than one way through the woods. You get the notion to run, that's your prerogative. But it would be unwise, the biggest gamble you'll ever take. You decide to do something like that, I don't want to know about it, hear? Now, let's go over the story again."

About a month later, Charlie drove to Salem, the seat of Dent County, near the banks of the Current River, where he would try a murder case. *State v Reynolds* involved a stabbing death stemming from a bar fight in the town of Cuba, two best friends going at it over some poorly-chosen words, amplified and made more insulting by copious amounts of alcohol. Charlie was defending Buck Reynolds, the last one standing in the blood-soaked battle. Of course he would argue self-defense. Even if Reynolds did strike the first blow—and that was in contention—the other fellow, Van Vliet, would have killed Buck Reynolds if he could have. Charlie had the ER doc on duty that day lined up to testify that among Reynolds' many abrasions, contusions, and lacerations, there were distinct signs of attempted strangulation apparent around his neck. There, in his Ferrari, eating up the road mile after mile, the rising sun at his back, Charlie idly made the comparison between Reynolds' situation and Burnham's. Both claimed self-defense. Reynolds' claim was not in doubt; Burnham's claim was in doubt. Reynolds fought hand to hand with his drinking buddy; it was up close and personal. Burnham, humiliated in front of everyone and seeking revenge at any cost, shot his guy from a distance, possibly —no, probably in the back. It was a chicken shit thing to do, but of course that wouldn't stop Charlie from pulling out every stop to defend the guy. If Charlie had to turn away every guy who claimed he was innocent when Charlie's instincts told him otherwise, then he wouldn't be in the lawyering business at all.

He was enjoying the fall morning, made even better by this winding stretch of road that the Ferrari took like a cat bounding after prey. Then he was passing through a piedmont, the incipient foothills of the Ozarks all around, and he saw a half dozen turkey vultures soaring, riding the wind currents 1,000 feet above. And, as he watched, those vultures became something else, something ominous, something recalled as vividly as the births of his four children. He was in the navigator position on the B17, the *Linda Ball*, manning a M2 .50 caliber machine gun, flying along in formation at 28,000 feet above a strong cloud bank. Almost immediately upon crossing the channel and entering German airspace, a swarm of enemy fighters came up to meet them. He noticed four of them, yellow-nosed Focke-Wulf-190s, sitting off the left nose at ten o' clock, just far enough away to be out of range of his fire.

Charlie felt his pulse quicken just thinking about it.

Even with fire coming from all directions, he managed to keep his eyes on the four Focke-Wulfs. Every now and then they would point their noses toward the *Linda Ball*, singling her out. Whenever they did this he, gave them a few bursts from the .50 caliber just to let them know he could bite. Then, all of a sudden, they peeled off one at a time and came right for the navigator's position. One after another, like bats out of hell at 400 miles per hour, they came head-on right for the ship and when they were about 50 yards away, they flipped over on their backs and rolled right through the rest of the formation, spitting lead all the way. He watched them dive down through the formation and disappear into the clouds. But before he could even breathe a sigh of relief, they shot back up like rockets, the same four standing off, getting ready to make a pass at the *Linda Ball*'s nose again. In they came, this time four abreast, and their wings seemed to catch on fire as all their guns opened up. He used his machine gun like a hose and sprayed lead into the F-Ws. He saw one start smoking and it dived down into the clouds, but he doubted that he'd shot it down because Jerry has a trick where he cuts his exhaust causing smoke to come from the fuselage to give the appearance of being on fire.

Somehow the crew got to the target and dumped their bombs, and with only a few battles on the return they managed to get back to base unscathed.

Charlie loosened his grip on the wheel. He knew these flash-backs were common among G.I.s who'd seen action, but 27 years later? Still, it wasn't something he dreaded. On the contrary, it was pretty damn interesting when it did happen. He'd seen the World War II flick *Command Decision* about bombing crews that left English bases to bomb interior Germany. That movie was in fact his life in wartime, so the occasional flashbacks were like scenes from a movie—the action-packed parts—playing out on the silver screen in his head. Coincidentally, Clark Gable, who played the dashing bomber pilot in *Command Decision*, was in fact a fellow crew member on the *Linda Ball*. Charlie and Clark Gable made five missions together, and there were times when the two of them sat side by side in their turret, Charlie firing the left nose gun and Gable firing the right, dealing death and destruction to anything in their sights. Gable chose to re-enact his wartime experience before Hollywood cameras, while Charlie re-visited his at 70 miles per hour along winding, rural Missouri roads.

He was lucky as hell to be alive—he knew that through and through—and the crucible of nineteen months in a German prison molded him into the man he was today, a man that other lawyers would go out of their way to watch in the courtroom. When discharged from the Army in 1945, Charlie, war hero that he was, found himself on the lecture circuit—local Rotary Clubs,

Optimist International, Moose Lodges and more. He was enrolled in Washington University at the time and the fees and honorariums earned from these presentations, modest though they were, offered a dependable stream of walking-around money for the student prince. Public speaking was easy for him, gregarious and charming to begin with, but practice makes perfect and before long his tongue had turned to silver. Dramatic when called for, comedic when the opportunity presented, Charlie spoke with a rich baritone that projected without apparent effort, as though he were speaking from a stage before an audience. Throw in a great smile and a charismatic demeanor, the man had honed his style to such an extent that Clarence Darrow would have looked up from his notes to listen to Charlie. That stint on the lecture circuit was to help him immeasurably in the courtroom.

He got to Salem just before seven-thirty and parked in the rear of Jack Gifford's law office across from the courthouse. Buck Reynolds was actually Jack's client but Jack had called Charlie, his friend since Washington University law school, and asked him to co-chair the case. When Charlie saw Jack coming out the back door into the parking lot he was again reminded of Andy Devine, the comic cowboy sidekick to Roy Rogers. When Jack greeted Charlie, pumping hands like a metronome, he was again reminded that Charlie struck a resemblance to the actor Tyrone Power. But first things first. They walked to a nearby diner and had breakfast. From there they were heading to the courthouse, the trial starting at nine.

"You know what I realized?" said Jack, digging into his hotcakes. "I realized that your reputation had been made prior to the changes in the rules of procedure. The discovery process kind of ruined the practice of law for you, didn't it? Like being forced to wear manacles."

"You might be right," said Charlie, a forkful of hash browns about to disappear, "but go on, why do you say that?"

"Because in the time before discovery, you'd get the police report and just walk in the courtroom and whoever talked the fastest and was quickest on their feet usually won the case. Now we just plod along, play it out by the numbers. The State does this, we do that. There are no surprises anymore."

"Oh, there're still surprises," said Charlie. "My bag is full of them."

Jack had his files with him and wanted to talk about specific points they should stress, but Charlie was more interested in the local harvest. Was it on schedule? Were the yields projected above or below average? But Jack didn't know the answers, he wasn't much into farming.

The trial in Judge Michael Harding's courtroom began on time and the first order was jury selection or *voir dire*. That would take up the morning. *Voir dire*—from the Old French, literally "speak the truth"—focuses on backgrounds and experiences of prospective jurors which may reflect on their abilities to be fair and impartial. In a criminal case such as this one, attorneys may want to know the juror's feelings on firearms, say, or the use of recreational drugs. They may ask if anyone has been the victim of a crime or knows anyone who has been. Counsel is provided with a pedigree of each citizen on the jury panel—name, address, age, race, level of education, occupation and spouse's occupation. Counselors study the juror's cards and may make assumptions about them, but to truly know whether they are going to hurt or help their client, they have to talk to them. The more time the lawyers have to talk to prospective jurors, the more the jurors volunteer of themselves—their manner of speech, intelligence, socioeconomic circumstances, biases—things which, when factored together, inform the attorney who is likely to swing your way when closing arguments are finished.

Of the *voir dire* process, Charlie liked to say that it was a little like getting to know the partners on your dance card.

Charlie was born and raised in St. Louis. His family was very successful in real estate. They lived in an affluent neighborhood, The Moorlands, and his father, Charles A. Shaw, was a multi-term Mayor of Clayton, the financial center of the metro area and seat of county government. Yet, for a city boy who had been offered every advantage in life, Charlie had a country air about him, a quality that he chose to play up in this rural community. Accordingly, he was "jus' folks" in his approach, winning over the panel of jurors with homespun charm and light banter.

"Well, Mister Adams, I see you're from Lenox and you belong to the KCs there. Do they have enough money to build their new hall?" Earlier, going over the juror's cards, Jack Gifford had mentioned the Knights of Columbus hall in Lenox. Jack himself lived in Lenox.

"We're working on it," said Adams, warming to the question. "I think we have forty-five thousand, a little over. We'll get there. We've got that fish fry coming up."

Jurors promise not to prejudge, to decide a verdict based solely on the facts, but they are human and therefore subject to bias, however subtle or inscrutable. If they take a like or dislike to the attorney, it can rub off on the defendant.

Charlie was the very model of concern for the juror's welfare. "Mister LeGrand, do you farm?" LeGrand says he does. "Livestock or grain?" asked Charlie.

"Just crops" replied LeGrand.

"And what are you doing this time of year?"

"Harvesting corn, corn and soybeans."

"Mister LeGrand, this trial may run for several days. If picked, would that cause a hardship on you as far as your farming operation?"

"It would," conceded LeGrand. "I ain't nearly done harvesting."

Charlie gave a sympathetic nod. "Are there other family members to help out in case you're picked for jury duty?"

LeGrand looked at Charlie in his charcoal gray suit, pressed white shirt with silver, monogrammed cuff links, string tie, and Western boots and said, "The wife, I reckon, but she wouldn't like it none." A chorus of chuckles from the jury pool.

By the end of the second day the trial was over. Buck Reynolds was a free man and Charlie was heading back home, eating up the highway in the Ferrari, the setting sun at his back. Charlie felt pretty damn good about the whole thing—the jury he'd gotten despite the prosecutor striking two of his first choices; the ER doctor's account of Buck having had signs of a death-grip around his bull-neck, testimony that hugely bolstered the claim of self-defense; and finally, the matter-of-fact pronouncement of Judge Harding, sitting under a replica of Gilbert Stuart's unfinished portrait of George Washington: "Not guilty." How he loved hearing those words, especially after that tortuous wait for the jury to decide, the suspense just scoring his innards, although to look at him—calm, collected—no one would ever guess. The sound of those words, in fact, went beyond the warm wash of exultation. They served to remind Charlie of why he'd become a lawyer—to defend the downtrodden, to insure the State didn't have the chance to railroad some poor slob into prison without decent representation, separate him from his God-given liberty. And he remembered the day he decided to go into law; it was day one of internment in Stalagluft III.

Tom Burnham couldn't ignore the presence of J.R. Moore in

his saloon. For one thing, the man was talking to his help, taking notes, pointing this way and that, nodding as if he understood what went down. It was Burnham's nature to thwart anyone attempting to pry into his business and he didn't much care how he did the thwarting, but now he had to grit his teeth and tell himself to let J.R. do his job. After all, the man was working for him, right? He watched J.R. move around the place, looking here in some corner, and there up toward the ceiling, studying things seemingly at random. It brought to mind the business of a building inspector, and Burnham hated building inspectors. And then he saw J.R. stop at a framed picture on the wall, a picture of Wild Bill Hickok seated in a chair, his partner Charlie Utter standing next to him, hand resting on Wild Bill's shoulder. The picture was taken in Cody, Wyoming, in the year 1874. Burnham had bought it at auction because he liked outlaws. Although Wild Bill wasn't an outlaw, he made his reputation with a gun and that was good enough. J.R. took interest in the picture with the busted glass in the upper right corner and there in the picture itself was a small hole about the diameter of a pencil. Some sort of projectile had drilled poor Charlie Utter in the forehead. Burnham decided to go on over and talk.

"Looks like someone didn't like this guy," said J.R. as Burnham sidled up.

"That's Charlie Utter," said Burnham, "and that's Wild Bill Hickok in the chair."

"Looks like a thirty-eight slug to me," said J.R.

"I'd say you're right and it's a shame, because I do like this old photo and I can't just run out and get another."

"You want to say how this happened?"

Burnham, twirling his mustache, looked J.R. in the eye and said, "I could say I bought it that way and that would be the end of it. But why bullshit, huh? The story is that strange things happen in a bar after closing, particularly when drunken off-duty cops are in the house. They like their target practice, what can I say?"

"I'd say those cops were more off-target than on. I mean, look here—more bullet holes, trailing up the wall. You let them do this?"

"Check out the ceiling," said Burnham. J.R. looked up and saw the old, ornamental tin ceiling punctuated with the same small holes, some of them ragged and elongated, coming at an angle.

"It's not just cops blasting away at the walls. It's you, too, isn't it?"

It wasn't really a question so Burnham didn't answer.

"I know Charlie—Mister Shaw—will tell you that if it gets out you're trigger-happy in your own bar it won't bode well for you in court. You'll be perceived as reckless, even dangerous. How many people know about this target practice?"

"Did you know I'm related to Wild Bill on my mother's side? Her great-grandfather was a Butler—that was his middle name, James Butler Hickok." Burnham lied about this just to see how it sounded.

J.R. met him eye to eye. "You can change the subject all you want. You've got secrets, you'd better uncork them."

Charlie had the medical examiner's report in front of him. Burnham was due to arrive any minute, and they would discuss the M.E.'s findings. Charlie absentmindedly gazed out the picture window looking west and there, at the bottom of the hill where the street ended, was a great expanse of turf and trees, sidewalks, too, with people strolling this way and that. Shaw Park, named after his father, the popular mayor of Clayton during the 1930s, boasted an Olympic-size swimming pool which became an ice rink in winter. The park was thronged nearly every weekend during clement weather, folks arriving early to claim picnic spots nestled in little groves, the large wrought-iron barbecue pits just waiting to be fired up. It was well-trafficked during the week as well, office workers emerging around noon to force fresh air into their lungs. Charlie thought that he might walk there, too. And he would try not to think about things, just enjoy the sun on his face, the primal act of ambulating. Problem was he didn't have time. So many people wanted a piece of his time and he tended to oblige, so much so that there wasn't much left over for him.

Burnham walked in the well-appointed office like he owned it. He doffed his Parrothead cap and placed it on the hat rack next to Charlie's Homburg, then he took a chair facing Charlie and with barely a salutation said, "Well?"

Charlie cut to the chase, too, telling him that the medical examiner found no trace of drugs, legal or illegal, in the kid's body, just booze with a BAC of one-point-three, a little over the limit of legally intoxicated. Furthermore, the bullet wounds were inconclusive, that is, it could not be determined whether the bullet entered the body from the front or back.

"This is good for us," Charlie said. "You say you shot him as he was charging you, raging mad, bent on taking your life. The prosecutor will say 'shot in the back, unarmed,' and to back that up they have the body found belly-down, laying head-first in a direction toward the car where he was heading. The jury doesn't like to hear about a guy being shot in the back, but as long as there's a serious doubt to that, which I will press, then you have a decent chance."

"Decent, huh? That sounds comforting—on the way to the fucking slammer!"

Charlie just looked at him.

"Oh, hell," said Burnham, exasperated, "don't take it personal. It's just that I think this thing is finally getting to me. I wish the trial were tomorrow. I feel like I'm in limbo."

"The conveyor belt of justice grinds slowly," said Charlie. "I can stop filing motions if you like, that will speed things up."

"No, file away. Do what you think you should. Know what happened this week? A group of guys came in my place, six of them, early twenties. It was after five, I happened to be in the bar. They sat there at a table, ordered sandwiches and drinks, and then just stared at me, malicious-like. If looks could kill."

"Friends of Cassise?"

"Friends, relatives, voodoo-practicing sons of bitches, I don't know, but it was unnerving."

"If it happens again, don't approach them, don't deal with it personally. You call me or J.R. and we'll find out who they are. If we can't get there before they leave then get their license plate, but that's all. If they are connected with the victim and there to intimidate it could affect the trial, maybe in our favor."

Burnham shook his head no. "I don't like letting others handle my problems."

"Anyone ever call you bull-headed?"

"I'm thinking you can do for me what you did for that stewardess."

Just then a feminine voice came over the intercom on Charlie's desk. "Charlie, there's a Kenneth Kwame on the line, says it's important." Charlie knew Kwame as a civil rights activist, most famous for leading a construction workers' sit-down strike for better wages—only problem was the sit-down was on the Interstate, halting traffic for hours, a federal crime. Once upon a time Charlie had defended Ike Turner for beating up Tina, and because of that, the Shaw number still rings, calls from the black community after 25 years. Charlie didn't doubt the call was important—to Kenneth

Kwame—but it would have to wait.

"Tell him I'll phone him in an hour or so. Ask if he needs to see me in person."

"Take the call," interrupted Burnham, rising. "We're done here."

Charlie furrowed his brow. True enough, the trial was six weeks off; whatever they had left to go over could wait. On his way out, Burnham stopped at the hat rack. He took Charlie's black Homburg and tried it on. He studied himself in a small nearby mirror, tilting the hat this way and that. Finally, he turned to Charlie, watching him the whole time and, with the hat angled absurdly like a burlesque house comic, said in an affected accent, "Not my cup of tea, old egg."

What an asshole, thought Charlie as he waved his client goodbye.

After speaking with Kenneth Kwame—an "associate" of his had been pinched for fencing stolen goods—Charlie took a walk down Central Avenue. He was tired of cigarettes at the moment and yearned for a good cigar. He entered the tobacco shop and said hello to the fellow behind the counter. Sterling Lee, the octogenarian tobacconist, beamed.

"Well, if it isn't my favorite barrister. How are you, my boy?"

"Well and good," said Charlie. "It's a fine day for the race."

"What race is that, Charlie?"

"The human race." Charlie paused, winked at Sterling and said, "I'm in the mood for a good cigar, a Dominican, not too big and not too small."

"Coming right up," said Sterling. "Here's a Cohiba that may suit your taste. Or here, under your picture, some choice Arturo Fuentes. I'll give you a nice price on the entire box."

Charlie leaned over the counter to better see the picture that

Sterling mentioned, a black-and-white, eight-by-ten photograph of Charlie and Clark Gable in their flight suits, arms around each other's shoulders in brotherly affection, standing before the nose of an aircraft—not the *Linda Ball* this time, but another B17, the *Cue Ball*. That photo had been on the wall for years, Sterling asking Charlie for a copy after he learned of its existence, Charlie obliging.

Charlie said, "You know that airplane is in a thousand pieces on the floor of the Baltic Sea."

"Talk about your harrowing experiences," said Sterling Lee. "But Clark Gable wasn't with you when it happened, right?"

"No, he'd been transferred by then. It was our last mission, you know. October 9, 1943, I was this close to going home"—Charlie held out a thumb and index finger, nearly touching—"I'd even written Joyce telling her to meet me somewhere in New York on Halloween. It was going to be a hell of a date, but it wasn't to be. Instead I got an extended stay in Northern Germany."

"You told it before, Charlie, but would you mind telling it again?"

Charlie glanced at his watch. He had a one o' clock docket in thirty minutes, but the courthouse was just two blocks over. "Yeah, sure, why not?"

Sterling handed him a Cohiba. "On the house," he said, and lit the cigar for Charlie.

Charlie took a few puffs and started out. "There were ten of us on the *Cue Ball* that day, ten that had flown twenty-four missions together, so naturally there was a good deal of unexpressed anxiety among us—our last mission, would we return in one piece and get to take a breather at last? My throat was dry. I sensed that other throats were dry, too, because this mission was the deepest the Eighth Air Force had ever penetrated into Germany The main target was the aircraft plant in Danzig, but we weren't going there. We were going into a little town called Anklam, northeast of Berlin, about thirty miles south of the Baltic coast. It was our job to feint a direct attack on Berlin then fade and get Anklam with the intent of drawing the enemy fighters away from Danzig. We were the decoys. *Cue Ball* was coming in on the coast, driving southeast from our base in England. Our P47 fighter escorts had limited range and had to turn back at the Belgian border. We were on our own. As navigator, I checked our course: right on target. Then, in my earphones, I heard the pilot's voice, 'Heinies at two o' clock!' *Cue Ball* trembled as the gunners opened up. We were being mobbed by a swarm of single-engine ME-109s and FW-190s. I jumped to one of the nose guns. The bombadier, Ben Fincher, grabbed the other. But we were close to target and Fincher left his gun and got on the bomb sight. A Messerschmitt attacked our starboard, very close. He sprayed and got away, leaving a wound in the wing the size of a gopher hole. That's all, I figured we were alright, thanked God and kept shooting. *Cue Ball* turned into the target. Fincher got ready to release the bombs when smoke started pouring out of our right wing. Jerry did get us after all, a direct hit in one of the fuel tanks, probably a .20 millimeter cannon shell. A terrific fire began. It looked and smelled like an oil well burning. The pilot slipped *Cue Ball* out of the formation, the bombadier hollered 'Bombs away!' *Cue Ball* jerked upward and we were free of the target. Our final mission, maybe we could get the plane home—our pilot, Harry Morse, was trying. Then, oily liquid fire gushed into the cabin. 'Bail out!' ordered Morse, and how we hated those words."

"I can barely imagine!" offered Sterling.

"Well, there's not much choice," said Charlie, puffing away. "The crew started to pour out of the plane. I pulled the cord on my ar-mored flak suit and the suit fell off of me. I noticed how clumsy my fingers were. I held my breath to keep from killing myself with hot

smoke and flame, made myself move deliberately. I picked up my chute and clipped it onto the parachute harness that I always wore. Then I was ready. The enlisted men were all out in the sky. Fincher went out the nose hatch. I followed him. It was my first jump. I hesitated, but the plane was on fire and the heat drove me out, head first, out of the sweat and dirt and smoke and engine noise, suddenly into the cool quiet. I was simply motionless in heaven— the strangest feeling—and then I zipped through a cloud and knew how fast I was falling. I was sharply afraid, but I gritted my teeth and hung on until I judged I had fallen five-thousand feet. I jerked the ripcord and it came off in my hand. Panic. But it was supposed to do that and in a maddening leisurely way the pilot chute trickled out and then the big chute emerged. There was a sudden jerk, so powerful that my head, which was down, snapped up. At the same time, my feet slung down so hard that my shoes came off. And now I was hanging from my parachute barefoot, swinging back and forth like a pendulum. I looked around and saw the rest of the crew like a flock of white sheep floating off somewhere, some above me, some below. Then, off in the distance, *Suzy Q*—the *Cue Ball*— pulled up a little and heaved over like a wounded elephant. She disintegrated in a fiery haze and a couple of seconds later there was the kick of the wind and the roar of the explosion and a red hot hunk of engine came sizzling past my chute. And it was all over, end of mission. There I was, floating in mid-air with German soil coming up fast and there was no *Suzy Q* and no crew and Halloween in New York shrank into a tiny speck and disappeared in the sky over the Baltic."

"And you're here to tell it, Charlie!" said Sterling Lee. "That's the amazing thing."

"There was another close call on the way down. I was directly above a lake and immediately I began to worry about falling into it, becoming fouled up in my parachute and drowning. Then the chill of rushing air on my bare feet reminded me of stories about broken legs on landing, even if you're wearing paratroop boots, and I wondered whether I ought to hope that I would hit the water. There were farmlands all around the lake and over to one side was Anklam. The town was hit, and hit bad. From my bird's eye view I could see a big column of black smoke rising from the center of town. Only a few minutes had passed since we dropped our bombs and already it seemed that every building in Anklam was shattered. Then, I heard this sound—*zuzzz!* I craned my neck this way and that, an enemy fighter had buzzed me and it was turning in the distance, coming back. Remember, I'm still several thousand feet aloft. What could I do? I set my teeth and shrank into myself, wondering whether it would ram me or machine-gun my parachute. But it didn't. It only buzzed me again like a curious bee, kicking me with propwash. This German was playful, toying with me, coming at me head-on then ducking under me, even waving as he went past. Probably radioing the position of the crew as they landed."

"All this as you're falling to earth," said Sterling Lee, shaking his head in wonder.

Charlie nodded and continued. "Now the lake was rushing up at me and, frantic, I began tugging at the chute's cords. Instinctively, I was going for dry land. Wind filled the parachute at the first tug, carrying me well beyond the edge of the water and directly toward a line of high-tension wires. Then it happened so fast—I was a hundred feet up, falling toward the wires. I kept tugging and I overshot them and hit hard. Almost instantly there was a rifle shot. After I finished rolling, I stayed down. I'd landed in a hay field and gradually I raised myself enough to look around and off in the distance I saw some people bunched together near a farm house. Pointing in my direction. Another shot, this one clipping the hay-stubble nearby. Too close for comfort. It won't do me any good to lie here, I thought, and anyway the collapsed parachute was trying to run away, pulling me with it. I went by the manual and hit a button which disengaged my chute. I was going to run, but first I took out my APO ID card and tore it into tiny pieces. Military security. For good measure I ransacked the wallet, tearing up phone numbers and addresses of friends back home, friends I wasn't going to see any time soon.

"Then I was ready. I looked to the farmhouse, but the people were gone. They had fired two shots, maybe it scared them. I saw the road, a brown band of dirt beyond a fence and some high hay. I started out, the hay-stubble cutting into my tender bare feet. I got to the road and started walking along the ditch next to it. I'm going home, I thought, knowing full well how foolish it was to even think that. But my exit from the hayfield gave the timid farmers courage. Three of them came running, shouting Halt! I halted. They came up on me breathless and seized my arms and shoulders, shouting incomprehensibly—mostly emotion, I'd say. Finally, one of them got hold of himself. Englander? he asked. Nein, I said. Amerikaner? he tried. Ja, I said. The farmers looked at each other, shrugging. They didn't like Americans, but Americans weren't as bad as Brits. However, I was a particularly ugly looking American. My flat-footed landing had banged my chin against my knee so that several teeth were driven through my lip and my mouth was bleeding badly."

"Too much," said Sterling Lee, riveted. "Wow. Double-wow. Go on, Charlie."

Charlie glanced at his watch. "I'm short on time so I've got to wrap it up. The thumbnail version of what happened next? Well, the local farmers rounded up the rest of the crew, all but Fincher. We were held at the farmhouse for a while and then they marched us down the road single-file toward Anklam. As we reached the outskirts of town, hordes of people lined the road, some on the narrow sidewalks, some poking their heads out of windows in damaged buildings, shouting angrily. In the town, they lined us under a great oak tree and brought out a rope. We were in for a lynching. Two men got up on a bench and began to make a speech to a gathering crowd, all flaming mad. My German was rusty, but I made out the word *terrorflieger*, meaning someone who bombs women and children, an act that's considered immoral, if not criminal, according to the law of war. The attack occurred just before noon. Apparently, one of our bombs had hit a schoolhouse and killed the children in it. Obviously an error, a bomb that had missed the target by a mile, but angry civilians don't weigh intentions. The burghers gathered around the oak tree were getting pretty lathered up—not that they needed much encouragement—by the rhetoric of the two men on the bench who talked around each other in a sort of point–counterpoint and who paused from time to time to look at the Americans and make, in dead earnest, throat-clutching, hang-'em-by-the-neck gestures. The menacing crowd was closing in, the orators were finishing up, the rope was ready, and it was a question of which one of us would get it first."

"I'd have shit my britches," offered Sterling Lee.

"I *was* afraid, no doubt about that, but apart from my fear there was a dawning realization that I was indeed a *terrorflieger*. One look around, it was shocking to see the damage we'd done. The buildings were ruined shells with flames spurting out of the windows. A big church steeple had been cracked in half and was hanging over the center of the street. The town was a complete shambles and I personally was the destroyer. Apart from its function as a diversion target, there was only one conceivable military reason for bombing Anklam: There was an insignificant munitions factory there. Well, I had personally bombed the factory and, while I was at it, I had bombed every other building in town, including the schoolhouse. I had navigated the plane deliberately, scientifically here. There were maybe five-thousand people in Anklam. It was October, Indian summer, the sort of warm days of autumn when people even in wartime are lazy-like, knowing that there's little chance of attack. It might have been a small factory town in Jersey or Pennsylvania, people going about their daily business, reasonably secure, until a flying warship released its bombs from 28,000 feet, setting fire to their homes, blasting their church, killing their children at their desks in their school. And it was all in a day's work, my twenty-fifth mission, and my wife back home waiting for Halloween in New York."

"It's only natural to have those feelings," said the elderly tobacconist, oozing empathy. "You'd never seen the destruction from the ground. You always were able to fly off, head back home. But the lynching, Charlie. Who'd they take first?"

"That's the funny part," said Charlie. "As though it were a comic opera, the orators orated too long and just as they were finishing, the Luftwaffe arrived. Two officers chugged up on motorcycles followed by a deuce-and-a-half with a dozen soldiers in back. They all jumped out and did an emergency-drill act, ordering the crowd to disperse and at the same time setting up their machine guns. The crowd scattered. The officers handcuffed us and bunched us around the oak. Then, after a bit, they herded us into the deuce-and-a-half and off we went, to our new digs, a fortress of a POW camp." Charlie paused, puffed on the Cohiba until the tip glowed, looked to Sterling and said, "Saved by the Luftwaffe, can you believe it? How's that for irony?"

Smelling like a cigar, Charlie walked down Central toward the courthouse. He would be a few minutes late for the motion docket in Division 36 but that was alright, the judge was often tardy as well. Walking along, he put his mind on the task ahead, convincing the judge that his subpoena served upon a six-year-old boy—actually, served upon his mother on behalf of the minor child—should not be quashed. By Charlie's way of thinking, the right to confront witnesses and to compel witnesses to come to trial, as set forth by the Framers reacting to their experience under the British yoke, was ironclad and not subject to exceptions. The Sixth Amendment Right to Confront the Witness meant, or should mean, that the State cannot just bring into court someone's statement in writing or allow another to give testimony by hearsay. The defendant has the right to have the jury see that witness in court, under oath, subject to cross-examination by the defense lawyer or by the defendant himself, if without counsel. This right, which Charlie deemed absolute, had been eroded in recent years by the State's use of wimpy statutes designed to protect certain witnesses from the supposed embarrassment of testifying. In fact, the use of these statutes or, in some cases, a court rule was becoming alarmingly commonplace, allowing into evidence, for example, a child's statement that daddy played with him and committed acts of perversion without the kid being in court. The State devises these so-called safe interviews where a social worker holds up a doll and asks whether daddy played with the pee pee. Then the social worker comes to court and says that Johnny said this to her in a confidential setting. The kid may have been prompted, subtly coerced, or even browbeaten to say such things, but at least he is spared the anguish of having to see dad in court and being cross-examined. This was the exact set of circumstances Charlie was about to confront. He would argue that his subpoena of little Johnny should not be quashed and that his motion to suppress the social worker's statements about what Johnny said about daddy, the defendant facing life, must be sustained.

In court, Charlie listened as the prosecutor got done with some windy argument about sparing the poor victim from the trauma of court. Now it was his turn. Charlie got up, banged his cowboy boot on the first step of the platform below the bench, stretched out his string tie, mopped back his black hair with his hand, and said, "Judge, what the circuit attorney has stated is sound law, great law … in Russia!" Those last two words were shouted. The judge ruled in favor of Charlie. As the next set of attorneys were shuffling papers and preparing to advance their particular arguments, the judge turned to the bailiff seated on his right and said, "This is *not* Russia."

The Burnham murder trail was nearly delayed because Tom Burnham had been arrested—*almost* arrested—for tearing up his own bar. Wednesday evening, about nine-thirty, two guys walk in, take a seat at the bar. They order Stag longnecks with Jack chasers. Burnham stands at the end of the bar, nursing a strawberry daiquiri, eyeing these two galoots because he senses trouble. Sure enough, not ten minutes go by before the one with the long hair sticking out from under his baseball cap tells the bartender to change the music. "Jimmy Buffet is for pussies," he says loud enough for Burnham to hear and get his hackles raised.

Burnham hears the next line as he's walking toward the two. "Put on some Hank Junior or Willie Nelson, and do it now while I'm in a good mood."

Bartender tells them straight-faced that Hank Junior went to the crapper about a half-hour ago. "Don't know when he's coming out, because he's so full of shit." That's when Burnham appears.

"Help you gentlemen?" The two pivot on their stools and glare.

"How in hell could you help us?" scowls the other guy, heavy-set, greasy blond-red hair, looking like Sammy Hagar after three weeks of KP duty.

"I could help you get the fuck out of here right now," says Burnham evenly, arms folded, girding for the obvious outcome. For a guy who liked frou-frou drinks Tom Burnham could be pretty damn pugnacious.

Long hair grips the neck of his Stag, squints at Burnham and says, "You the cocksucker likes to shoot people in the back?" That's all it took. Fists flying, bottles smashing, people shouting, jumping out of the way, Jimmy Buffet in the background singing "Cheeseburger in Paradise." The bartender leaping over the bar to help Burnham wrestle these idiots out the door. Burnham carried a sap in his back pocket, a gift from a cop buddy, and he brings it down repeatedly on Sammy Hagar's skull until the guy gets docile enough that Burnham and the bartender can toss him and his buddy outside and into the night. The old bum's rush. The two are picking themselves up, trying to pull their shit together, deciding whether to go back in to settle the score, when the squad car comes speeding up, lights flashing. The lone cop jumps out, sidearm in hand, sees Burnham standing at the door, sees the two guys near the entrance, unsteady on their feet, yet menacing. "What's the trouble here, Tom?"

Burnham tosses the sap into some shrubs and says assuredly, "Whatever the trouble was, it's taken care of now." The cop takes charge, talks to the two troublemakers, noting the bloody lumps on the one's noggin, talks to Burnham, calls for back-up. At the station the cops try to sort things out. They know Burnham from several other incidents at the bar, altercations where someone got hurt. They know he's feisty by nature. They know he attracts trouble. They also know he's close to going to trial for murder. They don't dislike him, they just wish he would cool his jets. They look at these other two and see they've got INSTIGATOR written all over their faces. They book Sammy Hagar and his pal for wanton battery, but decide to give Burnham a break and merely issue him a citation for peace disturbance. A fifty-dollar fine. The cops, thoughtful as they are, don't want to mess things up, prevent Burnham from having his day in court. But the incident makes the papers, the lead story in the *Post-Dispatch* Law & Order section the following day.

Charlie had Burnham in his office. He wanted to chew him out, but what good what it do if he was bent on fucking up his own trial defense by playing grab-ass with bar patrons? Jurors get wind of it, they see him as a vigilante type, Charles Bronson in those *Death Wish* movies. The guy was like a big kid, not thinking ahead when it came to the consequences of his actions. He would always be that way, it was his nature. "Listen," said Charlie, "I want to tell you something important." Burnham listened up. "The trial is four days away. I think it will last three days including jury selection. On the third day I am going to call you to the stand. I am going to question you and so is the prosecutor. To all questions you simply state the truth, don't hem or haw, don't be vague, don't be sarcastic, don't say anything more than what is required to answer the question. But above all, don't come off like you did when you first appeared in this office. You know what I'm talking about?"

Burnham frowned. "Arrogant? Conceited? Brash maybe? I've been called those things, but that's just another way of saying self-confident."

"I'm talking about you feeling proud of what you did. How did you put it? 'That nefarious cocksucker got what he deserved.' That's not going to fly. Any way you slice it, you killed the guy. Do you think you can appear to be contrite about it?"

"That's asking a lot," said Burnham.

"I said *appear* to be contrite. Think of it as acting. You're acting like you regret the whole thing, it's a tragedy but it couldn't be helped. You had no other choice, but still, you feel sorry it happened to begin with. Thing is, it's got to seem genuine. The jury can sense insincerity."

Burnham chuckled at the thought of pretending to be sincere. "What about these black belts having to register their hands and feet as lethal weapons? This came to me the other day. It was my lethal weapon against his and he had four of them, right? You going to bring that up?"

"Yeah, we checked that out already. That hands-and-feet lethal weapon registration is a myth, probably had its origin in the movies."

"The movies, damn right. Bruce Lee, Sonny Chiba, even white boy Chuck Norris, you tell me those guys can't maim and kill with their hands and feet. I hope you've got some kung fu fighter guy coming to testify what that training can do."

"As a matter of fact, we do have a martial arts expert coming in to testify."

"Good," said Burnham approvingly, "that shows me you're on the ball." He looked hard at Charlie. "I want you to do for me what you did for that stewardess," he told him.

Charlie knew what Burnham meant. In a celebrated case from several years back, he had defended an airline stewardess who shot and killed her boyfriend, a pilot. The stewardess was pregnant by the pilot and yet he had a wife and several other girlfriends, a real cad. The coroner's verdict of justifiable homicide went a long way in getting the gal acquitted.

"That was in out-state Missouri," noted Charlie. "We don't have coroners' verdicts here. You see, in the smaller counties in Missouri they have what's called a coroner's jury, a collection of his pals who get paid twelve bucks to sit and hear the circumstances and medical facts of a death. They render a coroner's verdict signed by the coroner. Justifiable homicide, the verdict pronounced in the stewardess case, is a bit of a contradiction, although it certainly didn't hurt our case. Why is it contradictory? It's akin to self-defense, but is killing an attacker in self-defense then a homicide? It is the mere killing of another, but not a crime—that's the way I see it. It can be abused, though. The coroner's jury and verdict is a way to sweep aside crimes in some instances. There's a story of a KKK murder in Mississippi where the decedent was found burned with fifteen gunshots in his body. Coroner's verdict: 'Worst case of suicide we ever saw.'"

"But my homicide was in self-defense, justifiable."

"And I'll be sure to drive that home," said Charlie. "Still, a favorable verdict of a coroner's jury, if we even had one here, would not hold sway if the prosecutor indicts the killer, which he did. In fact, the jury may not be allowed to hear the verdict of the coroner's jury in the criminal trial."

"All these fine hairs," said Burnham. "It hurts my brain to ponder it all, but you've got it all down, right? I've got to have faith in you. You're the best, that's why I'm paying you the big bucks."

"And speaking of that, I've got something for you." Charlie handed Burnham an invoice for $30,000 "services rendered." Another thirty grand.

Burnham glanced at it, guffawed. "That's all? Hell, I can blow more'n that on a good day at Fairmount Park. Horse Hookey, Tuesday afternoons. Ever go?"

"I've been, yeah," said Charlie, "and it's alright. But personally, I like my horses to take their time. I like to look at the scenery."

Jury selection in the Burnham trial. Thirty-six jurors were being questioned, alternately by Charlie and the prosecutor, a dapper fellow named Vincent Vas Dias with an East Coast accent. There was a break and the prospective jurors were excused to pee. Time passed, counselors checked their notes, Charlie conferred with Burnham about something. One by one, they returned from the restroom, filed back to their seats and the room got quiet when the bailiff announced that the court is now in session. Charlie led off the second round of *voir dire*, walking up to the jury rail. He looked right at the third guy in the front row and said, "Did Huck come back to St. Louis after the war?"

"Yes, Charlie, he did, all in one piece." The guy was all smiles.

"Thank God," said Charlie. Vas Dias jumped up. "Wait, Juror Number Three,"—prosecutor didn't think to call him by his name—"do you know Mister Shaw here?"

The guy shot a look that made Vas Dias think he was asking a dumb question. "Sure, everybody knows Charlie. He and my brother used to ride horses out in Jeff County as kids."

Then the prosecutor was up at the bench, so was Charlie, and one could hear the colloquy from the audience seats so it was a safe bet that the jury could hear it, too, what with Charlie's stage voice. And then the judge said, too loud as well, "Mister Shaw doesn't know this juror, he knows his brother. This is a small town. Go back to New York if you want someone who doesn't know some-one's brother."

After the effort at the bench where the State tried to strike Juror Number Three from the panel and the judge let things proceed, there was a collective sigh from the juror box and despite the judge's warning that they should disregard anything they may have heard coming from the bench just then, the admonishment had already sunk in.

The actual trial got underway on a Friday morning. The courtroom was packed to the rafters with friends and families of both the victim and the accused, stealing glances at each other from across the aisle that separated them. Sizing up, making judgments, one contingent convinced that the other contingent was essentially trash. In the front pews, newsprint scribes had their reporter notepads on their laps ready to take down what they saw and heard, hoping their version was more scintillating than the next guy's. Outside in the hall and even downstairs out in the plaza near the entrance, television crews waited for the principal characters to pass, coming or going, hoping against hope that one of them would answer their banal questions—"What do you think the verdict will be?"—or at least get some good footage. Burnham chewing his fingers, whatever.

And Charlie was gorgeous in the courtroom. He was very tough on prosecution witnesses. He would seize on little things and just drive a truck through them. Example: The State had one witness, a former waitress at the Opera House, who testified that Burnham kept guns in his office and had been seen out in the bar area with a handgun in his belt. During cross-exam, Charlie asked if she'd ever been around guns other than what she saw at the saloon. No, she had not. Would she be able to tell a real gun from, say, a toy gun? Well, not exactly. Had she ever seen Tom Burnham fire one of the guns that she saw? Well, no, but once she'd heard gunshots coming from his office. What did it sound like? Kind of like a firecracker. What time of the year was this? Summer, around the Fourth of July. And so it went, each response from the witness impugning her previous testimony under the prosecutor's direction. To top it off, Charlie asked why she had been terminated from her employment at Burnham's saloon.

"I wasn't terminated," she replied, "I quit because I found a better situation."

But J.R. had done his homework on this woman and Charlie had the goods on her. He went up to her, flipped-up blond hair, looking like poster-girl Farrah Fawcett, stroked his chin as if in deep contemplation, and asked when was her last day on the job. Right around the first of April last year. "Not long after your drug bust," said Charlie and this was not a question.

"I don't know what you're saying," she stammered.

"In that case," said Charlie, "I introduce Exhibit Twenty-three, the conviction record of this witness on charges of cocaine possession."

A lot of what Charlie Shaw did was Hollywood.

Over the weekend, Charlie decided to add more fence, stretching the barbwire taut from post to post, fixing the wire with industrial-strength staples driven by hammer. It was tough work, especially on the hands, but the work gloves that Joyce had bought for him were holding up nicely. Raymond Bess, the parolee, was helping him. It was a cold, sunny morning in early February. They were hoping to complete the job by Sunday afternoon, connect with the start of the fence some 400 yards distant. Then, finally, Charlie could let his horses into this tract—part meadow, part scrub with some woods and a pretty little creek. Charlie took good care of his horses, he liked making them happy. A horse definitely had feelings, and Charlie was convinced that if he treated them well, they, in turn, would give him their best out of sheer gratitude. Just this last summer he and some pals put four horses in a trailer and headed down to Gila Bend, Arizona, hit the trail for three days, roughing it. His four-year-old pinto, Zander, was exemplary on that ride; Charlie couldn't have been more proud.

Charlie and Ray worked mostly in silence. Ray was talkative by nature. In the Workhouse, they called him Motormouth. But if Charlie wanted quiet, so be it. Still, he knew that Charlie had some amazing stories in him and he wished he could find a way to get the man to open up, unpack a few of those tales. He didn't care for this work, a good conversation would make the time pass quicker. The opportunity came when Charlie nicked his wrist on a barb, tearing the skin in that small exposed portion between where the coat sleeve ended and the glove began. "Well hell, I'm leaking," said Charlie, putting point pressure on the bleeding wound with his other hand. "Is it bad?" asked Ray. "No," answered Charlie, "just go to the truck and get me the first aid kit, will you?"

Ray returned a minute later and watched Charlie apply some salve to the cut and wrap it with the biggest Band-Aid he could find.

"That fence'll bite you, that's for certain," offered Ray.

Charlie looked at him and smiled. "There was a time when I was doing the biting on another barbwire fence, using homemade wire-cutters."

Ray raised his bushy eyebrows, said, "Yeah?"

"Yeah," said Charlie. "You may already know this, but I was a flier in the war, shot down over Germany on my last mission, captured by farmers, along with the rest of the crew, turned over to the Luftwaffe, interrogated, and then taken to a prison camp."

"You did time is what I heard."

"Yeah, I did time," said Charlie, chuckling that Ray saw him as a fellow jailbird. "A bit under two years, first in a place called Stalagluft Three and later, as the war was ending, in another prison called Stalag Seven-A. There were thousands of us, couple hundred thousand maybe, all nationalities, but mostly Americans and Brits. They separated the officers from the enlisted men. I was a Captain, twenty-two years old, full of crazy ideas. I didn't much care for the accommodations so I tried to leave, but there was a fence in the way."

"Not your typical fence that you could just step over," offered Ray.

"Not in the least. Around the perimeter of this camp there were two big strands of curlicue barbwire about eight feet apart, electrified, but not all the time. And before you got to those, there was a warning wire. On all four corners, there was a guard tower, manned constantly by Germans with spotlights and machine guns, ready for anything. Plus, there was a guard pacing the perimeter at night, round and round, four-hour shifts, never stopping. Horrible job. But like I say, there were many of us who had nothing but escape on our minds and we were like industrious ants, always trying to tunnel under that fence, but we would get caught or the tunnel would collapse—the ground was very sandy there. And when we couldn't get under the fence, we tried to go over it, from the roof of the latrine. But that didn't work either. Finally, on my fifth attempt, I got out by going *through* the wire. The wire cutters did the trick."

"But the screws! The armed guards in the towers, the one on the ground, the electric fence."

"We had nothing but time on our hands, time to observe their routine and plot our course of action. We figured that we had two minutes to work without being seen. It was winter, and we were just waiting for the right night to try it when fortune smiled on us. There was a blizzard, a howling blizzard, and in the midst of it me and another guy, Steve, a cop from Toledo before the war, skulked out to the yard. We had white sheets and we covered ourselves with them and burrowed down in two feet of snow. It was the perfect camouflage. The guard passed us twice without notice, and we were able to wriggle past the warning wire and out to the fence. It wasn't electrified just then, probably they were saving some juice to ride out the blizzard. With these primitive wire cutters we were able to make holes in the fence and squeeze through. Then, we were in the unguarded camp of the German cadre. We still had to get through that, and we did. The few soldiers we saw at that time of night didn't pay us any mind. We got to a forest eventually, and we ran and ran. It was two hours before the guards discovered the hole in the fence."

Ray looked puzzled. "How'd you know it was two hours if you were gone?"

"Oh, we got caught. Three days later in a town named Katowitz near the Russian front. We were trying to get to the Russian lines, the Russians being the only allies anywhere around. We did get pretty far though, a couple hundred miles at least, hopping freight trains and laying low. We damn near froze to death several times. We had to play-fight, wrestle and box, to keep our blood up. When they caught us, they radioed the camp and the commandant there sent a sergeant to come get us. It took nine hours by train to get back to Stalagluft Three, and it was a bitter homecoming. When I got out of solitary confinement—a month that went by like a year—that's when I learned our escape hadn't been discovered for two hours."

"I bet they were pissed, the Krauts." said Ray.

"Oh, they meant business. They swarmed into our barracks, rousted everyone out of bed. They carried small ID pictures of every prisoner. One guard would prod an American soldier forward while another would identify him by his picture. They still weren't sure that a real escape had been made."

"Solitary. I been there, too, man. It's alright if you're into meditation, but otherwise it sucks. You're lucky that's all they did to you for escaping."

"Actually, they were planning to court martial us, me and Steve, and then execute us like they'd done to forty-five British officers who had previously escaped and were captured. Like I said, they meant business, but then the Russians broke through the Eastern front and they were advancing. You could hear the cannons off in the distance, and our commandant decided that we should all make a mass exodus, march hundreds of miles to that other POW camp I mentioned, Stalag Seven-A, near Munich."

"Bataan Death March, I heard of that."

"This was something similar. Only Bataan was done in the sweltering heat, this one in the freezing cold. A lot of guys died on that march, we hardly stopped to eat or sleep. There was no decent shelter." Charlie paused. "But that's a story for another day," he said, slipping on his work gloves. "That fence is waiting, let's get to it."

Raymond Bess went back to work with a new respect for his boss. Imagine getting shot down over enemy territory and then having the balls to escape from the prison they put you in. The man had more lives than a cat. He almost asked Charlie if the experience was anything like what you saw on *Hogan's Heroes*, the sixties sitcom set in a German POW camp during World War II, but now he was glad he didn't. That would have turned him off, thinking that he, Raymond, was trivializing what Charlie went through.

Charlie went back to his fence feeling slightly foolish that he had blabbed about his escape attempts. There were some things you just kept to yourself. His feelings while imprisoned in that camp were so personal, so intense, that to tell it now, well, it just didn't come out right. Back then, in that time and place, escape was all he thought about. It bordered on monomania. Never mind that if he were to get away he would be in hostile territory, no one to trust or ask for help. He would have to hide like a scared animal and if his identity was discovered he would be apprehended or possibly shot on sight. Still, he made six attempts and was either caught or something went wrong and he was able to get back to his bunk without being noticed. On the seventh try, he made it. Posing as an enlisted man, he got on a work detail filling in bomb craters in Landschutz, a war-torn town in Bavaria, and while the guard was distracted, he simply walked off. From there, by cautious starts and stops and yes, he did steal a bicycle along the way, he made his way to another town where he'd heard of an active underground. The Levasseur Trail, a network of sympathizers to the allied cause, proved to be real and, after vetting him carefully, Monsieur Levasseur himself gave him refuge. Charlie was put up on the prosperous farm of Oscar Steiger, the snow-capped Alps off in the distance, and there he was able to bathe, sleep in clean sheets, and eat decent meals for the first time in many moons.

Two weeks went by. The plan was to put him on a boxcar bound for Switzerland where presumably he would be safeguarded, but the Swiss weren't necessarily as neutral as thought to be, for officials there had turned over certain allied escapees to the Germans. It was near the end of the war for Europe, the allies were advancing. It would be days, possibly a week, before they came rumbling up the road leading to the Steiger *bauernhof.* He could've stayed put in his alpine idyll, not risked yet another perilous expedition, but the old monomania had not ebbed. He told his gracious host he was going to cross the lines and meet the American army while on his feet.

Two Serbs under Steiger, Bogo and Sabich, escorted him to a road and they walked toward the advancing division, witnessing along the way the spectacle of German soldiers deserting by the thousands. The kilometers ticked by, the question expanding in his brain—when? Charlie would never forget the feeling that washed over him when Bogo looked up the line and hollered, *"Komaraden!"* He meant that Charlie's comrades were coming and, sure enough, Charlie saw the big white stars on the tanks. He could scarcely believe it. Reflecting back on that moment, Charlie knew he'd begun to lose faith in everything; a couple years of prison will do that to you. You wonder whether your country is as good as you think it is. If it is the mightiest army on the planet, then why haven't they come before now, why has it taken so long? And yet here they were in his sight, the formidable armored brigade of the 44th Infantry Division, rumbling down the road, making the sweetest goddamn commotion he'd ever heard. They had liberated Frenchmen and Poles from prison camps. They had liberated Jews, living skeletons, from concentration camps, nearby Dachau being one of them, but Charlie was the first captured American they had seen.

He was interrupted from his reverie of Way Back When by the sound of clomping hooves. He turned to see Joyce approaching on her mare and leading a robust quarter horse all saddled up and ready to ride. "Look what just came in the mail," she said.

Charlie walked up to the new horse, stroked his mane and said hello. "You're a handsome fellow, aren't you? And a bit too big to come in a package."

"I heard a clatter in the drive," she said, "and I looked out. There was a pickup and a horse trailer. I went out and a guy was already opening the back and, before I knew it, this wonderful creature was standing in front of me. The guy said, 'Here, this goes with him,' and he handed me a card. I didn't read it, so here you go."

Charlie took the card and unfolded it. "Mr. Shaw," it read. "I am walking around today a free man because of you. A sunset, the taste of an apple, a baby's cry, believe me, I take nothing for granted these days. The money I paid you wasn't enough so please take this horse with my deepest gratitude. Sincerely, Buck Reynolds."

Joyce said, "Can we keep him, Daddy, please?"

"Let's see what he can do," said Charlie, Joyce nodding enthusiastically. "Ray, you take the truck back. The fence'll wait until later."

The trial of *State of Missouri v Thomas Burnham* was wrapping up on Tuesday afternoon. Charlie consistently argued self-defense. The victim was a karate expert who had already demonstrated extreme prejudice toward his client, kicking him in the head hard enough to stun. By his martial arts training, Paul Cassise's hands and feet could be seen as lethal weapons even if they weren't officially designated as such. Soon after that, seeing Mr. Burnham in the parking lot, the victim charged at him, intent upon "finishing the job," as he himself had put it. My client feared for his life and had no choice but to use deadly force.

This morning, Charlie had the medical examiner on the stand saying that in regards to which direction the victim was facing when shot, toward Burnham or his back to Burnham, the bullet wounds were inconclusive. This afternoon, however, prosecutors brought to Missouri from Atlanta a star forensic witness who testified for two hours. The expert said that blood patterns on the ground near the shooting meant the victim was shot in the back as he fled. During cross-exam, Charlie walked up to the forensic witness, studied him for a moment, and announced he had just one question. Was it possible that the impact of the bullet from a high-caliber firearm, a .357 Magnum in this case, could have spun the victim around? That is, shot in the chest but landed belly-down? "It's possible," the witness said. Looking at each juror, Charlie slowly walked back to the defense table.

Closing arguments concluded, the jury was instructed and they went out to deliberate. The clock on the wall said four thirty-five. The counselor and his client sat at the defense table, Charlie doodling on a legal pad and Burnham rubbing his lucky buckeye. In a whisper Charlie said, "Well, I guess you decided not to turn rabbit and run. That's a good sign."

"I am on fucking pins and needles here," said Burnham,

whispering out the side of his mouth. "The suspense is killing me. I feel like I want to tear something up."

Charlie was pretty tense himself, although he didn't show it. He could see that Burnham was indeed on the verge of losing it, an aura of anxiety enveloping him. "I know it's hard," he said, "but try to calm down. Do some deep breathing. I've got a good feeling about this."

Number Three, Huck's brother, ended up being elected the foreman. Around five twenty-five a note came in from the sequestered jury of twelve that they had a question. The judge read the question: The foreman of the jury wanted to know if they should go ahead and vote now to acquit the defendant or go to dinner first.

As they were leaving the courthouse, crossing Central to go to Powers' and celebrate, Burnham dropped some papers in the street. As he stooped to gather them, he took too long for one motorist who blew her horn at him, a very irritated-sounding horn. *Honk! Honk!* Burnham scooped up the remaining papers from the asphalt, walked over to her, put his face on the other side of her partly open window and screamed, "Your horn blows, how 'bout you?" Charlie had to laugh. The guy was absolutely incorrigible—and best of all, he was no longer his client.

The following day, all over St. Louis, when people read the verdict in the morning *Globe* or the afternoon *Post*, they were either outraged or amazed. Charlie Shaw had done it again.

Tom Burnham moved his family to Key West, where he started a new bar with a Hemingway theme—mounted Marlins on the walls, fishing nets hanging from the ceiling, and over the bar, a big picture of the author at work, typing away on an old Smith Corona, a cat on his lap. Well, the Smith Corona was not old when the picture was taken just down the road at Hemingway's villa, now a tourist attraction. An endless stream of Jimmy Buffet poured from the bar's loudspeakers and, if anyone dared complain, they could just get the hell out right now. Burnham was in the house about six hours a day, often seen holding court at the end of the bar, a piña colada or margarita in hand, his back to the wall just like Wild Bill Hickok. For years, he told the story of that shooting to anyone who'd listen. The story grew with embellishment—the kid he killed becoming a made member of "the organization," there being a bounty placed on his head even now, and so on. He never regretted what he'd done, and he never failed to state how grateful he was to Charlie Shaw for getting him off the hook.

Charlie Shaw continued to practice law in St. Louis for 20 more years. His stature never stopped growing. Today, the Missouri Association of Criminal Defense Lawyers confers annually an award honoring those who "exhibit outstanding trial skills and a passion for trying cases involving the innocent accused." It is called the Charles Shaw Trial Advocacy Award.

Through a Serbian church in South St. Louis, he corresponded with Bogo and Sabich, the Serbians who helped him hide from the Germans and later escorted him along the road leading to freedom. In the 1990s, during the civil war in Bosnia, when President Clinton ordered the bombing of Serbian cities, the pastor of that church, Fr. Bogdan Rinkevic, who for years now had been translating Charlie's letters and mailing them, said to Charlie, "How is it that my people can help you in time of need and yet your children bomb my country?" Charlie thought about this and said he didn't have a good answer except that war is the most idiotic excuse for conflict resolution ever invented by man.

He died in 2001, at the age of 79. By coincidence, his funeral was held the morning of September 11, at the same time hijacked American airliners were crashing into buildings filled with innocent people, an act of war for a new generation. If such things really could happen, Charlie would have sat up in his coffin and said, "Well, here we go again."

Bobby and Lamont
THE **LINDELL BANK** JOB

CEDRIC STOKES DIDN'T WEAR HIS VEST THAT DAY. For one thing
it was too damn bulky. It restricted his movements and made him
feel like he was in a suit of armor, which would have been close
to the truth. Although the protocol in the Allied Barton Manual
called for it, insisted on it, Cedric wore or didn't wear the vest
based purely on whim, the same whim that governed whether or
not he snapped his seat belt before heading into traffic. It all boiled
down to two things: How lucky he felt that particular day and how
much disdain for the rules he happened to be harboring at the
moment. For Cedric Stokes was a contrarian by nature, a security
guard with a strong dislike for authority. To not wear the vest was
to strike a blow against the pin-heads that ran the agency which
employed him.

Not that his sartorial decision on the morning of March 17,
1997, made a mouse fart of a difference in the outcome. There was
no way Cedric Stokes wasn't going to be wasted. When two guys
walk in a bank just before noon, wearing ski masks, toting AK-47s,
and barking commands at two dozen terrified customers and
employees, you know fucking well they mean business. The first
thing they do is take out the one guy that could spoil their plan.
And if they shot him in the chest and the vest that he might have

worn did its job—hell, before he could even draw his Smith & Wesson, they'd have blown his head off.

They had checked out the building a month in advance, one of several banks in the offing. What they liked about this one, the Lindell Bank & Trust, was the security guard who sat at a desk in the rear of the big lobby. Reading a magazine and sipping coffee when they were there, the guy could could've been in a cafe instead of a bank. The tellers were all women, mostly young, fresh faces, probably hand over the money easy and not try anything stupid. Plus, the bank, a box-like rectangle built in the early 70s, was located at Clayton Avenue and McCausland, an area called Hi-Pointe, and it was next to the highway. Afterwards, they quick jump on Highway 40, blend into traffic, be gone like they were never there.

"That bank, somethin' about it," said Bobby behind the wheel, driving off.

"Jus' cryin' out to be robbed," agreed Lamont.

"Feels right."

Lamont nodded, pulling a joint from his shirt pocket. "I got the same feelin', bro. That's one accommodatin' bank. Why else they goan have free coffee and cookies?"

After it all went down—four people dead, the bank shot up like a country stop sign—the papers called it a copycat robbery. The reason? The job had similarities to another bank robbery in Los Angeles two weeks before. Two guys armed with automatic weapons and wearing body armor botched the job and then they turned a suburban street into a war zone, firing at bystanders, police, and television helicopters. Those assholes were finally shot and killed, but not before they wounded more than twenty. Fact was Bobby and Lamont were aware of that fiasco, they read the papers like any other informed citizen, and they'd already made their plans before the LA ruckus. Still, they felt free to critique the actions of their rapacious brothers across the continent.

"Shoulda got out while the gettin' was good," said Lamont. "Can't understand why they wanna make a stand with nothin' to gain."

"Maybe they so goddamn pissed they didn't get the money, they jus' decide to take it out on anyone happen to be there at the time," offered Bobby. "Go out in a blaze of glory, like they say."

Lamont shook his head no. "Waste a good ammo, you ax me. You fuck it up, you get the fuck out and try it again another day."

"That ain't goan be our story," said Bobby emphatically. "We like a machine, a bank robbin' machine—precise, efficient. In and out in five minutes."

Lamont knew exactly what Bobby meant. They had both been on the Soldan High School drill team, handling weapons way back then. The drill rifles weren't real of course, just dummies, but, still, you got the feel of it.

They were sitting at the bar in Sadie's Personality Lounge, Union at Wabada. It was five days before the robbery. Bobby had a High Life in front of him and Lamont was working on a Remy and Coke. Just a couple other guys in the bar over near the door. In hushed tones they were going over the scenario. It was their plan to park the van close to the door, the entrance being at the east end of the building, facing a quiet parking lot. They would put on the ski masks, walk briskly to the door, carrying duffel bags for the cash, weapons concealed beneath the long duster coats they had bought for the occasion. This was one of the dicey parts. During that short walk from the van to the bank, if anyone saw them wearing those get-ups, it'd be pretty obvious what was going down and, if they were of a mind, they could flag down a cop or call 911. If they had one of those cell phones, they could call right then and there, cruisers screaming up before they knew it. But there was no way around that initial exposure, they conceded, and they just had do their best to try to time it when no citizens were around. Same thing if someone was leaving the bank when they were entering. That unlucky person would be shoved back in, lined up against the wall with the rest of them.

Once inside, the first job was to take out the guard. There was only slight debate about this, Bobby saying they could get the draw on him and disarm him. Lamont saying, "No way, man, those guys are trained to react. He sees our masks, he pulls his weapon— fuckin' shoot out at the OK Corral right there in the lobby. We got to do him and do it quick."

Quick could be a problem they both knew, the guard's desk at the far end of the lobby, facing the entrance. They couldn't just stroll up to him, so they'd have to fire from a distance, maybe 50 feet, spray the motherfucker. But then he might not be at his desk reading a magazine like before, he might be chatting with a teller or in the can. The guard was a bit of a question mark, but they'd deal with it alright.

Killing the guard would set off panic and they would have to take control immediately. They would order the customers to shut the fuck up or they'd be shot. They would move them plus any banking officers over to one side of the lobby and have them face the wall. There were four teller counters, but not all would be occupied. Anyone behind the counter would be told to put the money in bags, if it wasn't already in bags, and hand it over. Lamont would be positioned mid-lobby, ready to load the duffel bags, at the same time keeping his eye on the people facing the wall and watching the door, should someone walk in. Bobby would be at the counter making sure the tellers did what they were told. The whole time their AK-47s would be trained on this one, that one, their demeanor and body language unmistakably conveying the grim business at hand.

When they had what they came for they would back out, make for the van, and head for the highway—so close, just a left turn out the parking lot and then a quick right. There were security cameras on the side of the bank building. Big Brother was watching; let him watch. Bobby and Lamont had concealed identities and the van had stolen plates. There was a place over on the East Side, Washington Park, a back room in an old trucking depot, that they rented. Once there, the door locked and bolted, they would lay out the loot and celebrate. It was old school, their plan, but it would work.

"Yow! Ow! Ow!"

"What're you yowing about, Obie?" asked Jimmy.

"*Ooo-ooohoo!* I just smashed my thumb," cried Obie, sucking the affected digit, big baby that he was.

"Spud, take that hammer away from Obie, will ya? Before he does something really stupid."

Spud walked over to where Obie was standing, a pile of scrap lumber, plywood and two-by-fours, at his feet. "Obie, why don't you string the crepe paper? That's a good job. Rolls of green, white and orange, get creative with it. I'll finish up this end."

The float was nearly done, and just in time for the big Hibernian parade in Dogtown. They were in the back of The Irish Immigrant Pub, a century-old, wood-frame building on Sutton, near the Union Pacific crossing in Maplewood. The bar was owned by Jimmy's uncle Mike, a teamster, who each year allowed his flatbed trailer to be transformed into a rolling advertisement for the pub itself. Jimmy, Spud, and Obie did the work in exchange for beer, although Jimmy got his beer free anyway, him being the bartender, bouncer, and janitor rolled into one.

After a half hour more of pounding and sawing and cussing they stepped back to look at the float, a rudimentary frame with pinewood rails and plywood panels on each side. The panels were painted with leprechauns and shamrocks and lettered to read IRISH IMMIGRANT PUB · ERIN GO BRAGH—OR ELSE! At the mid-rear, on an elevated deck, there was a great chair with a high back: the throne. Jimmy would occupy that throne, posing as Finn McCool, the Irish warrior of legend, while Obie and Spud and a dozen other regulars would form the rest of the clan. They were going to paint their faces blue—"just like the ancient Celt dudes"—and wear bathrobes as period tunics; Jimmy's bathrobe had a fur collar sewn to it. Always girded for battle, McCool and his intrepid band would be armed to the teeth—broomsticks whittled into pointy spears, kitchen knives for daggers, baseball bats as war clubs. "It's a thing of beauty," pronounced Jimmy, holding out his Busch longneck for a toast. Three Busch longnecks clinked.

"It is gorgeous," agreed Spud. "Only thing that bothers me is the porta-potty. It's green, sort of, but not Kelly green."

"We ran outta that paint," said Jimmy. "And besides, what do you care what color it is when you're *inside* of it puking your guts up? Doofus. But we do need to go over the checklist. Provisions, right? Very important."

"How many coolers?" asked Obie.

"We got ten cases of beer, so probably six," said Jimmy. "And we'll need peanuts and chips and stuff to munch on."

"Me and Obie'll be heading to Shop 'n Save," said Spud. "You want us to get the cabbages there, too?"

"Cabbages *and* potatoes," corrected Jimmy. "Get what you can, but the grocery store won't have enough. We need boxes of 'em. You're gonna have to go to Produce Row and buy in bulk. You do that early. Go see the Cusumano boys, they'll take care of you, and then meet back here around eight. We'll load up and head out. Parade starts at noon, but I want to be in line by ten."

"It's gonna be a great day for the Irish," said Obie whose real name was Oswalt Biermacher.

The first thing that went wrong was Lamont didn't like putting the ski mask over his hair which had just been sheened at Dozier's Tonsorial Parlor. "You put that fuckin' thing on," ordered Bobby. "You know you gotta wear it for the job, so why even bitch?"

Lamont handed Bobby the joint and put the thing on. He looked at Bobby now, the ski mask covering his skull tight as a condom, just his eyes and mouth showing. "I hope I don't look as silly as you, but somethin' tells me I do," he said.

"Jus' think of it as Halloween," said Bobby. "We trick or treatin'. We goan pull some tricks, get a bag of treats. You ready?"

They were sitting in the van, parked almost in front of the bank. This was the moment of truth. They were poised, ready to enter the bank and wreak havoc on hapless persons just going about their humdrum day without any inkling of imminent danger. If they were edgy it didn't show, their nervous systems dulled by pot and booze, a pint of Captain Morgan's Rum consumed between them in the last twenty minutes. To add to the mix they had taken oxycodone on the way here, washed it down with a 32-ounce High Life. This regimen only slightly more prodigious than on a regular day.

"I gotta use the toilet," said Lamont.

"Fuck that," said Bobby. "This is it, let's do it."

They burst through the doors, scaring the shit out of anybody with any sense at all—shouting, pointing weapons, gesticulating madly. Lamont saw the guard sitting at his desk, eyes wide, mouth open, like a guy who'd seen something horrific. He fast walked over there and just as the guy was getting up, about to draw his side-arm—*pop! pop!*—he shot him. The guard slumped back into his seat, a look of stunned disbelief on his face, and that was that.

The second thing that went wrong was the fat blonde. Disobedient cunt. Everyone else doing what they were told, lining up against the wall and she's got to break for the door, screaming like a crazy person. Lamont had no choice, really. Two down. The rest went off without problem. Just some small aggravations that they might have expected—people whimpering, tellers not moving fast enough, one woman saying the Hail Mary over and over. They gave that to her, what the hell.

They left with their duffel bags a lot heavier than when they went in.

"I'll be goddamn if that wasn't *under* five minutes," said Bobby, exultant, putting the van into gear.

"We done good," agreed Lamont. "Now let's get the fuck out."

"We there already," said Bobby, turning left out the parking lot, then running a red light for an immediate right. They'd just taken their ski masks off when they heard the sirens. "Here it comes," said Bobby, chuckling. "But guess what? We gone!" Off to their left, they watched the two white city cruisers approaching, speeding, lights flashing, in the westbound lanes of the highway.

"This ain't right," said Lamont.

"They ain't goan see us," said Bobby.

"No, I mean this ain't the highway. This some street alongside the highway. You took the wrong turn, you stupid motherfucker!"

Bobby didn't say anything at first, just kept driving but a bit slower. He saw they were in a neighborhood. He saw the highway about 50 yards away, a big chain link fence and grassy median between them and it. "Well, fuck me," he said.

"Turn around! Do something!" screamed Lamont.

Too late. They were already in some kind of traffic jam, cars stopping, cars parking, people everywhere, carrying lawn chairs and coolers, all moving in one direction like some biblical exodus.

"What is this shit?" wondered Bobby, laying on his horn. An arm appeared from the driver's side window of the motionless car in front of them and a hand at the end of that arm gave them the finger. Bobby looked in the rear-view, saw a line of cars stopped behind them. The oncoming lane next to them had stopped cars in it, too. They were boxed in.

This was the third thing to go wrong, and it was a big one.

"You done a lot of stupid shit in your life, man, but this the stupidest," chided Lamont, voice rising. "We even practice the getaway! How you be this fuckin' stupid?"

Bobby shot him a look. "Shut up, fool, lemme think."

Lamont, patently disgusted, got out of the car and slammed the door. He came around back and looked down the street, studying the situation. He got back in the car. "Nothin' moving," he told Bobby, "but theys a cop way down there directing traffic."

"Nothin' moving, but *we* got to move," said Bobby, trying to maintain composure. "We not even a half mile from the bank, this place goan be full of cops anytime now."

"What we need is a flying car," said Lamont.

Bobby conked his head as if to dislodge that incredible statement and said, "I'm thinkin' of jumpin' that sidewalk there an' goan through the yards."

"How you goan do that when the whole street's lined with parked cars? You goan plow right through? We stuck here, man—and I still gotta piss."

Bobby was a man of action, even if that action was desperate in the extreme. He looked at his partner and said, "Well, there's only one thing to do."

Mayrose Gannon had just turned the corner from Louisville Avenue onto Oakland, her dachshund Teddy straining at the leash, when she saw them coming. "Oh, sweet Jesus, help me!" intoned Mayrose, crossing herself. She was an old bird, had lived in Dogtown all her life, and never before had she seen two Negroes sprinting down Oakland, carrying laundry bags, coming right at her. Mayrose was a woman of habit and that habit involved walking Teddy every day. She and Teddy got their exercise as recommended by both physician and veterinarian and, as they walked, Mayrose said the rosary. At this particular moment, the two men fast approaching, she had a baggie of dogshit in one hand and a rosary in the other. They came at her like she wasn't even there, bowled her over, and kept on going. Grunting and groaning, Mayrose picked herself up, checked Teddy for injuries, looked at the dogshit that had somehow gotten smeared on the front of her dress and wondered when the neighborhood had started going to hell.

The Hibernian Parade in Dogtown is always held March 17, the real St. Patrick's Day, as opposed to the larger parade downtown with its tricked-out floats and colossal inflated leprechauns—the one that occurs on the Saturday previous to March 17. A true Son of Erin may go to the downtown hoolie, sure, but he will not miss the Dogtown party. He will skip work if he has to. He will dig out his favorite green shirt. He will plan on drinking and carousing starting no later than noon and carry on well into the evening.

The staging area for the parade starts at Tamm and Oakland and backs up across the Highway 40 overpass and onto the street that runs along the south side of the zoo. Jimmy and his crew had arrived early enough that they were given a prime position, less than twenty units behind the lead. They'd been settled in since ten and already into their second case of brew. The weather was decent, sunny, in the 60s, a more than slight breeze. The boys were in high spirits, play-fighting with their homemade spears and daggers, blasting The Chieftains and Tommy Makem from a boombox. At the fore of this party boat were several bins filled with potatoes and cabbages. Jimmy had got the idea from the Mardi Gras parade in Soulard, watching the crowd snatch the beads thrown from the floats, doing anything to get those dime store trinkets, the girls going so far as to lift their shirts and show their ta-tas, nipples turned to raisins in the cold. Well, cabbages and potatoes were the staples of the Irish diet—today, in fact, there were corned beef and cabbage dinners being offered at every bar, restaurant, and church hall within a five-mile radius of Dogtown—so Jimmy reasoned that these items, so easily tossed, would really impress the crowd. They might even take them home, make their own St. Paddy's meal and, saying grace, they would remember the thrill of catching a nice cabbage or potato and they would thank The Irish Immigrant Pub.

Precisely at noon, a shot was fired from a starter pistol. A dozen members of the Invera'an Pipe Band, in full regalia, began to step out. They marched up Tamm Avenue, high-stepping, the base drum laying down a beat to a rousing bagpipe rendition of "The Minstrel Boy," and one by one the floats followed. Finally, it was their turn. The guy driving Uncle Mike's Ford F-150, a pipefitter named Timba, stepped on the gas, the flatbed truck lurched forward, and Obie fell off the back.

"Doofus! Get back on the truck," called Jimmy. "You're lucky you didn't fall on your spear."

"That woulda been a great start to the parade," added Spud,

wearing a football helmet with antlers protruding out the sides.

Obie picked himself up and began jogging painfully, catching up. He got himself back on board and received a can of Busch for the effort. They were crossing the overpass now, the crowd coming into view, a sea of green lining both sides of the street. As soon as they passed McDermott's, they began throwing the produce. Lobbing the cabbages, zinging the potatoes. The crowd seemed appreciative, catching them good-naturedly, holding up the cabbages triumphantly, calling out for more. At the same time they were clowning, jabbing thin air with their spears, doing muscleman poses like Charles Atlas on the back of an old comic book, saluting the big white-green-orange flag fluttering from the cab of the truck. Blue faces calling, "You want some more? Let's hear it for The Irish Immigrant Pub!"

Then Obie got beaned with a potato, some ungrateful dog acting out. He picked up the offending potato, held it out dramatically and bellowed, "Oh, you wanna play, do you?" Obie chucked that potato sidearm-style as hard as he could, into the crowd, hitting a pretty red-haired woman square in the chest. The thump was heard back to the float. "Oops! Sorry," called Obie, "didn't mean to."

Jimmy, sitting on his throne, sized up the situation and gave a regal command. "Jesus H. Christ, you're sposed ta throw the potatoes to the nice people, not *at* them."

"They started it," countered several regulars itching for a fight.

"Yeah," said Obie, pointing to an oozing abrasion on his forehead, the result of his fall, "they started it."

Jimmy shrugged. "Well, if they started it, we'll finish it."

The stuff flew like guided missiles, every man except Timba at the wheel tossing potatoes and cabbages at the crowd, hitting people at random in the torso and head, laughing like buffoons, and ducking when the objects were thrown back with equal force.

Some spectators were amused, but more were incensed. If it weren't for a waist-high series of interlocking metal barriers holding them at bay, they would have stormed the float like rioting prisoners.

They left their dusters in the van along with their AK-47s, too conspicuous to carry in plain sight. They each had pistols, though—a 9 millimeter Glock for Lamont, and a Taurus snubnose, detective model .38 for Bobby. They rounded the corner on Tamm and saw more people in one place than they had ever seen.

"What's this bullshit?" said Lamont, out of breath.

"They all wearin' green," said Bobby, "got to be the Saint's Day— you know, guy with the big hat, hates snakes." Bobby had attended St. Teresa of Avila Grade School for five years, and he knew his saints.

"The fuck you talkin' bout?" said Lamont suspiciously.

"We in the middle of a parade," said Bobby. "We got two choices here: We move on, steal a car, catch a ride, whatever, or we stay an' get lost in this crowd."

"You ain't notice that we the only niggas here? How we goan get lost?"

They did not butt heads very often, mostly they were too drunk or high to expend the effort, but when they did disagree, Bobby usually won out. They would work their way through the crowd— tens of thousands it looked, maybe a hundred thousand or more— and they would come out the other side wherever that was and make their escape. When the van was discovered, the cops would figure they ducked into the neighborhood here. But unless the cops had a bird's eye view, a helicopter, they would be hard to spot. They decided it would be smart to carry just one duffel bag so they went into a secluded area between two houses. There, behind some

bushes, they hunkered down and quickly consolidated the contents, their eyes taking in the green, much of it loose but some of it
bound with paper bands that read "100s," "50s," "20s," and so on.

"Oo-wee!" confirmed Bobby. "That's what I'm talkin' 'bout."

Lamont took a sizable wad of bills and put them in his jacket.
"Pocket money," he explained. Bobby followed suit saying that's
how he liked his money, all crumpled and used, not clean and crisp
and probably marked. They crammed the empty duffel under a
shrub, Lamont slinging the full one over his shoulder, and off they
went. They headed up Tamm, following the floats, not knowing
they were heading for Clayton Avenue, five blocks up, a large,
jam-packed intersection and ground zero of the parade.
Forward motion was slow and halting. Crushed in rollicking
humanity, glancing at the floats rolling by, hearing the lilting strains
of bagpipes, they forgot for a while that they were wanted men.
The crowd was protection, protection and anonymity; they were
merely bees in a vast hive.

It was going well for them, Bobby looking like a man with a
plan, when they heard the shout. It came with a pointing finger
directed at them specifically, and it said, "Hey, those guys aren't
wearing green!" Bobby and Lamont looked to see a band of big,
dumb-looking white guys standing in front of them, blocking the
sidewalk, each one with can of beer in his hand. They then gazed
down at their own attire—combinations of dark slacks, khaki
jacket, charcoal gray pullover, Lamont sporting a beige, wool ivy
cap, Bobby in a boonie hat—but no green, no sir.

The biggest, dumbest-looking one, wearing a large pin that read
FUCK ME – I'M IRISH, shouted, "Get 'em!" As a unit, they rushed
toward the two. Bobby and Lamont knew how to think on their
feet. They weren't afraid of no white boys and they could've just as
soon shot them dead in their tracks, but bottom-line they didn't

need the attention of a scuffle of any kind. "Run," said Bobby, and Lamont was down with that. But it was a moment too late and the FUCK ME guy had already grabbed Bobby by the arm. He was winding up to hit Bobby when Lamont jabbed him hard on the nose. Bobby broke free, elbowing the guy hard in the ribs. They saw the others circling, moving in, they looked at one another and knew what they had to do. Stiff-arming anyone in their way, they jumped the barricade, Lamont losing a shoe as he went over. Now they were in the street among the floats, exposed, sticking out like tinfoil on a telephone pole.

"You believe that shit?" said Bobby, pretty worked up. "I been discriminate against for bein' black, but not wearin' a certain color? This some fucked up parade."

"This ain't good," said Lamont. "We gotta get back in the crowd."

"Look there," said Bobby, motioning up ahead. Two city cops stood in the intersection, watching the parade, there simply to keep order. And that meant keeping the spectators behind the barricades.

Lamont shifted the duffel to his other shoulder and replied, "They ain't necessary lookin' for us."

"Yeah, but they got radios and they hear what went down. They got a description."

"How they know we black?" asked Lamont. "We wear gloves and masks. All they see is our eyes and mouth."

"That's enough, trus' me," said Bobby. A float rolled by, a pickup pulling a flatbed trailer, and it almost bumped them. At the same time, the crowd was starting to get annoyed at the two interlopers, yelling for them to get out of the parade. Someone threw a potato at them. "We got another move," said Bobby. "C'mon."

It could have been O' Sullivan's School of Irish Arts with two dozen prepubescent girls jigging in their best wigs purchased from

Celtic Curls. It could have been Riordan's Plumbing Supply with old man Riordan and his platoon of kin, throwing Tootsie Rolls and suckers to the children along the route. But out of all the floats in the Hibernian Parade, they had the very bad luck of choosing this one to party crash. The float moving at the pace of a brisk walk, Bobby grabbed the rail at the rear end and hoisted himself up. He then got the duffel from Lamont, set it next to him, and gave Lamont a hand up. It was only when they stood up and took stock of their surroundings that they saw what they had. A bunch of guys in bathrobes with blue faces all staring at them, primitive-looking assholes.

"This ain't good," said Lamont.

"Who the fuck are *you?*" demanded the one sitting in a big plush chair with a high-back. The Big Cheese, obviously.

Lamont looked to Bobby. Bobby held his hands out, open-palmed, a show of appeasement, gave the guy his best grin. "Who the fuck are we? We the Black Irish, man, come to party wit' you."

"No way," said this one big honky moving in on them. "You get your own float."

Bobby, still thinking on his feet, hoping to just hitch a ride past the cops in the intersection. "Our float got away from us," he told the scowling guy in front of him. "We jus' need to chill for a li'l while—you know how it be. Tell you what, we lay down up there behind that big chair. You won't even know we here."

"Your ass!" said the big man so close now that Bobby could smell his bratwurst breath.

Bobby saw they weren't getting anywhere. He went over the big man's head, called out to the guy in the chair, "Look man, one brother to another."

But Jimmy wouldn't listen. "Obie, give these guys the boot."

Obie came at Bobby and Bobby did this thing he'd picked up as a kid growing up in The Ville—a simple move, really, where you kick your leg behind the assailant's leg, somewhere below the knee, shove him back and he falls flat on his ass. Obie, surprised to find himself prostrate on the deck, started grabbing at ankles. He got one with no shoe, just a thin brown sock, and he held on tight, jerking at it, trying to topple its owner. He felt feet stomping his back, he heard his pals rush in to help, and he knew there was a donnybrook in progress. Still gripping the ankle, Obie took the foot and put the big toe in his mouth, biting down as hard as he would on a particularly tough pork chop.

Lamont screamed. "Oh, don't *even* do that!" But it wasn't just this chump-ass down there on the boards doing him, there were lots of other guys all over him and Bobby, trying to shove them overboard. Bobby was busy fending off a couple of them, trying to hold on to the duffel at the same time. Same with him, Lamont, these guys crawling over him like monkeys, punching his face, twisting his neck. Lamont reacted by pulling out his Glock and shooting one of them, a guy with some weird headgear, point-blank in the belly. The guy fell, writhing and moaning. Obie, in the process of rising, looked at Spud, doubled-up, staining the boards, and said, "This fucker is mine." Spud understood.

Before Lamont could get off another shot, Obie was on him. From his boot he pulled a dagger—the precision-forged Wusthof kitchen knife his ma had bought from Famous-Barr and would skin him with, if she knew he'd taken it—and he stabbed Lamont below the shoulder blade.

Lamont couldn't fucking believe it, the guy was trying to kill him. "Oh, I'm goan get yo ass for sure," he promised. "I'm goan make you cry!" Other followers of Finn McCool rushed in and began jabbing both Lamont and Bobby with spears, swinging baseball bats. Now Bobby had his gun out and he was standing there, at the very rear of the float, one step from falling off, and, for the moment, holding the blue faces at bay. Lamont had no such leverage. Obie had him in a headlock and stabbed him again, this time in the ribs. Almost simultaneously, a spear caught him in the groin and he felt the point go deep. He'd once seen a picture in a Natural History book, a color plate of some giant beast stuck in quicksand or something, and surrounded by cavemen armed with spears. The beast already had a lot of spears sticking out of its hide and it was about to go down, one more notch on the cavemen's clubs. Lamont was this beast, but before he went down he sincerely hoped to take a few of these assholes with him.

This spectacle of mayhem electrified the crowd. Thinking it was a dramatization of some bygone battle, they clapped and cheered wildly.

The big man now had him in a bear hug from behind, squeezing the breath out of him. Another spear point gouged him in the thigh, and Lamont found himself actually wishing the cops would come and save him. Someone hit him in the shin with a baseball bat. Each insult finding a new plateau of exquisite pain, and Lamont crazy with frustration that he had a gun in his right hand but couldn't get his arm free to take a shot. Then Lamont heard the man in his ear, a whisper, saying, "Why won't you die?" Lamont was pondering this question when the blade went into his right eye socket. There was a white explosion in his skull, and he knew he was ruined. He screamed, a godawful sound that turned heads.

Bobby looked at poor Lamont, blood pouring from his face, eyeball hanging out like a movie monster. He started to say something, but a gunshot interrupted. Lamont's nervous system, gone totally haywire, caused his extremities to twitch. One of those twitches found the trigger on the Glock and squeezed off a shot which hit

Obie in the foot. Obie released his vice-grip on Lamont and began hopping around, cursing and yelling. Then Lamont was reeling, staggering side to side, wildly off-balance, his left hand pressed up against his right eye, his right arm holding out the Glock. He began firing indiscriminately.

All this while the float kept moving. They were now in the big intersection, Clayton and Tamm, wall-to-wall people, all of them in the same *rah-rah!* mode as high schoolers at a pep rally. The two cops, Jackson and Johnson by name, had just heard a gunshot and they began moving in, handguns drawn.

The Dogtown Massacre, as it was later dubbed, climaxed with Lamont shooting up the place like a drunken cowboy in old Dodge City. He had 16 rounds left in the magazine, and he fired them all in 22 seconds. Lamont tended to aim high. Mostly he hit the sides of buildings, brick fragments raining down, and some rounds just sailing off into the blue, maybe hitting something a half-mile away. But by sheer volume he did manage to hit a beer cooler; Jimmy's throne, behind which Jimmy, as Finn McCool, was hiding; the plastic barber pole outside the Happy Medium Barber Shop; the side mirror of the F-150, sprinkling shards of glass into Timba's 64-ounce Strawberry-Banana Slurpee; and the big plate glass window of Seamus McDaniels' Tavern. One fateful stray round caught a guy standing on a balcony, hit him in the mouth. He was a college student who'd driven in from Rolla just for the parade. One second he was in high spirits, standing among friends, and the next second he was dead. His body crumpled and the top-heavy torso flipped off the railing, falling some 24 feet to the pavement but first landing on another young man, causing cervical injury that would plague him for the rest of his life.

For a few seconds there was dead silence—hard to imagine with the streets thronged like that. Lamont kept firing, but with his magazine spent. Obie, who had the sense to lay low during the shooting, now rose and with one quick motion plunged his dagger up under Lamont's chin. Lamont, arms flailing, began gurgling and at the same moment a bullet fired by Officer Johnson tore into his chest. Lamont's consciousness switched off like a TV screen. Bobby looked on horrified, saw the blue faces menacing, saw the cops coming, pointing their guns. Inspiration comes at odd times and what Bobby did, he reached into the duffel and began tossing wads of currency, fives, tens, twenties, even hundreds, tossing it everywhere—at Jimmy and his drunken mates, at the spectators on the other side of the barricades, high into the air where the breeze scattered it. Pandemonium reigned, people scampering madly to get theirs, some snatching the bills as they wafted down. Free money! People leaping the barricades at first and then simply unhooking them and pushing through. Free money! Bobby saw his chance and leaped off the float, slipping away in the confusion.

"What're you doing in those shrubs, Teddy?" Mayrose had Teddy on a long leash and she did not object if he stopped every so often to check out a bush or a hydrant as they walked along. She drew the line at dead animals, however. The dachshund had once rolled in something dead and it took her a week of scrubbing to get the stink off. "It better not be a dead possum," she cautioned. By then Teddy had gone in the shrubs and pulled out what looked to be a sack of some sort. Coming closer, Mayrose saw it was big and made of canvas.

"What in the world have you found? Some dirty old thing." Teddy sniffed at it cautiously and then looked at Mayrose expectantly. "Oh, I see. You want to take a look at what's inside. It is kind of curious, isn't it?"

She pulled the thing out all the way. It was what her late

husband, Art, used to call a gunnysack. She and Teddy were actually on the side of someone's house. If the gunnysack was in their shrubs it might belong to whomever lived here, but she was pretty sure they didn't know it was even here. Mayrose stood the gunnysack upright, moved the flaps aside, held the mouth open, and peered in. She saw only darkness, shadows. She gave the big sack a couple of shakes.

"Hmm, I'd say there's something in there," she told Teddy, "but I'm not sticking my hand into something I don't know what it is." Glancing up and down the street she saw no one; today she and Teddy were out quite early. She took the sack away from the house, out of the shade and into the light. Again she opened the sack, this time the sunlight illuminating the interior. Way down at the bottom she saw bills, with Ben Franklin on top. "Oh, my!" she uttered.

Maxie Touhill came to the door in his skivvies, eating a banana. "What is it, Mayrose?" he asked, scratching his behind. Mayrose was his neighbor, a nice enough woman who had undoubtedly cast her vote for him in the last Aldermanic election, but all the same a bit of a busybody.

"I want you to see what I've found," she told Maxie, holding out the gunnysack.

"Something good by the look on your face," he said.

She nodded. "It's best if we do this inside."

Maxie said to give him a minute while he got his pants on, and he padded off. Mayrose and Teddy stood outside, waiting. Maxie came back wearing baggy, rumpled trousers and a striped rugby jersey. He opened the door and waved them in. "I would apologize for the mess," he told her with a wink, "but then you might assume, wrongfully, that otherwise it's clean and neat."

"Oh, I've seen bachelors' homes before," said Mayrose, winking back.

This remark scared Maxie into thinking Mayrose was coming on to him. He went to the big table in the front room, took a seat at one end, telling Mayrose to sit at the opposite end. He cleared his throat, swallowed the phlegm, and said, "So what's this important business? Now you've got me intrigued."

"I'll show you," she said. And with a dramatic sweep she took the canvas bag and turned it upside down, dumping the contents onto the table.

Maxie gawked at the cash in front of him, Mayrose enjoying the scene. "I'll be a monkey's uncle," said Maxie, "where'd you get this?"

She told him where she found it and they both agreed it had to be connected to the craziness that had occurred the day before, those poor people getting shot and stabbed right in the middle of the big parade, money in the air. "Too much hoopla," Mayrose concluded. "Shameful, a bad mark on the neighborhood."

"What I'm thinking," said Maxie, "is they stashed this in the bushes thinking to come back for it later."

"Pooh," said Mayrose. "They had the one bag filled with cash and that got out, as you know, into the crowd—"

"Lord, I saw it from the open window of Dempsey's law office, over the music store, his yearly shindig, my eyes popping out, just wishing I could've got down there in time to get me some. I damn near jumped out of that window."

"What you call a windfall," added Mayrose.

"Literally," said Maxie, "and today half the palookas in Dogtown will be out spending their share of that windfall." He paused to give Teddy a scratch behind the ears.

Mayrose nodded knowingly. "Well, my theory is they each had one of these—I know so because they ran into me, literally knocked me over, running down the street—and they decided two bags was too many, so they put everything into the one. But they accidentally left some in the bag they were leaving behind."

But Maxie, ogling the money on his table, was barely listening. He picked up a hundred dollar bill and held it up to the light for scrutiny. "Did you happen to count it?" he asked.

"No," said Mayrose. "I just now found it. Thought I'd bring it to you straightaway, that you'd know what to do."

"You did right," said Maxie. "I'll take care of it. The police will be very interested in this bag."

"Maybe it'll help catch the one that got away," offered Mayrose.

"The one that got away. Like he's a big fish, huh? Well, maybe he is. But it's a big pond, too." He rose from his chair, their business concluded. "Now you get back to your walk. I can see Teddy's getting restless."

At the door, Mayrose hesitated and Maxie could see she had something on her mind. "What is it?" he prompted.

"Oh, it's just that … well, my nephew Frank, he was picked up for DUI the other night. And then I guess he had some words with the cop and now he's in the Workhouse until someone bails him out. He's basically a good boy, a little wild at times. You know how these kids are. My sister don't have money for bail and her husband, he don't even care. He says let Frank cool his heels for a good long while. It's breaking her heart."

Maxie, oozing empathy, gave her a pat on the shoulder. "Don't you worry, Mayrose, I'll take care of it. That's what Aldermen are for."

Once alone, he went back to the table and began counting. He arranged the bills in piles according to denomination, all the while singing a catchy show tune: "We're in the money, the skies are sunny, I'll take some money—oh yeah!" He let out a jolly

laugh, large sums of money always made him giddy. Altogether he
counted three-thousand, four hundred and fourteen dollars, about
a third of that in loose hundreds. The piles in front of him reminded him of play money from a Monopoly game. He took a bill from
each pile. That amounted to only one-hundred and eighty-five
dollars. He frowned. "Hell, that only buys St. James Place." Maxie
took some more off the top, then he took a little more. Now he
had eight-hundred and twenty dollars. "Well, that's a little better,"
he told himself. "Now I can sweep the railroads." He took another
hundred for good measure. After the money was all put back and
he was showered and shaved and ready to open the bar, he dipped
back into the bag and took another hundred and sixty for extra
good measure.

Sergeant Scanlan blew through the door like a full force gale.
He seemed perturbed that Maxie had called and said to get over
there now if he wanted "a scoop on the big holdup." But then Scanlan's usual state of mind was one of perturbation. So many things
bothered the big ruddy cop it would take a 70-page college-ruled
notebook to list them all. The first thing Maxie did was to shoo
old Red Rush off his barstool, telling him come back in a half-hour
and there'd be a free beer waiting. Red, indignant, saying make it
a beer with a whiskey chaser. Second thing was to lock the door
behind Red. The third thing he did was offer Scanlan a drink, and
being that it was two in the afternoon and no one in the bar now
except him and Maxie, Scanlan took a schooner. Maxie poured
himself one, too.

"What's this about the robbery?" said Scanlan with a shudder.
"What a fuckin' mess that was."

"First things first," said Maxie, holding out his glass. Scanlan
seemed wary, but he went ahead and offered his and the two glasses
clinked. They drank and put down their beers. Scanlan looked to

Maxie, all smiles, and said, "What the hell are we toasting?"

"Well, we could be toasting a milestone of Digger's Hideaway," said Maxie. "Come June it'll be twenty years of being in business."

"A good run," agreed Scanlan, "but something tells me that ain't what we're toasting."

"And that something would be right," said Maxie, moving behind the bar and pulling out the canvas duffel. He turned the thing upside-down and currency poured out.

Scanlan's immediate reaction was anger, or at least severe annoyance. "So you're tryin' to bribe me now, are you? What is it you need, a three o'clock license? Christ, man, can't you be more subtle?"

Maxie had to laugh. "C'mon, Tom, this ain't no bribe, and besides, I can hardly keep the doors open past eight much less three in the morning." Maxie motioned to the bills laying on the bar. "This cabbage is homegrown. My neighbor found it in some bushes down along a side street off Oakland. It's got to be connected to the holdup."

Scanlan, now disappointed that it wasn't a bribe, said, "You're right about that. It's the same bag as the other we found. Good going, Maxie."

"Yeah, thanks," said Maxie. "I tried not to handle it too much, thought you might be able to get some prints off'n it."

"Unfortunately, paper and cloth don't take fingerprints, but good thinking all the same."

"Still, one more piece in the puzzle, right?"

"You got it," said Scanlan. "The evidence techs will examine everything there is to examine. A fine tooth comb, as they say."

"The one still on the loose? Any leads on him?"

"We got the big net out as we speak," assured the cop. "We know his name. We know his associates and relatives, his haunts, and we got men watching. The FBI is in on it, too. It's only a matter of time."

"You'll probably find him hiding in the attic of his mama's house," said Maxie.

"That wouldn't surprise me," Scanlan said, "and when we do catch him he'll wish he'd never been born. Causing all that carnage, scarin' the bejesus out of decent citizens, it almost makes you want to lose faith in humanity—oh, wait, that's already happened!" And he laughed at his own joke.

"Another beer?" asked Maxie.

The cop shook his head no. "Thanks anyway, I'll just get this evidence over to the station. Did you happen to count it?"

"No, Tom, I didn't do any kind of accurate count, just eyeballed it and it looks to be over two-thousand."

"No specific number? That's alright, we'll get it counted and return it to its rightful owner. All in a day's work, eh?"

"You guys are the best," said Maxie, pouring himself another draft. "Say, did I ever tell you why this place is called Digger's Hideaway?"

"No, but I think you're about to."

"Well, Digger was this three-legged dog belonged to my ma when she bought this place and this animal, he liked to lay under the porch and—"

"Another time, Maxie, got to go now."

"Alright, Tom, you know your priorities. I respect that. Oh! Just one more thing, take a second, okay?" And he gave Scanlan the name of Mayrose's nephew, said no big deal, just that the kid's mother was on her deathbed. Scanlan said he would see what he could do. If there was one thing Maxie Touhill was good at it was calling in favors.

Bobby had been looking at cornfield stubble most of the
morning. Planting was still a month off. Every twenty miles or so
he would see a town off in the distance, probably only a half-mile
from the Interstate, and the way he would know there was a town
nearby was by the gray monolith seen poking up through the still-
bare trees. Like a church steeple, only it wasn't a church, it was a
grain elevator. This emptiness of landscape was alright with Bobby,
wanting to see and feel the countryside all around him. He was of
the firm belief that a rural setting where a traffic jam is ten cars behind a tractor was just what the doctor ordered. He'd had enough
excitement back in the city to last a lifetime.

He had played the scene in his head many times, the escape
from almost certain death. He always knew he was resourceful,
but that kind of quick thinking, that deserved a reward. Well, the
fact that he was a passenger on this bus, each minute putting miles
between him and St. Louis, maybe that was reward enough.

After Lamont had been slaughtered like an animal and he,
Bobby, had made it rain money—all those people in the street
providing cover—he jumped from the float and ran like hell. He
saw the breach in the barricade and got onto a side street, rounded
a corner and kept on going. It was a solid neighborhood with more
parade people standing around on porches and in front yards,
partying, boisterous, watching the black man sprint by. He skirted
around one knot of people on the sidewalk and in his wake he
heard, "Run, nigger, run!" And the thought came to him: *That's just
what I'm doing.* He ran hard and in five minutes or less he made it
out to Hampton Avenue where the traffic flowed freely without
detours or roadblocks due to the parade route. He saw a bus stop
with six people waiting, three of them black, and he joined them.

The bus pulled up a minute later and he got on, not knowing or caring where it was headed. But he knew his way around and after a series of strategic connections involving Bi-State buses and the new MetroLink railway, he ended up over the river at the terminal in East St. Louis. From there, he walked to the Greyhound station over on Bond Avenue and he bought a ticket for Barnwell, South Carolina. Then, for a half-hour, until the bus left, he sat in the lounge area, that morning's *Post-Dispatch* covering his face. When the loudspeaker called for boarding of the bus departing for Louisville, Knoxville, and points East, he got up and stood in line. It was that easy.

The destination was not chosen arbitrarily; still, he was glad for the name. Barnwell. It sounded uneventful, not too big and not too small, the kind of place he could blend in. He knew there were blacks living there because Odessa lived there. Bobby met her last year on the Blues Cruise, a three-hour riverboat excursion with live music. Odessa was visiting relatives on the Northside, had never been to St. Louis, and Bobby played tour guide, showing her the sights from the starboard rail. They danced, nuzzled, and laughed their way through the hot July evening. Bobby was smitten, like-wise Odessa. But come Sunday, she had to get in the Fleetwood with her family and drive back home. A long-distance romance ensued, the two lovebirds talking on the phone some nights until one. Bobby didn't mention this to anyone, partly because he was very private about his feelings for women and partly because Odessa was nothing to brag about anyhow—those missing front teeth, the psoriasis, and her being, in her own words, "chubby."

"That jus' means there's lots of you to love," he told her one night over the phone and she allowed how that was a good thing because she was hungry for love.

And now he sat in a Greyhound bus, gazing out the window at

strange terrain, covering ground at seventy per, thinking how he'd been handed a fresh start. Sure, there was an all-points bulletin out, had to be, but what kind of description could it have—black male, mid-30s, five-eight, medium build, short black hair. Shit, that's half the guys he knew. He had eight-hundred, eighty-two bucks in his billfold, what was left, after buying the bus ticket, of the bills that he and Lamont had hurriedly stuffed in their pockets, just in case. That would carry him for a while—groceries, beer, little gifts for Odessa, bonbons and shit. She talked about Moon Pies, two for a buck. Odessa lived alone and had a good job at a mattress factory. If she would put him up or find him a crib, he'd just hole up like a possum under a junked car, watch TV and work jigsaw puzzles. Nobody knew where he was going, and he sure as hell wasn't going to profile himself in this new town. If anything would give him away, it was accent. He could learn to start conversations with y'all, but he would have to work on his drawl.

Illustrator Ben Tegel was born and raised in St. Louis. He studied painting at Washington University and, following graduation, left for Los Angeles to start a rock n' roll band. He did that for a while, then started doing other things, including illustrations. He now lives with his wife and two small dogs in the Brookside area of LA, where he enjoys tofu hot dogs and watching the fights on TV. Samples of his illustrations and sketchbook work can be seen on www.baloneyboy.com

In a checkered life, Wm. Stage has been a tree-trimmer, ambulance driver, and public health officer. He holds a Bachelor of Philosophy degree from the long-defunct Thomas Jefferson College, an "educational experiment" run amok in the cornfields of south-western Michigan. He is a Vietnam-era veteran of the Army Medical Corps, and, in 1991, he was called into active duty with the Air Force Reserves during Operation Desert Storm. He has written newspaper columns for three decades, and, more recently, his commentaries can be heard on KWMU-FM, the National Public Radio affiliate in St. Louis. He has taught photojournalism at Saint Louis University, and his camera work can be seen on www.pixofpeople.com and www.paintedad.com. *Not Waving, Drowning* is his ninth book, and the first one that is entirely fiction.